CURSED
WITCH

CURSED WITCH

CREATURES OF THE OTHERWORLD

BROGAN THOMAS

Brogan Thomas
BOOKS

CHAPTER ONE

Eight years ago.

I sit slumped in the chair outside the headteacher's office as I wait for someone from my coven to arrive. My hands twist in my lap as I pluck at a ragged thumbnail. I wrinkle my nose. Every time I move, a whiff of my failure flies up my nostrils.

I smell like burnt toast and plastic.

I tug at the sleeve of my charred blazer. Parts of the navy jacket are yellowish brown, the polyester fabric has shrunk with the heat and the whole left arm is crispy. My once smart white shirt is smudged with black. I look a state.

At least I wasn't seriously hurt; the quick actions of my teacher saved me—well, physically. Mentally, I'm a mess.

The door leading to the corridor is wrenched open, and she stalks into the room. The door slams behind her. Her violet eyes—the same colour as mine—scan the room until they land on me. "Tuesday," she whispers in horror.

My skin prickles uncomfortably and the secretary drops her paperwork and sits straighter in her chair.

The woman standing before us is a tiny powerhouse, bubbling with authority. The best witch in her generation. Dressed in an immaculate grey suit, her blonde hair is tied back in a severe knot.

"Hi, Mum." I drop my eyes to my lap and wrap my arms around myself. I feel like a ten-year-old.

"Are you okay? Did they heal you?" She leans down and her hands flutter in front of me. She finally tucks a strand of burned violet hair behind my ear. "I can fix your hair," she mutters as she pats my head. She drops her hand and roots through her big, brown handbag, which contains a plethora of potions.

"Mrs Larson?" the secretary interrupts. "The headteacher can see you both now." The lady smiles kindly at me.

Her kindness makes me uncomfortable—hell, everybody's kindness makes me feel uncomfortable.

Poor, poor Tuesday.

It's not anything they say, it's that look. The pity. Every day it gets worse—silent pity wrapped in poorly veiled disappointment. It seeps into my pores and messes with my head.

It coats my soul with its filth.

I am never going to be good enough. Oh, and the witch community won't cast me out.

No, they *love me.*

Endless love and understanding. The whole "our love will fix you" thing. It's nauseating. It drives me fucking nuts.

I hate them for their kindness, which makes me a total shithead. Is it wrong to wish someone would just be angry with me for once? I think I could deal with the anger instead of facing the pity in their eyes when they look at me. *Ha! Says the sheltered girl who is yet to live,* my inner dialogue helpfully pipes up.

Mum doesn't pity you.

No, behind closed doors and away from prying eyes, she hates me.

I jump to my feet, almost running away from that thought, and beat my mum to the office door. I'm keen to get this over with. I rap my knuckle against the glass and when I hear the muffled reply, I open the door and head inside.

The headteacher sits behind a heavy wooden desk, and when she sees me, her brown eyes crinkle with concern as she rises from her seat. "Oh dear, the colour-coded ingredients didn't work then." She nods at mum and thrusts her hand out. "Carol." A spark of purple magic zaps from her index finger. It meets mum's answering spark. The witch equivalent of a handshake.

It's another item on the long list of things that I cannot do. I tuck my hands behind my back and fidget.

"Please, both of you, take a seat." Once we're seated, the headteacher returns to her chair. She folds her hands on top of the desk and, with eyes full of sadness, studies me intently.

"Tuesday shouldn't be doing any dangerous magic," my mum angrily starts. "Why would you have her doing such complicated spells? She could have been seriously hurt—"

"It was a Don't Hear Me Now potion."

Mum deflates, and with a cringe, rubs her face. "Oh."

"There was no way to predict this would happen. It's unprecedented." The headteacher stares at my mum meaningfully and then both women scrutinise me. "I think we can agree that Tuesday's magiclexia is too much for spell work, and it gives me no joy to tell you her educational needs are becoming disruptive. Carol, it isn't fair to the rest of the class."

They are talking about me as if I am not in the room. It doesn't matter what I think, what I feel. My hand drifts to my sleeve and I pick at a particularly crusty bit as my thoughts drown out their voices.

Magiclexia.

I roll my eyes. It takes everything I have not to throw my hands in the air with exasperation. For them, it always comes back to my brain. It's never anything to do with my shitty magic. They are convinced I have cognitive difficulties and their poor witchy minds cannot conceive a *Larson* is simply low on power. That I am a magical dud.

No, there must be something wrong with my brain.

I'm sick of this shit. Sick of the whole "come on Tuesday, if you could just try harder" lecturers, followed swiftly by the sickly sweet "we believe in you, Tuesday."

If I try any bloody harder, my head is going to pop off. I wish they would all bog off.

Today just proves, yet again, how useless I am. Even with all the help in the world, I still can't get a simple basic spell correct. I rub my dirty face—crap, I'm missing half my eyelashes. Who's ever heard of such a benign potion exploding? I am bloody cursed.

I slump further and stare out the window at the school grounds beyond. *I wish I could go home and have a shower. I can't believe I'm sitting here, wearing my shame.* My left knee jiggles, and I grind my thigh into the chair to stop the movement. *I wish I never had to come back here again.* I hate this school.

A crunchy piece of my jacket crumbles in my fingers and flutters to the floor.

What sixteen-year-old can pinpoint the exact moment her life fell apart? I can. Everything was going okay until I turned eleven and had to do the entrance exams for this damn school. Yeah, that went well.

For so long, I masked that I was struggling. Magic is hard. It isn't effortless like it is for my sisters—it makes little sense to me. I just can't get it. How everyone describes their power doesn't feel the same to me.

As a kid, I covered up my issues like a pro. I kept my head down, and no one noticed. Looking back, I don't know how the hell I got away with it. I must have been committed. I found ways around things. A new basic spell at school? I'd, urm, *borrow* an advanced one from home. The potions were all over the house. It was easy to do a switcheroo, and bam hey presto, my spells were perfect. I smile bitterly.

I only did it a few times. I didn't see it as being dishonest, not really. I just wanted to be normal. It was a knee jerk reaction. I was just a little girl. Disappointing my mum and being teased by my friends was the worst thing imaginable.

Or so I thought.

I frown and rub my chest. My coven was horrified I'd hidden my issues from them.

I made my mum cry.

They threw money at the problem and hired a specialist teacher. But my wonky, crappy, low powered magic wouldn't play ball.

Those first few years were so hard, and the damage was done in the eyes of my coven. I went from being a normal kid to a child with special needs.

Worse, I was a thief and a liar.

A rogue tear runs down my cheek and I surreptitiously rub it away.

I swallow and take in a deep breath. The smell of my scorched uniform tickles the back of my throat and I choke a little to stop a cough. What does it matter if my magic is crap? What does it matter in the scheme of things? Yet each failure gets harder to stomach. Each day gets harder to believe—to believe in me.

I hate it.

I HATE IT.

There's not a day that goes by that I don't wish I was human.

With these witchy expectations piled so high on top of my chest, I can't take a full breath.

As if I don't hear the whispers: *She was bred for greatness. What the hell went wrong?* Yeah, I am shit. I get that, thanks.

"We can put her in a different class. Perhaps we can try portals next?" With those words, I lift my head and focus back on the conversation. My mum sighs and leans forward as she runs her fingers through her blonde hair.

"Stop," I whisper. It is as if some demon has taken over my mouth. "Please, just stop. I can't do this anymore." My bottom lip wobbles and I viciously bite it, holding it still.

My mum casts me a withering glance. "Tuesday, don't you think—"

"NO!" I yell.

The word echoes around the room as I throw my hands in the air in frustration. My entire body shakes. "It's like I'm a fish and you're asking me to climb a tree. I can't do it. I am a fish, not a... I'M NOT A FUCKING MONKEY!" I slap my hand across my mouth in an attempt to push the swear word back in.

Oh no.

The awkward silence in the room is palpable as both women sit open-mouthed and stare at me. The headteacher, with a shake of her head, snaps her mouth closed.

My mum visibly swallows, and her face goes red. "Tuesday Ann Larson, I will wash your mouth out with a potion if you swear like that again," she threatens. "I apologise, headteacher, my daughter has been brought up better than that." She scowls at me.

Doesn't she understand how frustrated I feel?

"I can't do this anymore. I won't." I vigorously shake my head. "I'm sorry. I'm sorry that I've let you all down." The chair scrapes against the floor as I push away from the desk and stumble to my feet. "I'm out. I'm done. I give up." My arms flop to my sides and my chest and throat burns with pain. What they expect is suffocating me.

"I am a fish," I mutter as I back away.

"Tuesday, what on earth are you talking about?" Mum asks as her beautiful face scrunches up with confusion. She looks at the headteacher as if she can interpret my crazy.

"Everybody is a genius. But if you judge a fish by its ability to climb a tree, it will live its whole life believing that it is stupid. It is a quote from Albert Einstein," I croak, as my vision goes hazy with tears.

I do my best to blink them away, but a sneaky one rolls down the side of my nose and plops onto my dirty shirt. Through a huge burning lump in my throat, I rasp, "Mum, I can't be your monkey. I can't do this anymore. I am not... I'm not good enough. I am not strong enough.

"I am not a witch." With that firm declaration, I turn on my heel, and with as much dignity as I can muster, I walk away.

CHAPTER TWO

Crap. So much for the grand exit. I have to wait for my mum to finish in the office. I can't sit. I'm too wound up. So I stand in the corner by the window with my back to the room and the still smiling secretary.

Outside, it's a perfect winter's day, cold but with a bright blue sky. My eyes are drawn to a robin sitting on a fence post. His red chest is puffed with pride as he guards his territory. A gentle breeze ruffles his feathers.

With the way I feel inside, shouldn't it be raining? I sniffle and use my sleeve to wipe my nose.

The burned bit scrapes my face.

I felt guilty for so long. It's the first time I've ever said no, the first time I've stood up for myself. I swallow as I remember the expression on my mum's face. I think people don't like it when you tell them no, especially parents.

I lean my head against the cool glass. I had to say something. I can't keep doing this to myself. I can't keep spectacularly failing. What about my self-esteem?

What everyone seems to forget is this is my life and I need to live it my way. I'm sixteen, so it is not like they are going to let me stop my education. I am not that naïve. But everything here is set up for me to fail. This path that everybody wants me to take isn't my path. I know it deep inside; I can feel it in my bones.

Every time I attempt a spell, a rune, or try to do an incantation, it feels wrong... like I'm on a greasy tightrope wearing shit shoes without a safety net. Splat. I fall to the ground every damn time.

They flush my self-confidence down the drain over again as they try to make me into someone I am not. Just once, I needed to be honest with myself, to be honest with them, even if I fail and they ignore me. *Please don't let them ignore me.*

I might as well flush my entire head down the loo. It would feel the same.

I'm drowning.

Fate must be pushing me to do something else—something I can actually do. One single thing I can excel at... Just one small thing. This can't be my life, forever the disappointment, forever on the outside. I have to believe there is something more. Some kind of purpose.

It's not giving up if your time could be spent doing something better.

Right?

I sigh and close my eyes.

Ten minutes later, the office door opens behind me and my mum exits the room. The little hairs on my arms rise as a wave of anger radiates from her. Her heels clack ominously towards me.

Oh no. I duck my head and hunch against the glass. I know there is no getting away from her. I gather the remaining scraps of my tattered courage and when I turn to face her, she glares. Her violet eyes are spitting mad.

"You're excused for the rest of the day," she snarls, and with stompy heels, she strides away. "Come on."

I nod, and like a good little girl with my eyes fixed on the floor, I scuttle behind her as we head outside to the car.

I sit with my arms wrapped around me as we drive home in uncomfortable silence. Wow, I suddenly understand the expression, "you can cut the air with a knife." My mum is livid.

With a sharp "go to your room" when we get home, I leave her at the front door, and hurry upstairs.

I strip out of my uniform and throw the whole thing in the bin before getting into the shower. Hours later, when Dad gets home from work, I sit on the stairs and listen to them whisper-argue about me as I fiddle with a piece of burned hair. I don't know why they don't use a privacy potion. I guess they don't care. After about twenty minutes of heated debate, I am called downstairs. I take each step as if I'm on my way to face a firing squad.

I peek into the room and my heart drops into my stomach as I take in Mum's still angry body language. Looks like she hasn't calmed down, and from what I've already overheard, it appears she also hasn't understood a word I've said.

"Matthew, tell your daughter that she will not be leaving school," my mum says as I enter our bright yellow kitchen.

With a shaky hand and fortifying breath, I pull out a chair and sit at the table. I'm getting a headache from the stress.

I clear my throat. "I didn't say that, Mum. I know I can't just leave school. I am asking not to do any more practical magic classes. It's for everybody's benefit, for everyone's safety."

"So, you've decided you don't want to do magic classes. Explain to your father that you, in your teenage wisdom, have also decided you are no longer a witch." I purse my lips and sensibly keep my mouth closed. "No longer a witch," she scoffs. "Have you ever heard of such stupidity? Did you blow that potion up on purpose?" she asks.

I flinch. Wide-eyed, I shake my head. "No. No, Mum, I did not."

Mum harrumphs. "What is wrong with being a witch? What's next? Are you going to decide you want to be a vampire?" She throws her hands into the air. "Your sisters are all outstanding. They are incredible. If you would just try harder—"

"Carol," Dad quietly reprimands. "That's unfair." He watches me with sad eyes as I hunch in the chair. "You know she didn't do it on purpose."

My mum sniffs and rubs her face. "Do I? Well, she has lied before. We have spoken about this, Matthew. She is not leaving that school. She doesn't get to do what she wants. What would the community think?" Her eyes widen.

Fuck the bloody witches.

This time, I say nothing. Acting out won't win me any prizes, and they have already made up their minds.

Familiar frustration bubbles in my chest and makes my heart hurt. It makes me dizzy. I take a deep breath as I battle with the overwhelming need to throw myself on the floor like a toddler and sob my heart out.

"No. It's not happening. It's. Not. Happening. Tuesday, I am your mother, I know what is best for you. One day, you will thank me."

I doubt it.

Come on, you ninny, say something. I try a different tack. "If you want to keep paying for me to go to school for the next four years to learn nothing, that's your choice."

She slams her hand onto the table and growls like she has a shifter trapped inside of her. Both Dad and I jump. "You are a witch. You will have a witch's education." The violence she excludes makes me wish I could take my words back. Pull them back from the air and let them dissolve on my tongue. "I cannot deal with her when she is like this." Her chair scrapes against the tiles with a screech as she gets to her feet and storms away. The cupboard doors open and slam closed.

Normally I'd get up off my butt and help her. But I'm not going anywhere near her today, not with the mood that she's in. The anger coming off her in waves makes me want to curl into a ball and protect my squishy bits. Oh, she's never hurt me physically—no, my mum's weapon of choice is her words.

The plates clack together as she shoves them down on the dining table in front of me. "No daughter of mine will quit." I cower. My dad winces, but he doesn't say anything to contradict her. When my mum has her back to us, he leans across the table and sketches a rune onto my hand. My eyelids tingle.

"To fix your hair and eyelashes," he explains.

"Thanks, Dad," I mumble.

Magic fixes everything, doesn't it? The bitterness I feel is like a rolling blackness inside me. I square my shoulders and lift my chin. "So, I must keep going to school, keep taking the magic classes that I can't do. Okay..." I nod. Oh heck, I am nuts. I don't know when to shut up. "If I sit there and refuse to do the practical lessons, what then, Mum?"

Mum stops viciously chopping up a carrot and points the knife at me. I sink further into my chair. "That is down to you, Tuesday. If you do not try, you will fail, and I will never forgive you."

Then I will fail.

It's going to be a long two years.

Thank goodness witches are legal adults at eighteen. As soon as I hit that birthday, I am out of here. Independence starts with money. This weekend, I plan to get a part-time job.

Fuck you, Mum.

"Another thing—your swearing." Uh-oh, it's like she can read my mind. "She said the F word, Matthew. At the headteacher. The *F* word. I have never been more embarrassed in my life."

"I didn't swear *at* her. Well, not really." I cringe and rub my mouth. "I'm sorry, I was upset. I didn't mean to. I'm sorry I embarrassed you."

"Upset?" Mum huffs as she throws the knife down on the chopping board and storms toward me. "*You* were upset? What about me?" She prods her chest. "I am upset. You—you do not know the meaning of the word. But I will give you something real to be upset about." She pulls something from her pocket. A potion vial clacks on the table and with her index finger, she pushes it towards me. "While I was waiting for your father to come home, I made this just for you. Drink up."

Made it with love, Mum?

The purple liquid inside sloshes. Purple is... I mentally flick through the catalogue of potions in my head. Mind control? A blocking potion? Uh-oh. Purple is not good.

"It's an anti-profanity potion. I told you I would wash your mouth out with a potion," she says smugly. "So here it is."

Horrified, I stare at Dad for help. "Dad?"

He shrugs.

He shrugs. Thanks, Dad. I shake my head. No, this isn't happening. It's not bloody happening. I didn't think she'd—

In the past, she's always threatened me and my older sisters. But that's all it's ever been—a threat. An empty threat.

I swear a lot. It's a Northern English thing. Where we live in Lancashire, we practically use swear words as punctuation. I've never used a bad word in the presence of anyone distinguished before today. I'm not normally that much of a heathen. I understand why she is upset. But to magically gag me? She has finally lost the plot.

Mum impatiently taps her fingernails on the table and the expression on her face makes my hands tremble. *Looks like I don't have a choice.* I don't even bother to glance at Dad again—there will be no help from him.

I pick up the bottle.

"How long will it last?" I rasp.

"A few weeks. Just long enough to get through the winter solstice celebration. I do not trust you to behave and your father's job with the Hunters Guild is far more important than you, your potty mouth, and your silly tantrums."

Silly tantrums? Wow. Nice.

At school, was I really being dramatic? I don't think so.

Damn it, I should never have spoken up. I should have just kept my head down and my stupid fears to myself. Let the grown-ups sort things out.

I cannot believe I felt guilty all this time about hiding my problems with magic. Now I see my younger self was the smart one—smart to keep my issues to myself. All Mum cares about is her reputation. She doesn't care that, each day, I am dying a little bit more inside.

"I will not ask again. Drink the potion."

My eyes flick to Mum and then Dad. This is both my parents breaking my trust on a whole new level. I promise myself here and now that I will never ask for their help again.

I am done.

The vial in my hand is warm from being in her pocket. I roll it between my fingers, and with a sad sounding sigh, I dig my thumb into the cork. It comes out with a slight pop. Without preamble, I tip it to my lips and drink.

I gag when the liquid hits my tongue. It is vile. Potions do not have to taste bad, which means Mum has made it taste awful on purpose. I wipe my mouth with the back of my hand. She has gone out of her way to make it extra gross.

Made with hate, right, Mum?

The potion will only last two weeks. It will not be that bad.

CHAPTER THREE

Eight years later.

There is a whoosh of magic that makes the little hairs on the back of my neck stand on end, and then the ward protecting the building fails spectacularly. Seconds later, there is a crash as the lobby door gets kicked in.

I sit up with a jolt and the crumbs stuck to my pyjama top spill around me. "Oh fiddle-dee-dee" comes out of my mouth instead of the "oh fucking hell" my brain was aiming for. *Umm, yeah, thanks for that, Mum.* Bloody two weeks my arse. Eight years and counting and I still can't swear.

In my head, it is all good, but as soon as I open my mouth, those sweet, naughty swear words transform into torturous embarrassment. The quirk has made me odd, and with the weird way words bubble up out of my mouth, people apologise if they say a bad word around me. Apologise to *me* as if I'm pious.

Honest to God, they think I'm the swear police.

How can I explain that my mum magically gagged me? And that the spell is so strong, and my magic is so weak, it can't be broken?

I can't.

There is no way I am going down that rabbit hole to explain my coven drama. Oh, and I have this laugh—it makes me almost want to punch myself in the face. It's this small, fake titter, and I do this bizarre wave as if I am the Queen and I'm waving away their bad word. Absolving them. Yeah, I look like a right dick.

A crumb still stuck to my top catches my eye. Ooh. I hum the Hasbro commercial for the Hungry Hungry Hippos board game as I drop my chin to my chest and, without thinking, hoover it up. It takes me a second. Eww. I wrinkle my nose and cough—that wasn't toast. I prod my mouth with my tongue. I don't know what the hell that was. It was gritty and now it's stuck unpleasantly to my teeth. Gross.

Mental note: do not eat strange random crap stuck to you.

Bang-crash-bang. "Crikey. Stealthy, the intruders are not." It must be a heck of a fumble for me to hear them three floors up. And it is nothing to do with me. My neighbours are a rough lot and the building gets raided at least twice a month. It's no biggie.

I yawn and lazily stretch, my wrists crack, my left shoulder pops, and my lower back aches. Ow, I really need to get off this sofa and move around more. My sedentary lifestyle during my time off isn't doing me any good. I flop back and roll onto my side. The zip of the cushion digs into my hip as I glance at the dusty exercise bike rammed into the far corner. I will start an epic fitness regime... *next week*, I promise myself.

If I'm not here, vegging on the sofa, doing my version of a couch potato, I am working. I force myself to be manager Tuesday for over sixty hours a week. So, when I get home, I get to be lazy Tuesday in all her glory. I wiggle and point my toes. The evil cushion pokes at me again. Bloody thing.

My eyes drift to the floor as the ruckus downstairs continues. "Why can't people behave themselves?" I grumble. It's after ten at night. I shouldn't have to listen to this. No, I should watch instead.

I lean down and, with my tongue clamped between my teeth, I slap my hand about on the floor—without looking—in search of the remote. It dropped on the floor a while ago. I ignore the gritty texture of my carpet. Gross. I need to clean under there at some point. Aha, it's disappeared halfway under the tiny blue sofa, so I hang upside down and coax it out with my fingers.

As I sit back up, I spin it around, and with a *pew-pew-pew* sound, I point it at the television and turn it on. I'm so glad I don't have to get up to find out what's happening. As I am so nosy, I love the cameras my sister Ava installed in the building. But though I find watching random people fascinating, I have a rule: no camera time near bedtime, with a cut off at nine. But I have Sunday and Monday off this week, so a few extra hours are no harm. I click the app for the building's security cameras. *No one needs to know.*

Cross-legged, with an excited shiver running down my spine, I stare at the TV. The intruders are dressed in skin-tight black suits with stripes of colour along their shoulders and arms. Their faces are hidden behind full headgear. I can't help snorting. *What the heck?* They resemble evil Power Rangers. I lean forward. *How embarrassing.* A bad Halloween costume crossed with a military scuba suit.

"Those tight suits have got to chafe." I tilt my head to the side. No wonder they have their faces covered, as I can only imagine the ribbing they'd get from their friends if they were seen in those getups. Oh my, this is so much better than watching TV.

My eyes drift to my kitchen. I wonder if I will miss anything if I grab some popcorn...

"Flat eight, on the third floor. Harris, you take point," says the gruff voice of the Red Power

Ranger. My eyes widen and with a squeak of shock, I drop the remote.

What? That's me. I live in flat eight. Uh-oh. Whoever they are, they are coming for me. "No-no-no." Adrenaline gushes through my bloodstream as I scramble up from the sofa and dash around my tiny flat as if my bum is on fire. *What the heck do I need to do? What do I need? What do I need?* I screech to a halt, panting.

"Stop freaking out." Helpful. When has telling yourself not to freak out ever bloody worked? I need to decide what to do first. My eyes flick frantically around the room as my hands shake. My fear and panic are making me dizzy.

I tuck a strand of violet hair away from my face. You would think they'd at least knock rather than destroy everything in their wake. How the hell did they find me? I have been so careful. I nibble on my thumbnail. Heavy footsteps and muffled voices are now *outside* the door, and my heart skips a beat. They are here. A flash of magic has me scrambling away. The flat's ward—done by my sister, Jodie, who's one of the best witches that I know—*groans.* Oh yeah, that's a great sign. I stare at it with wide eyes.

I bounce from foot to foot and mutter, "This isn't happening, this isn't happening." What the heck did I do wrong? Whom have I pissed off? It can't be about the old lady with the out-of-date fish. Even when she slapped me in the face with it, I gave her a refund.

I am way too young to die, I mentally wail. With that fun thought, I dash towards the huge safe room, which takes up a vast amount of space in my tiny flat. In living alone and away from the coven these past six years, this fancy safe room was something Dad had insisted on. It is one of the best on the market. I cringe when the front door is hit with another blast of magic and the ward lets out another awful groan. I thought this stupid, expensive thing was overkill. I guess they weren't wrong with all their warnings.

In the world I live in, magic is commonplace, with all manner of supernatural creatures: shifters, demons, witches, vampires, and an abundance of fae. Our world is all about the strong against the weak. It is all about power. If you're not powerful or you don't belong to a powerful group that can protect you, you're as good as dead. With a clank, I brace my feet and drag the heavy safe room door open.

This raid has got to be something to do with my dad. The next big war is brewing, and my dad is high in the Hunters Guild. The creature police. They oversee all the other councils.

I shimmy out of my red silk dressing gown and matching pyjamas, and then stuff my feet into my socks and wiggle into my beige thermal bottoms. Since I left home at eighteen, I am no longer protected by the coven. If someone wants to hurt my dad, well, I'm the easy target.

I cluck my tongue as I yank my sports bra on. My nostrils flare with indignation. It makes me so mad. Why can't I be left alone? I haven't done anything wrong. My skin is a little damp from my panicked state, so instead of the bra just sliding down, somehow the fabric sticks to my back and then twists.

I blink in shock. *Is it stuck?* "Cheese-on-a-cracker," I mumble. I tamper with the urge to scream as I attempt to tug the bra back up. I am bloody stuck. Ha. "Oh, this is bad. So-so-so bad." I wildly eye my flat door and the groaning ward.

Oh no. Any second now they're going to bust through the door and I'm going to be standing here, a sweaty mess with my arm stuck and my bra twisted, one boob in, one boob out.

Surprise.

I let out a wild, panicked laugh. What a heck of a surprise that would be! Who could think this stuff up? This? This is a bloody nightmare... This could only ever happen to me. *One step at a time, Tuesday,* I mentally berate myself. *Stop messing about and get your bloody bra on.* I wiggle and tug and just when I think I will have to get my feet involved, one good yank and I free myself from the sports bra.

Phew.

My arm throbs and with a quick glance down, I see I have a bright red line across my left breast and my head itches where I've pulled out a chunk of hair. *Good times.* I grip the evil bra in my fist, glare at it and grind my teeth. I take a steady breath and put the bra on again, *slowly* this time, giving it the respect it demands.

"There, okay, I got this." Boobs sorted, I put my top on. As the base layer slides down my torso, I hurry back into my living room and pull out the padded rucksack for my laptop. I use my bubbling anger at the mercenaries to wash away my fear. Frightened people do silly things and react without thinking. I can't let my fear rule me. I won't. This isn't my fault, and it isn't Dad's fault either.

No, it's the fault of the wanker who sent the bloody Power Rangers to break down my door.

I continue to layer my clothing and top everything off with yellow hi-vis waterproof trousers, a matching coat, and chunky boots. I catch myself in the mirror as I shuffle past and wiggle my eyebrows. Ha, I resemble a bright yellow version of the Michelin man or the giant marshmallow guy off the classic film, *Ghostbusters*.

A big, luminous body with a tiny, violet head sticking out.

Sexy.

My door shudders and I hunch. Bloody mercenaries.

I dump my discarded pyjamas on my bed and swing the heavy door of the safe room closed. With a blinding flash of magic that tickles my nose, the safe room protections engage. As I stand *outside* the safe room, I nod my head with satisfaction. The multi-layered ward crackles menacingly and the energy coming off it makes me shudder. That will keep them busy.

I smirk at the red sash of my silk dressing gown as it peeks out of the door. *Oh, looky here, Tuesday has run into her safe room. Please spend hours trying to crack it.* My lips twitch into a wide grin. It is perfect.

I shuffle back into my living room, and with a groan, drop to my knees. "Daisy, come on, we have to go." Thanks to the idiots breaking down the door, she's hidden underneath the sofa. With my cheek resting on the carpet, I can just see her if I squint. Yellow eyes with vertical pupils glare at me, and her third eyelid tracks across the eye from side to side. "Come on, zig-zag, let's get somewhere safe." I hold my hand out and wiggle my fingers.

A low hiss comes from between a mouthful of razored teeth.

"Hey, don't you hiss at me, young lady," I reprimand in the perfect, if not creepy, imitation of my mother. Her claws dig into the carpet, and she wiggles further back, out of arm's reach. "Look," I huff. "I'm not the bad guy here.

The bad guys are currently smashing down Auntie Jodie's ward. Come on now, you scaly little beast, we have to go."

Daisy narrows her eyes and her nostrils flare. She must smell my desperation as, after a long assessing blink and a put-out sigh, she finally crawls towards me. I scoop her up into my arms and she puffs a smoky cloud of hot air into my already warm face. Her tail wraps around my wrist, front claws dig into my collarbone, and she wiggles underneath my chin. "What a brave girl."

I see a flash of red out of the corner of my eye. Blimey, the ward is struggling... Who the hell is out there? There must be a strong magic user. *Someone I do not want to meet.*

Oh no, the ward! I want to slap my forehead. My sister is connected to it, and she'll know that something is wrong. Goosebumps rise underneath my ridiculous outfit and I swallow down a lump of nerves that wants to crawl up my throat. I juggle Daisy into one arm and grab my phone. I quickly send Jodie a text that I am okay and to keep away from my flat. There are already a few messages that I've missed. But with what is happening outside, I haven't got time to read them.

I unzip my jacket and carefully pop Daisy inside. "What a smart, clever girl," I coo as she snuggles down into the specially made pocket across my chest. I can feel her heart beating with fear, so I take the time to rub the base of her horns and stroke her beautiful, soft scales. "There, that's better Daisy. You are safe."

Daisy was brown when we first met, her scales sore and flaky. But after a few weeks and a fortune on lotions and potions, the little dragonette moulted and her true colour emerged. Gold. Her scales are a bit tarnished on top and lighter on her abdomen, feet and underneath her tail. She is so beautiful.

My waterproof outfit rustles and squeaks as I hurry into the kitchen and grab a potion ball from a drawer. It's the size of a marble and it swirls with a goopy green liquid.

My sister Diane is the genius behind this spell. It is a protective bubble for Daisy. It is designed to maintain oxygen, temperature and to cushion her from any blows. This fabulous little potion will make sure she is one hundred percent protected while I get us to safety. I stuff a good handful of dragonette mix into my coat to keep her occupied while I whisper the easy incantation. The protective bubble pops around her. Perfect.

Then I load up. I stuff random potions that my sisters keep giving me and things Daisy will need into my pockets. I finish with a few good handfuls of dragonette mix. If Daisy has food and her water dish, it is all good.

The ward flashes again. I am running out of time. What I can't do is fight a dozen magical Power Rangers. I'm not a ninja. So it's time to get the heck out of here.

CHAPTER FOUR

I scramble to the door that holds the flat's heating boiler and—being mindful of Daisy—shove myself inside. Gah, the space is tight. I barely fit. As I wiggle, air from my puffy coat tickles the back of my neck as it compresses. I press my thumb to the hidden panel on the left and the electric lock disengages, causing the panel to pop open.

With a groan, I drop to my hands and knees. I drag my laptop bag behind me as I crawl into the dark hidey-hole.

When my dad set this emergency exit up, I laughed and laughed. I mean, who needs a hidden exit? Not me. As I close the door, I burn my hand on the hot water pipe, causing me to hiss. *Bloody thing.* Yeah, I thought my dad was crazy, and along with the stupid panic room, it was a complete waste of money. I'm not laughing anymore. The escape hatch, as I lovingly call it, is now the best thing ever. It's a hidden ladder that runs perpendicular with my building's lift shaft that will take me safely down to the ground floor and into the maintenance room.

With a little more room to move and in almost total darkness, I strap my laptop bag onto my back. *Crikey, I wonder how many spiders are in this area at the moment?* Perhaps not being able to see is a good thing. I try to ignore the feeling of cobwebs tickling the top of my head and face. I shudder.

Oh shit, on top of everything that's happening, I am going to have to grovel to Dad. I will have to listen to an epic "I told you so" lecture. *Well, if I get out of this alive...* I roll my eyes at the thought. If all goes well, I should be able to sneak out of the building with no one seeing me. *Bye-bye, mercenary Power Rangers.*

I swing myself onto the ladder. My heart jumps in panic and I yelp as my clunky boots make me miss the step. As my left leg dangles into the black abyss, I scramble to curl my arms around the ladder and hang on for dear life.

Shit, what a time to find out that I don't *do* climbing.

I get my shaking foot back where it should be as my chin digs into the rung above me. Perhaps putting all my gear on before I escaped wasn't such a good idea. A bead of sweat runs down the side of my face and my cheeks radiate heat. Nope, not a good idea. Not at all.

Frozen in fear, I hang on the ladder. My heart thuds and my knees knock together. I lick my lips. My mouth is as dry as the Sahara. Gah, I feel sick.

I drop my eyes and peek at Daisy. She seems perfectly content. I can hear her nibbling on her food. I grit my teeth and force myself to move my right leg. I can't hang around here all night. As long as I don't look down and I take my time, I'm going to be fine.

I screw my eyes closed and blow out a breath. With a clang, I slide my right foot off the rung and toe the next one below. I make sure my boot is completely balanced on the rung and then I cautiously let go of my death grip on the ladder and allow myself to step down.

Okay. I am okay.

I keep doing it, counting each step in my head as I go. It seems like it takes forever. When my boots hit the solid concrete floor of the maintenance room, my knees buckle and my entire body shakes with residual adrenaline. I'm alive. I am alive. I want to cry and kiss the ground at my feet. But I refrain, 'cause that would be minging.

I look up at the never-ending ladder above me with a shudder. Nope, I never want to do that again. It's like I've just climbed down Mount Everest. My arms and hands are aching.

Fuck you escape hatch.

When I move away from the ladder, the whole thing shimmers and disappears. It's hidden by a long-lasting Don't See Me Now Potion.

With a cautious peek out the fire exit to see if the coast is clear, my boots teeter on the step as I pause on the threshold. Oh crap. *I hope there are no bad guys out there.* I take a deep—if not shaky—breath and coax myself to move outside. *You can do this, Tuesday.* My whole body tenses as I move, and the outside air whooshes around me. I am in a tight alley at the back of the building. I flatten myself to the wall.

No one is here. *I am okay. It's okay. No one is out here.* I push the door firmly closed and my back scrapes against the red brick as I hug the wall, my bright yellow trousers rustling as I move.

With a smile, I glance down the tiny gap of my jacket at my girl. "So far, so good."

Three doors down, the alley opens into a tiny, private car park. I dash towards the building and open the back door.

The smell of food hits me, and my stomach gurgles. Yum. Chinese. I wave at Wendy, who is standing at the front counter, taking a phone order. Adamantly, I point to the lockbox that holds the keys for the scooters that they use for the takeaway deliveries. Wendy nods and gives me a thumbs up. I grin at her and mouth, "thank you," then grab a helmet from the side and stuff it onto my head.

"Ew." I gag and wrinkle my nose at the smell. You haven't lived if you've not stuffed your face into the padding of someone else's sweaty helmet. My skin itches. I grab a set of keys and mince my way to the back door.

"Oi, Tuesday!" shouts a voice behind me. My heart jumps and for a second, I freeze. I turn to see Wendy as she hurries toward me with a bag of food. "I don't want you going hungry. Nice to see you. It's been way too long."

"Thanks, Wendy," I say, my voice muffled by the helmet. "I'll get the bike back to you tomorrow." She pats the top of my head and rushes back to the ringing phone.

Outside, I head to the yellow and red scooters. I jiggle the keys and squint at the number etched on the key ring. When I find the corresponding scooter, I open the storage compartment under the seat, grab the gloves nestled inside, and pop in my yummy food. I throw my leg over and insert the key.

While I am safe in the car park, I use my phone to book a hotel room nearby. I might as well hide out in style. With that all accomplished, and a last check on Daisy, I stuff my hands in the gloves and rock the scooter off its stand. I turn the key, twist the throttle, and zoom into the night.

* * *

I nip the scooter into a designated motorbike parking space and grab my soon-to-be midnight dinner from underneath the seat. I slip inside the hotel and shimmy across the lobby like a proper weirdo, the helmet still firmly in place as I want to keep my face covered. The professional vampire on reception doesn't bat an eye and I check in without issue. Key card in hand, I head straight for the lift.

Once safe inside my room, my entire body sags with relief. I am proud that I made the three-mile journey to the hotel without freaking out. Buzzing down the main road on a scooter at night is scary. Wow, I've done something epic. For sure, along with the Mount Everest ladder, it's another fist pump moment. I evaded the bad guys, and both Daisy and I are safely tucked away.

The best escape ever and as a bonus, I have Chinese. Whoop.

The hotel room is nice—full bathroom, a king-size bed and a seating area that leads onto a balcony. I tug the smelly helmet off and stuff it in the cherry wood wardrobe near the door, rubbing my ear on my shoulder. My head itches with the need to wash my hair and face.

Carefully, I unzip the jacket and gently pull

Daisy out. Her nose twitches. "Look at this nice room, zig-zag." I place her on the floor and grin as she slowly stretches out one wing and then the other, then her back legs kick out with a thump as she excitedly bolts away to explore. She disappears around the side of the bed.

I shed my waterproof layers and throw them onto a chair. I'll use the thermal base layers as pyjamas—my outfit of choice.

I hunt down the welcome tea and coffee set, slide the tray from underneath and pop it in the bathroom with a handful of clean shavings for Daisy's loo. Then I quickly set up an area with her food and water. I turn the television on low and slump on the bed with what feels like a hundred cushions behind me, then I munch on Wendy's chicken chow main. I love that Wendy gave me a fork. As I am eating, I bite the bullet and ring Jodie. I need to check if my coven is okay.

"Tuesday." I scrub a hand down my face when Mum answers my sister's phone.

Great.

"Hi, Mum," I say through gritted teeth.

Mum is silent. That isn't a good sign.

I hunch and stuff more food into my mouth. When she still says nothing after that first mouthful, I do my best to appease her. I don't enjoy silence. "Some mercenaries came to my flat. I have no idea why I was targeted. Please don't send anyone; they have a heavy magic hitter. I'm sure they'll leave when they find out I am not there. I'm urm... at a local hotel stuffing my face with Chinese." Silence. "Is urm... is everyone okay on your end?"

"Tuesday Ann Larson," she growls. Uh-oh, my full name. I almost choke on a noodle. Oops, I'm in trouble. "Your lack of planning for your emergency is not my crisis."

Okay, thanks for that Mum. My bad. I should have planned for a group of mercenaries to bash down my door with someone strong enough to rip away Jodie's ward. I'll get right on that and do an entire A-to-Z emergency plan next time. I groan. I work in retail for spell's sake. It's not like I'm a practising witch or anyone special. I thought I did quite well. I had a plan; it might have been Dad's, but it worked.

"You should have come home immediately." *Home.* Their house isn't my home. "Why did you not come home? I have called the full coven for an emergency meeting. You need to come home right now so we can protect you— Matthew, she's at a *hotel.*" Her phone rustles as she huffs, and she drops her voice to an angry whisper. "I will not have our magicless daughter attacked by thugs."

I roll my eyes. Does she hear herself? *Magicless.* Yeah, and woe betides anyone who messes with me. It would be a lovely sentiment *if* she wouldn't take this as an opportunity to gain control of my life. She doesn't recognise that she is the worst offender and the reason I avoid everyone in my coven.

"Mum, I am fine. Please don't bother everyone. I didn't want to bring this minor issue home with me." The word *home* gets stuck in my throat.

"Well, it isn't just about you," she snarls. "Why are you so selfish? They also came here, but our wards and powerful magic kept them at bay. After an attack on our coven, do you think I have time to be running around after you? Selfish girl. Look Tuesday, I know it's not something you want to hear but being without magic makes you an easy target. I knew I shouldn't have allowed you to live on your own," she mutters.

Oh, so my older sisters who can stir up a potion are fair game? They sure as heck don't live at home. To Mum, it is like being able to mix a potion makes you a superhero. And as for her saying she shouldn't have allowed me to live on my own, I moved out at eighteen, on my birthday. She didn't allow me to do anything. I'm now twenty-four, for spell's sake. I have never asked her for a bloody thing.

Yet it is all my fault? And I am the selfish one?

Don't say anything, Tuesday.

"Another thing I shouldn't have allowed was for you to work in that shop," she continues. I am a general manager in a big department store. "You can work with Jodie." I wonder if she will ever conclude that she is wasting her breath. I mean, she is like a broken record. If I didn't take her oh-so-helpful advice the first dozen times we had this exact conversation, I certainly won't suddenly turn around and say, "What a great idea Mum!" after the hundredth.

"Heaven knows that girl needs a break. She works so hard. Honestly, I do not know why you insist on working with humans when you can help your sister." Perhaps it's 'cause humans are too busy trying to stay alive and keep their families safe than be bothered with me? It's so frustrating. I know Jodie is busy running the magic shop and working as a nurse, but I work hard too. Apparently, what I do isn't good enough.

I make a noncommittal sound in the back of my throat and stuff a piece of chicken in my mouth, so I won't say anything I'll regret. No wonder I avoid her like the plague. She can't help herself.

My lack of magic—she can't stand it. She takes it as a personal affront. I shake my head as I angrily chew. I've found it best not to argue, as what's the point? She never listens. The sad thing is, I don't care what she thinks anyway. Not anymore.

I lock away my hurt, channel my inner manager, and dig deep into my epic customer service training. I smile widely. I hope the shape of my mouth will be enough to change the cadence of my voice. "I am sorry, Mum. I didn't know that there had been an attack on the coven. I'm sure this misunderstanding will get sorted out, and I will be back in my flat in a few days. So please, don't worry."

"A misunderstanding?" my mum screeches. I wince. Oops, bad word choice. "Breaking down your sister's ward is far from just a misunderstanding, young lady. If you answered your bloody phone once in a while, then you would have known that there was a security issue. What you cannot seem to grasp is that we are witches, and our coven protects our weakest members. Now, you will come home this instant so we can protect you, while the Hunters Guild deals with the problem."

My fake smile slips and I stare down at my food. I'm always going to be the coven's weak link. I poke at my noodles, and with a sigh, I push the box of food onto the bedside cabinet. I am no longer hungry. I bring my legs to my chest and hug my knees.

"I must insist that you move back into the fold," she continues. "You need to come home." *I'd rather shove my head in a washing machine.* "We can get you a nice, normal job." A job suitable for a witch, she means. "And get you some help…" My mum continues and her words fade into the background, drowned out by my emotions.

My hurt.

I don't care. I don't care. I don't care what she thinks.

Yeah, right. I'm the only one deceived when I try to convince myself. The hurt makes my throat tight, leaving me to swallow against it.

Times like this, I wish... Gosh, how I wish I was super strong, my magic dramatic, with lots of bells and whistles. Instead of meh, non-existent.

I clear my throat. "I appreciate that you're only trying to take care of me, but Mum, you are smothering me. I have a well-paying job—"

"At a clothing store," she scoffs.

"That clothing store has paid my bills for the last eight years." I ignore her as she splutters and plough on. "I have never asked you or Dad for anything. I'm safe. I love you all and I will ring you next week." *More like next year.*

"Tuesday, don't you dare hang up—" I end the call. My tummy flips, and the Chinese food lies heavily in my stomach. I hug my knees tighter.

Today has been a nightmare.

CHAPTER FIVE

Daisy's claws dig into the carpet as she scrabbles around the bed. How can one small dragonette make such a racket? When she gets to my side, she stands on her hind legs and her front claws rest against the box frame. She wiggles her nose. I smile, lean down, and gently scoop her up. She settles next to my leg in the centre of the crisp white duvet and the softness of her scales helps to calm me.

I close my eyes for a second and force myself to breathe. I survived another fun phone call—that must count for something. At least I didn't tell her to fuck off. Not that I can, with the anti-swear mind control.

"I love you, little zig-zag," I whisper. My voice cracks and I rub my face.

Gosh, I shouldn't have let the conversation end like that. Every time we speak, I always seem to mess it up. I love my mum. Guilt churns in my tummy like black sludge. I know she is worried, and rightly so. Gah, I sink into the pillows. I could have handled that better. Perhaps I should have gone straight to the coven? I glance around the hotel room and shrug. It is telling that my first action was to go to a hotel. Not a friend, or my sisters, but a hotel. *Okay, Tuesday, enough of the coven drama. You need to check what's happening at home.* I drag my laptop bag, which is at the end of the bed, towards me and log into my building's security cameras.

I start the feed before the mercenaries enter the lobby. The building's ward chimes with distress on the computer's small speakers and then the main door crashes open. A puff of plaster dust rents the air as the door hits the wall. Like I've seen in countless action films, the group of men—dressed head to toe in their odd gear, so they can't be identified—tactically rush the building.

My face scrunches up in a frown as one guy doesn't conceal himself. He follows behind the others at a nonchalant pace, his hands stuffed in the pockets of his trousers. It's as if he's out for a winter stroll window shopping. "What a cocky motherfudger." Where did he come from? I can't believe I didn't spot him when I was watching at home.

Heck, how could I have missed him? He certainly stands out, and it appears he is the boss of the motley crew. I pause the footage and take a few stills, then email them to my Dad.

Why does this man feel comfortable showing his face when his colleagues don't?

"Flat eight, on the third floor. Harris, you take point," says the gruff voice of what would be the Red Power Ranger.

Two men stay on the ground floor, while the rest head upstairs. They clear each floor— military style—and make their way slowly up the building.

They move fluidly, like shifters... or vampires? I rub the back of my head. To guesstimate their height using the door frames of the hallway, they are big, so perhaps I was right the first time and they are shifters.

The guy—the boss?—doesn't rush. No. He slowly makes his way, strolling along without a care in the world, still shopping. I grind my teeth as I follow him with the cameras.

Who are you?

I speed up the footage until the group of mercenaries finally get to my flat and I watch as they clear the way for the boss guy. Look at that—they move aside and let him deal with the ward. My eyes widen. He is the magic user who took down the wards?

Well, I am surprised. He's a witch? I lean closer until my nose presses against the screen. He doesn't resemble any witch I've ever seen. I tilt my head to the side. The witch community is small, and male witches are incredibly rare. I would have remembered this guy.

With my mouth slightly open, I watch as he rips my sister's ward apart. 'Ecky-thump, the guy is packing some power. The ward is complicated, yet he rips it apart like it's tissue paper. He could have at least made it look difficult. What should have taken him hours, took him, what, fifteen—I check the timestamp—no, twenty minutes?

Nerves flutter in my belly. Crap, I'm lucky I got out of the building when I did. With a swipe at my keyboard, I copy all the footage and again email it to my dad. The Hunters Guild will want to see this.

What the heck is he? Who is he? I nibble a nail.

I need to find out more about him, about all of them. Where did they come from? I skip the footage to the camera in the street before they entered the building, but—no, that can't be right. It can't. Something is blocking the security feed. I stab at the keyboard, but nothing I do fixes the issue. I growl in frustration and glare at the mysterious man. I send the entire file to Ava. Tech is her thing. I will have to let Ava, Dad, and the hunters deal with this. I'm okay with computers, but I am not an expert in CCTV.

I skip to the live camera inside my flat: Daisy Cam. I only have it so I can check on Daisy when she doesn't want to come to work with me.

Wow, they've already broken into the safe room. Shocking. It's also kind of disappointing that what should have taken them all night, took this mystery guy only forty minutes. I shiver. The other mercenaries I can hear through the camera are tossing my place. The laptop bumps against my abdomen as I wave my hands in the air and squirm on the bed. *Monsters.* They are breaking my shit.

"Nice to see the Hunters Guild has rushed to my flat," I grumble. *Everything can be replaced. It's only stuff.* I concentrate instead on the witch. He turns his head towards the Daisy Cam and smiles.

He smiles at me.

I yelp. What the friggity-fig-frig was that? I jerk away from my laptop and slam the lid closed. But not before I see him disappear. The witch *Stepped*.

Stepping is an old, powerful fae thing. A teleporting thing. Witches don't bloody Step. "Not a normal witch," I squeak out. "Not a witch at all." With my heart pounding, I shove the laptop back in its bag and shoulder it. I scoop Daisy into my arms and cradle her against my chest as I scramble to my feet. "We need to get the hell out of here. We are not safe."

Every instinct I have is lit up and screaming danger. I don't know why, but I am sure he knows where I am. The guy is coming for me. Did he trace the security feed? My phone? Both are encrypted. It shouldn't be possible.

Yeah, it also shouldn't be possible for him to rip through wards like he's walking through cobwebs. Or Step.

Oh no. Oh no. Heart pounding, I grab my yellow jacket and trousers and stuff them underneath my other arm. I snatch my boots off the floor, the laces biting between my sweaty fingers. I will put everything on when I get the heck out of this hotel. I yank the room door open and narrowly avoid ploughing into a muscular chest.

"Where do you think you're going?" says a deep, heavily accented voice.

An *eep* sound slips out of my mouth and everything I am holding—except Daisy—thuds to the floor.

I scramble backwards. My bum hits the bathroom door, and it smashes back into the tiles with a crash.

Oh my. He is here.

He strolls into the room and, without taking his blue eyes from me, kicks the room door closed with his heel. I gulp. Without breaking his stride, he walks over my discarded outerwear. My panicked heart pounds in my ears.

How is this possible?

Daisy snarls and snaps her teeth at him. A puff of smoke comes out of her left nostril, and a lick of orange flame comes out of the right. I can feel how frightened she is with the rapid beat of her heart as it thuds against my palm. I love that she's being brave and trying to protect me, but I cannot put her in danger or allow her to be hurt.

Without taking my eyes from the stranger, I carefully squat, place Daisy on the tiled floor of the bathroom, and click the door firmly closed. I wince at her angry yowl. She growls and scratches at the door, then there are a few thuds.

"Hello, little lost witch," he says. His full lips tilt up with amusement. "I am told you're a dud, but you're more than that, aren't you? Your coven has hidden you well."

What? What on earth is he going on about? I haven't got a scooby. When all he gets in response is my dumbfounded expression, his mouth clenches and a muscle in his jaw jumps as if he's grinding his molars together. What is he expecting, a confession? My eyes drift away from his ticking jaw, and it's then that I notice his pointed ears.

Aes sídh, he is fae, an elf.

His short hair threw me. They normally wear it long with these pretty traditional plaits. He's a strong, old fae if he can Step.

"It's been over a century since I've met one of your kind in the real world. Stupid of you, really." My gaze darts from his ears and I take in the predatory gleam in his eyes. I smell bullshit. He is trying to butter me up. *One of my kind?* I wrinkle my nose.

It doesn't take a genius to work out I hate being a magical dud. *Nice one, Tuesday, that you know your place.* Yeah, I'm the secondary character, even in my own damn story. I swallow down a strange lump in my throat. I know I'm a silent internal badass. I don't have to be anything more.

But then why do I always feel so disappointed? My bottom lip wobbles, and I suck it into my mouth and chomp on it. None of that.

No. If this elf thinks I am going to fall for his total rubbish spiel of me being some kind of *chosen one*, ha. He has messed up. Boy, has he ever messed up.

A rush of angry heat washes away my fear and I see red. In the back of my head, I am utterly terrified, but I'm also too reckless to care. I've tipped over into madness. I don't cower like a normal person. No, when I am frightened, I get mad in a psycho way. It's another weird Tuesday thing, one that I presume is hereditary. Thanks, Mum.

I can feel my temper bubbling. It's warm in my chest and it spills out of my mouth with a vomit of words. "What?" I scoff as I narrow my eyes and lift my chin. "Are you nuts? Has your magic fried your brain?"

I hold my hand up and wiggle my index finger. "One, you and a bunch of mercenaries broke into my home and trashed it. Two"—a second finger joins the first—"you chased me across the city and forced your way into my hotel room." My hands go on my hips and I glare at him.

Shut up, Tuesday, a small voice in the back of my head begs. But I ignore it as I'm on a roll. My nostrils flare. At least my angry rant makes me feel like I am in control. "As if I would believe a single thing you say, sausage head."

Or not.

I meant dickhead. *Dickhead.* I groan.

He smirks and takes another menacing stride toward me. His bright blue eyes shine with mirth. "Yeah, that sounds about right," he drawls.

"You are delusional." I clench my fists. I've never hit anybody before, yet I'm struggling to tamp down the urge to punch him in his smug face.

Thumb out, right? Hit with the first two knuckles and twist your hips... I glance down at my small, balled fists then back at his smug face. I wince. It looks kind of hard.

"You're coming with me."

"Oh, heck no." I shuffle back and glance around wildly. There must be something in this room to brain him with. I'm not a victim. Mournfully, I glance at my heavy boots that are now behind his bulk. They would have made a fine weapon. The helmet would have also come in handy, but there's no way I can get past him to grab it. I tilt my head. He's a big bugger for an elf. He must be well over six feet, towering over my five-foot-four frame.

Lamp? I want to smack my forehead. *Magic. Bloody heck, Tuesday.* I have a knockout ball in the hidden pocket of my thermal trousers. It's a close contact spell and, well, we can't get any closer than this. One second, I'm about to grab it and the next, his weight is crushing me into the bed. Oof. I groan as his body knocks the breath out of me. His weight pushes me into the soft white covers.

'Ecky thump, this guy is built like a shifter. Crap, I wish I had listened to my dad about those self-defence lessons. He'd be snoring on the floor now if I'd used the potion sooner.

One hand grapples both my wrists together and slams them above my head. He reaches down between us... I panic. *Is he... is he reaching for his zipper?* A frightened whine escapes my throat, and I do my best to wiggle out of his hold. Before I can scream bloody murder, he pulls his hand back out, and in it is a nullifying band. It is made to remove every spell and shut down every trace of magic. It works on every creature but is mainly used on criminals.

Why does he want to use that on me? Why bother? My magic is non-existent. I try again to wiggle away, but his hand presses my wrists harder into the bed with bruising force and the clunky ring on his finger digs into my skin painfully. The damn thing is hot, and I wince as it burns me.

With a flick of his hand, the nulling band snaps out and wraps around my wrist. Something inside of me crashes. Disappears. Ouch. *What the heck?* I don't have magic, but the jolt of the band hurts me down to my very bones.

"I don't feel well," I mumble.

"You'll get used to it," he says. His fingers sweep my tangled, dark purple hair away from my face. He tugs at a strand. "Huh. Not magic. I didn't expect that." The nulling band is making me batty. He didn't expect what? Did he expect me to turn into a frog? I hate magic. Why would I use a potion to change the colour of my hair? Everything is me.

"I can't breathe," I whisper. The elf smirks and digs his elbow into my ribs. I groan. Yeah, that helps. What an arsehole. Thinking I have been appropriately cowed, he lets go of my wrists.

With a scowl, I slowly lower my hand, the one without the null band, to rub my ribs. Inch by torturous inch, I work my hand down until I slip my fingers into my waistband. With my thumb and forefinger, I pull the potion ball out.

Then slowly, ever so slowly, bring my hand back up, and I aim for the skin on his neck.

He jolts when there is a crash behind us, and the room's door is unceremoniously kicked in.

"Hey, welcome to the party," my voice slurs. "Ahh, here comes the cavalry." I hope.

He grunts, and his weight is yanked off me. There is a slap of a fist meeting skin—I hope it's his face—and the bed shunts to the side. The sharp movement of the bed whips me sideways and the potion ball flies from my fingertips and rolls off the side of the mattress.

Gah, for fuck's sake.

I try to move so I can find where the potion has landed. But I can't. What the heck? My head swims. Without his weight on me, I should be able to breathe, right? Yet each breath is getting harder. Like I am breathing through a twisted straw. It's too much... It is way too much. Why can't I bloody breathe? Did the bloody elf break something?

A body thuds to the floor. I hope that's the bad guy. My thoughts are fuzzy, and I can no longer open my eyes.

Come on, Tuesday, get up... darkness.

CHAPTER SIX

My aching bladder wakes me and, with one eye firmly shut and the other open the barest of a crack, I zombie shuffle to the bathroom. The rules are: if I don't open my eyes, I'm still asleep.

To save me valuable seconds in the bathroom— the joy of living alone—I tug my thermal leggings down my thighs as I move. When I get to the toilet, I slam my bare bottom down on the seat and groan as I pee like a racehorse.

Once finished, with my eyes now firmly closed, I bump into the counter and quickly wash my hands, then without peeking—on my first attempt, go me—I grab the fluffy towel. Hotel towels are so fancy.

All sorted and with my leggings back in place, I continue my weird shuffle back to bed.

"Morning," says a gruff, amused voice.

"ARRAHH!" I jump a foot in the air and clutch my chest. I tremble and my heart pounds as my now wide-awake eyes fixate on the strange man in the chair across the room.

I blink.

Oh no.

Some new guy is sitting in the chair like a James Bond villain. His long legs are spread wide apart, with Daisy and a small pile of dragonette mix on his abdomen.

"Don't worry. She is fine." His steady eyes are weirdly comforting. The light colour stands out against his dark hair and skin tone. His entire expression is kind, and I believe him. Daisy is fine.

Me? Yeah, not so much.

My now adrenaline-fuelled, wide-awake brain helpfully reminds me about what happened. The elf. I touch my empty wrist. The null band is no longer there. Huh. It's then my brain whispers, *did he see my bare bum?*

A small noise slips from my lips. I can still feel my body tremble, but my mind is oddly blank. I rapidly blink and then, in my head, I carefully run through my toilet shuffle, step by step. Then I factor in the chair's angle.

I allow myself a second to close my eyes. Mortified, my face heats and I want to sink onto the floor. Oh bloody hell, he saw my bottom.

My bare bottom.

Oh no, why me? I mentally whine. I rub the back of my neck and my hand catches on my long hair. Phew, my hair is down. It's long... It must have covered most, if not all, of my lily-white-arse. Right? Right.

I open my eyes and cringe as I take stock of the situation. There is nothing I can do about it now. Hopefully, he will be a gentleman and ignore the whole thing. Like I will. It never, ever happened. I cough to clear my throat and examine the guy. Wow, if I thought the elf was big, this guy is on another level. He has got to be a shifter.

The man's massive hand strokes Daisy as she delicately nibbles at the food on his abdomen. She is happy, the little traitor.

"Never saw the appeal of a dragonette as a pet, but I have to say, I've changed my mind. She is absolutely adorable." His rumbly voice is like velvet.

"Yes, she is. Though she is less pet and more best friend." But that's beside the point. I rock from foot to foot. Who the hell is this guy? "The elf?" I husk out. Might as well get to the point. I need to see what he wants and then get rid of him sharpish.

"I'm sorry. He Stepped before I could get a good grip on him," he replies gruffly, his eyes apologetic.

I shrug. "It's okay, as long as I don't see him again." I hope the elf is gone for good. His strange comments about my magic threw me. When you've been told all your life you are the magic equivalent of a garden pea and some dickhead lies, making it out like you are some hidden marvel, it gets you questioning yourself. I am not too proud to say, shamefully, that I wanted to believe him for a hot second.

"He was creepy. Thank you for your help." I point to Daisy. "Urm… do you mind?" All my instincts say he's a good guy, but I still have a strong urge to rescue my dragonette.

The stranger nods. "Of course." I tuck my hair behind my ear and shuffle forward, intent on scooping Daisy off his flat abdomen. I hold my breath as I lean forward, doing my best not to stand between his legs or touch him.

It isn't until I get closer and study him that I get the full effect of this man. At first glance, he is humongous, and dare I say, forgettable. Just another shifter. A soldier with his black hair shorn close to his scalp. But then as my eyes trail over his perfectly symmetrical face—the words *ultra masculine* scream in my head—with strong elegant lines, high broad forehead, straight nose, good cheekbones, square jaw peppered with stubble, and a full mouth...

Carved without any weakness.

The shifter oozes raw alpha male. He is all testosterone and metaphysical fur.

Rich, dark skin and soulful eyes—a stunning grey—take my measure. Huh. I've never seen a guy with such thick eyelashes. He is incredibly handsome.

Ridiculously handsome.

I breathe him in. He also smells fantastic, of cinnamon and vanilla. I frown. That's right. I sniffed him like a freak. I don't think I've bothered to smell a guy before. Oh my goodness, I am so weird.

I have Daisy, but as I get lost in his pretty grey eyes, I stupidly gather up the remaining food. They are the kind of eyes that shine with intelligence and confidence. He doesn't look— he watches. My fingers brush against his bumpy abs. I gasp, and my heart misses a beat.

'Ecky-thump, now I am assaulting him. Oops. "Sorry," I mumble. I spin in my socks, and we hurry towards the bed. Red-faced, I perch on the edge and pop Daisy down beside me. Is it hot in here? I tug at the neck of my top. Thermals in a hotel room aren't the best.

"Your dad sent me."

"Oh." That was something I should have established. I guess I am still a little thrown from the bum incident. "Thank you for saving me. Are you a hunter?"

"Hellhound," he replies matter-of-factly. The carefully hidden hellhound power ramps up and hits me square in my chest.

I gasp and feel my red cheeks instantly pale. Born of pure instinct, fear grips me. This time, crazy Tuesday, who valiantly mouthed off at the elf, scampers away in my head and hides. Whoa, I feel woozy. I wobble to the side and grip the white cover to ground myself.

Shifters alone are a scary lot. It's not them turning into animals that produces the terror, it's that if you get bitten when they are in animal form, and you are a witch, a human, or even some of the weaker fae, you are so screwed. You will die.

Men have an over fifty percent chance of becoming a bitten shifter. They can't shift themselves, but they gain extra things like a longer life span, an eight pack, and strength.

But women always die.

There's something wrong with the magic. It obliterates the X chromosome. There's no healing spell, no medication, and nothing in the world can stop it from happening. So, when you add an old shifter and then the power of a hellhound to the mix... it's an *oh crap* moment.

Hellhounds are scary. Like a monster under your bed scary. They aren't from hell or anything like that. They are powerful old shifters with fire magic. Nature literally sets the strongest of the poisonous biting machines alight and gives them extra strength.

Yay.

The shifters reacted to the magical phenomenon by training these scary beasts into killing machines. Of course, they did. It really adds to the entire fear factor. They are the terminators of shifters and I have never met a hellhound before, as they are rare. They are the Hunters Guild's elite fighters. Elite soldiers. They are the shit-has-hit-the-fan last resort.

And I have one in my room, a hellhound with pretty grey eyes and he is staring right at me. A predator, a fire wolf, looks at me from inside his eyes.

Hellhound. Hellhound. Hellhound.

Thank goodness I am sitting, and that I've already been to the loo. Why are the bad guys always mouthwateringly good looking? It doesn't seem fair.

"Hey-hey, you are okay." He takes hold of my hand and drops the potion ball that had fallen to the floor earlier into my palm. Gently manipulating my fingers closed, he holds my hand until he is sure I have it firmly in my grip.

A big-ass knife appears from out of nowhere and he places the hilt in my other hand. The blade is heavy; I know they do something technical to the silver to make the soft metal hard like steel. In seconds, in an attempt to make himself smaller, he is kneeling in front of me. The hellhound angles the knife in my hand, so the tip presses against his chest.

My heart misses a beat.

The hellhound has given me the means to protect myself against him. At least I can swallow down my chaotic, frightened thoughts and listen to what he has to say. I peek up through my lashes.

His grey eyes are so earnest.

"Hey, Tuesday, you are okay," he coos at me. "Sweetheart, you are safe. I am not gonna hurt you. Breathe, you are okay. I promise you are safe with me." His giant hands come up to cradle my face. His hands are so warm. "My name is Owen. I am a friend of your sister, Jodie. Your dad sent me to help you. I'm sorry if me being a hellhound scared you." It's a silly reaction but, I think, a normal one.

Why did my dad send a hellhound?

I take a deep breath and whisper. "My coven?"

"They are safe." I close my eyes and drop the knife. My hand is trembling so much, I don't want to risk catching him and cutting off his nose by accident.

No, accidentally stabbing someone is not on my to-do list.

"Everyone is safe. You are safe. I'm not with the guild anymore. I work in Ireland with the fae. I've been hunting your elf for the past three months."

"He's not my elf," I grumble.

"No, he is not. He's a bad man. When your dad received your emails, he got in touch with me. He gave me the heads up and instead of going to your place, I traced you here as I had a feeling the monster would come after you. I'm sorry I was late, and that he put his hands on you." Owen's thumbs brush gently against my cheekbones, and he huffs out a self-deprecating sound. "I thought my being here would be comforting. I'm sorry I got that wrong, that I frightened you."

I blink at him. His eyes, this close, have a dark blue ring around the outside. So pretty. There's a knock at the door. I flinch.

"That would be for me," he says gruffly. Owen lets go of my face. With a tight smile, he pats the bed and then rises elegantly from the floor and prowls to the door.

I lean forward to peek around the jutting bathroom wall that's blocking the bed from the view of the door. I huff. I can't see, as the hellhound's bulk takes up the whole entrance. There's no getting past him. Saying he just has wide shoulders, a narrow waist, chiselled chest, and washboard abdominals does not do the hellhound justice. He is big. He must be almost seven-foot tall.

"I got the scuba guys," says a rough female voice. I cover a snigger with my palm. I'm not the only one who thought their combat gear was stupid. "Rat shifters. Where's the elf?"

"Stepped."

"Ah shit. What's the score, Nanny Hound? Ten-nil? You're slipping." Looks like I am also not the only one to pick up that the hellhound is on babysitting duty. *Nanny hound*. Great.

"Old wolf, ya need to catch up. Next time, I'll handle the damsel and you grab the bad guys. What? Bad day at the office? Are you losing your touch?" The hellhound growls and the woman's throaty laugh threads through the room.

The laugh raises the hairs on my arms and an unshakeable sense of foreboding creeps along my spine. Along with that laugh, came the trickle of her power. She is so loaded up... My lips buzz.

"How's the girl?"

Fuck that. I scoop up Daisy and wiggle to the head of the bed, which is as far away as we can get from her without going through the window. To keep my hands busy, I scratch a finger between Daisy's horns.

"Safe."

"Good. I bought the stuff you wanted. You know I am no good at this female crap, so don't blame me if I got the wrong stuff. She should be able to brush her teeth and there are at least a few changes of clothes. I might have forgotten knickers..."

"Thanks, Forrest."

"Soooo, do I get to meet her?"

Oh no. No, thank you. There's a rustle of clothing and the floor in the hallway squeaks as if she is bouncing on her toes.

"Not today."

"Oh, come on, Owen. Jodie said I'd love her little sister. I've met everyone in the coven but this one. Please?" she throatily whines.

"No," he growls back.

Forrest. I am sure I've heard that name before, but not from my sister. There is a bump and a scraping sound against the door. I strain my ears at the sound of... wheels. He must have pulled a case inside the room. "I will see you in an hour."

"Nice to meet you, Tues—" Owen slams the door in her face.

Wow, rude.

And I am so glad. I shiver; I can understand why he didn't want me to meet her. Owen is on protective duty, and he's taking his babysitting seriously. His shifter nose must have caught the stench of my fear. The way my body reacted when she laughed. Oh boy, and the power she has. Bloody hell, it comes off her in waves. I've never felt anything like it. Instinctively, I wanted to climb out the bloody window. She is dangerous. I rub my arms and do a full-body shiver.

Crap, if she feels like that in the corridor, I can only imagine what it would be like standing next to her. I don't know what the heck type of creature she is, and I don't want to find out.

The fact she could arrest, um—I frown—take down the huge Power Ranger rat shifters by herself? Yeah. She is beyond scary.

I lift my eyes. Owen is standing silently in front of me. While I was stuck in my head, he brought me a suitcase.

"Thank you for all this," I croak.

"Are you okay?" I nod. "Did you hear all that?" I nod again. "Okay, find something to wear in here. You're going on a trip. While you were sleeping, your dad arranged a safe house. Oh, and the guild has contacted your work and explained what's happening. You're on emergency leave until this mess is sorted."

I puff out my cheeks. Great. I guess my department managers can handle things for a few days. Being hunted by some psycho elf takes priority, I guess.

"Okay, thank you," I mutter.

"Unfortunately, there isn't a portal nearby. So, Flash, if you think you're up for it, we are going to have to drive."

My brain grinds to a halt... Flash? Owen's face is carefully blank, but I can feel the growing horror race across mine. Is that a twinkle in his grey eyes? My chest and neck prickle with embarrassed heat. Oh bloody hell, he's talking about my bottom.

Flash. I'm a bloody flasher. Ha.

Once again, I am absolutely mortified. Daisy's scales rub against my hand, and I pick her up from my lap and gently clutch her to me.

"I can drive myself to the safe house. I'll be fine," I squeak.

CHAPTER SEVEN

"I can drive myself to the safe house. I'll be fine," I grumble as I grip the leather steering wheel so hard my fingers cramp. Yep, great job there, Tuesday. Leave the hottie hellhound with the biceps as big as your head to travel almost seven hours and three hundred and seventy-five miles, alone.

In my usual stubbornness to avoid help of any kind, I insisted I could drive myself. "What could go wrong? I will be fine." I sniff with self-disgust.

I have spent hours driving in a state of heightened alert, with my hands locked in a death grip onto the steering wheel in a ten-and-two driving position and a nervous sweat beading on my brow.

I dare to take my left hand—frozen claw—off the wheel for a second, to rub my tired eyes. I want my boring life back. I would rather deal with a nightmare shoe sale display, one where a kid has mixed up not only the left and right shoes but also the sizes. Matching hundreds of different shaded shoes is preferable to this.

I am so stupid. The last time I drove a car was the day I passed my test, and I never left my home city. Dad taught me to drive when I was seventeen. Once I had my pass certificate, as a rite of passage and for my first and last solo trip, I drove my dad's car through a McDonald's drive thru. That was seven years ago. I rub my thumb against the steering wheel and swallow. I loved learning to drive with Dad, but the whole car thing tainted the experience. All three of my older sisters were gifted their first car. With blatant unfairness, and in a sweeping statement by my mum, I was informed that if I wouldn't behave like a proper witch—I was refusing to attempt any magic—I had to walk.

I lift my stiff shoulder. It was fine. Who was I to dictate how my parents spent their money? I enjoyed walking and school wasn't far.

I am sure it was a naff attempt at reverse psychology by Mum, but instead of pitching a fit, I drifted further away. I wanted nothing from them anyway, so it was probably a good thing. In my teenage mind, it only highlighted again that my parents and magic just brought me pain. It made me more determined to be successful on my own terms. *Away from magic.*

I didn't drive a car again until today. I push the unhappy thoughts to the back of my mind. It's in the past and I am no longer a teenager. I'm an adult and I am adulting perfectly.

I quickly peek at my phone. According to the driving app, I am only thirty minutes from my destination. *Nothing is going to go wrong.* As if fate is listening to my thoughts, the fancy hire car shudders, and the headlights dim. *Oh, no.* There is a burst of warm air from the heater, and then the dash lights up, blinding me. I take my foot off the accelerator just as the car goes dark. Slowly, we roll to a stop.

"Motherclucker."

The engine ticks and my heart pounds as I sit wide-eyed in the dark on a country lane in the middle of nowhere Scotland. I gulp and my shoulders creep towards my ears. The fear that is rolling inside me makes me feel sick. I was pooping myself just driving. This is on a whole new level. The dead car is on a bend with no lights, and we are surrounded by thick hedges.

Oh no.

With shaking hands, I put the car in neutral and let go of my death grip on the wheel. *Get a hold of yourself, Tuesday, and think about what you need to do. Don't you dare freak out,* I berate. Crikey, the voice in my head sounds like Mum.

If I can deal with sixty-two staff and our wonderful array of customers, I can deal with this. I am the best problem solver. My not-so-sneaky staff call me Scary Poppins when they think I'm out of earshot. I roll my tense shoulders and flex my sore fingers. I am spoonful-of-sugar nice until things go wrong, then I can get a bit bossy. *I am a retail manager badass.* I snort.

I unclip my seat belt and, channelling my inner Homer Simpson, I frantically push every button on the dashboard, but nothing works. The phone Owen gave me is also dead. It must have cut out at the same time as the car did.

Uh-oh. That is not creepy. Not at all.

Magic normally raises the small hairs on my arms and tickles the back of my neck. I don't feel that sensation. But that doesn't mean much. Why would the car and the phone die at the same time? I shiver and then turn my head to scrutinise the passenger seat. My girl, who is safe in her fancy extra-large protective travel bubble, is fast asleep. I think. I tilt my head and narrow my eyes. Damn it, I can't see her. My eyes can't pierce the thick darkness. Why does tonight have to be so dark?

"It's okay, Daisy. I'll get us out of this," I say, in case she is awake and is looking at me. I aim for brisk confidence, but my voice wobbles at the end.

With a disgusted huff at myself, I crack the car door and the sound of the night rolls in. I blink into the darkness. I am so used to city sounds and the never-ending artificial light. I have never seen the outside world so black, so vast. It's jarring. I hold my breath and listen.

There are strange clicks from random insects. I frown and tilt my head. Wow, I didn't even know we had clicky minibeasts in the UK. I have no idea what the hell they are. I strain my ears for any other signs of life. The wind rustles in the trees and that's it. Absolute silence.

At least I will hear if a car comes, well, urm, unless it's electric. Great. I nibble on my lip and wince. I've been chomping on it for hours and desperately need some lip balm. My bottom lip probably looks a chapped mess.

"I wonder if this car has a warning triangle?" Gosh, my voice sounds loud to my ears. I grab the keys, rotate my stiff body, and boldly shove the heavy car door open. I use the door frame to help me clamber out onto the road. My knees knock together, and I whimper as I straighten. I've been driving for so long, my poor body has moulded to the shape of the seat. I was too nervous to stop and take a break in case I had to turn the car around or drive in a small space. The thought of reversing gives me heart palpitations and makes my top lip sweat.

My feet crunch on the ground as I head for the back of the car. When I reach it, I trip on the uneven road surface and almost go down, but a wild grab with my hands and my fingers dig into the roof trim. I hang on a second longer to steady myself and then squint down at my feet. What the heck is that?

"Oh my goodness, please don't tell me I hurt some poor creature." I toe something squishy and I squeal. "Oh no, oh no, am I a murderer? I was driving super slow." I feel sick.

No, it's not a dead body. Is that… Is that grass? I stop myself from dropping to a crouch and touching the ground as a trickle of memory tugs at my brain. A flash of the road before the car died. I lean against the car with relief. The rural road had a strip of grass running down it and I now distinctly remember I had been mindful to keep the tyres straddling it while praying no one came the other way.

Now, will the boot open with the key alone? These new cars are so fancy and reliant on technology. I feel along the back of the car, the dirt from the road gritty underneath my hand. I aim for the middle and… Aha! I find the lock. I trace it with my fingertips and then blindly aim the key.

The boot whooshes open and I puff my cheeks out as I methodically feel my way around the boot. Nothing. It's bloody empty. No crappy triangle, no warning spell. I haven't got anything to light up the car. I drop my head in defeat.

I am doomed.

I slam the boot closed and shuffle my way to the front. Hands on my hips, I peer at the road ahead. Why is it so bloody dark? As I turn back to the car, the moon peeks from behind what I can now see is thick cloud cover.

As the clouds break, the full moon shines down, granting me much needed light. I tip my head back in thanks and give the moon a grateful smile. Between the heavy clouds, I can see a slice of the night sky and a smattering of stars. Wow, they are so pretty. I quickly glance about before the light disappears and I see—I tilt my head—is that a break in the hedge? Just around the bend... Is that a driveway?

I dash forward, being mindful of the uneven road, and I find a driveway and a sign: THE SANCTUARY HOTEL.

Well, isn't that convenient? A warning bell in my head is going off like the clappers.

Creepy. Creepy. Creepy.

But what choice do I have? I glance back at the dead, stranded car and pull a face. Creepy hotel or wait until it gets light? The way the car is positioned on the road, I could kill somebody if another car comes around the bend.

Mind made up, I ignore my screaming self-preservation instincts and turn back to the car. It shouldn't be too much of a push. Right?

As I hurry back up the grassy road, I realise there is a slight incline I didn't notice. That's handy. I might be able to freeroll the car into the driveway. That's if the fancy car's steering works without power. Otherwise, I'm going to overshoot the driveway and find myself stuffed into a hedge.

So much fun, I think with a manic smile as I clap my hands. "In for a penny, in for a pound," I mutter. I will say a lot about Mum, but she raised me and my sisters to be tenacious. All the Larson women are stubborn as hell. So, thanks to Mum, I am not a damsel in distress.

I dump the keys in the closest cup holder so my hands are free, and I take a peek at Daisy. Her hot breath fogs in adorable puffs against the travel bubble. She is curled in a ball, and thankfully fast asleep.

Then, like I've seen in films, I brace myself against the open door frame. *Come on, Tuesday.* My boots dig into the uneven tarmac as I give the car a good push.

Nothing happens. I groan, jump back into the car, and put the car in first gear. That might help. I get back into position. *Films make this look so easy.* I growl, get a little mad, and *push* the car with all my might. Just as my poor shoulder begins to scream in protest, the wheels move, inch by tiny inch, and then the car is rolling.

Yay, it is moving!

It quickly picks up speed. Crap, it's rolling pretty fast! I squeak and fling myself into the driver's seat. I am almost settled inside when the car door slams closed, cracking against my right shin, which is still dangling in the road. Ouch. The stupid bloody thing. I stuff my leg inside and ignore the urge to give it a rub.

Instead, I grit my teeth and tug like mad on the steering wheel. The wheels dry grind on the tarmac and the car *eeks* its way to the left. *Come on. Come on.* Without meaning to, as my eyes are firmly on the looming menace of a hedge, I clip the kerb and the bounce puts us dead centre on the hotel's driveway.

We roll into the empty car park. The front wheels bump into another kerb, stalling the car's now slower momentum, and the car settles into a parking space. Perfectly between the lines.

Wow.

CHAPTER EIGHT

My heart is pounding from the adrenaline of my epic car push and coasting antics. I lift my arm and kiss my bicep. I am so She-Ra. I have the urge to bellow "I have the power" while wildly waving my arms about. Oh, or was that He-Man? My face scrunches in a frown. Meh, who cares? I bet few people have pushed a car by themselves.

The car park is dimly lit with ground level lights that highlight the crumbling path up to the hotel. Why didn't I see the lights from the road? The hedges weren't that thick. Even though the lights are dim, they should have been visible.

I vigorously rub my forehead. I find this all hard to deal with. Nothing makes sense. I know something wacky is going on, but I have no idea what, and interpreting this shite is beyond me. I am almost at my limit. I've spent hours driving, frightened half to death that I am going to crash the car, and my whole body aches. The need for a locked door, a bath, and a good night's sleep thrums through me.

In the light of day, everything will be better.

Hottie hellhound mentioned my coven will meet me at the safe house, so my mum is at the end of this wonderful drive. Yeap. I huff. I am not in the mood to deal with her, and I can't be arsed with her passive aggressive bullshit. So, if I can leave that confrontation until tomorrow... now that would be a billy bonus. I can so risk a stay in a creepy hotel to avoid Mum.

Perhaps Dad can come and get me in the morning? Something inside of me dips and I rub my thigh and pick at some imaginary fluff on my black jogging bottoms. No. No, he won't. I will ring the hire car company in the morning and get them to fix the car. I lean across, and from my yellow jacket hung on the back of the passenger seat, I grab a handful of potions and stuff them into my pockets. I need to be ready for anything.

Typical spaghetti western music *bow-wow-bow-wow-wow* chimes through my head as I then pull out a plastic blue and orange toy gun and blow on it.

No longer She-Ra, I'm now Clint Eastwood.

Instead of underwear, Forrest left this and a bunch of weapons in the suitcase. With a helpful scrawled note to add a sleep potion to the foam bullets.

Wow, just wow.

The woman is a scary, evil genius.

I am glad I added the potion before I left, so the gun is good to go. Many creatures carry weapons, but not guns. Guns are licenced and heavily regulated. There is also this strange thing of honour between creatures where it's all blood and blades. Oh, and not to mention the many spells and nasty potions that will melt your face clean off and turn you inside out. Go witches.

For all our technological advancements, I don't think we've ever made it out of the dark ages. So, guns are a big no-no. Not that this is a real gun. My grip tightens on the plastic. I have no idea if a toy gun wielding a sleep potion is illegal. If caught with it, I might be in a huge amount of trouble. Like I care. I don't know how my aim will measure up anyway, but I am willing to try anything if the shit hits the fan. I'm not a fighter, and I am a crap magic user. But after meeting the scary elf, I will take whatever I can get.

I slide out of the car, and as soon as I put weight on my right leg, my poor calf throbs. I glare at the offending car door and slam it closed a little harder than necessary. *Bloody door.* I nod, feeling vindicated with the car now suitably chastised. I hobble around to the passenger side to get Daisy.

Like I've seen in films, I stuff the toy gun within easy reach behind my back, tucked into my waistband. When I take a step, the elastic pings and the gun slides down the back of my trousers and clocks me on the ankle. I roll my eyes, stand on one leg and jiggle until it pops out of the bottom and clatters to the ground. I tighten the string on the jogging bottoms and put it in my pocket.

"I have the power," I grumble as I struggle to lift the small suitcase from the footwell. With a grunt, I drag it out and then tap Daisy's travel bubble. The magic swirls and it rises from the seat. As I move away from the car, it floats in the air behind me.

I wish I had the same magic for the suitcase, I think as I hobble down the wonky path. I hobble, smack, hobble, smack. With each stride, the damn thing bounces in the ruts and smacks against my leg. The sore one. I grit my teeth, lift my eyes, and take in the hotel. The Sanctuary appears to be a gatehouse to a stately home. A squat, mini castle. It even has—I'll have to Google the name—a flat roof with the castle-like square spikes along the pitch. I bet it once had a turret.

Even in the dark, I can see the rundown state of it, which makes me sad. The place could be incredibly beautiful, but it would take some serious money to restore it and give it the modern twist it needs, while retaining its history. That might be why someone turned it into a hotel, in an attempt to get it to pay for itself. But the whole place screams money pit.

About twelve feet from the door, the heavens open and I am pelted with freezing cold Scottish rain. I'm instantly drenched. I can't feel my face. With rain dribbling down the back of my neck, I mournfully think of the warm waterproof coat I left in the car as I scurry the final few feet to the door. With relief, it opens and I hurry inside.

I wrinkle my nose as I am instantly hit by the odour of feet. Nice.

The interior is as sad as the exterior; they have ripped the heart out of this poor old building. I see touches of grandeur peeking out, screaming for restoration. I shake my head and hobble to the wooden reception desk and ring the bell.

As I wait for someone to come, my eyes drift back around the room. What a waste. If I could draw, or had an aptitude for math, I would have loved to have been an architect or a designer. I guess life impedes your passions.

I smile and shake my head. Whenever a new housing development pops up, I can't help having a nosy at their floor plans.

I can spend hours on the internet going through the drawings and analysing the room shapes, mentally redesigning the layouts or appreciating clever designs. I know it's nuts. Looking at building plans is a weird hobby, but I like it. I once spent an entire month studying a manor house that had been converted into fancy apartments. Wow, they did an incredible job.

Building my own home is definitely on my bucket list. Sometimes to get to sleep when my brain is too busy from work, I build houses in my head. It's a quirk. I guess everyone has some strange thing they do. I haven't got the skills to build a house, but it doesn't stop me from mentally doing it anyway. It comforts me enough to sleep. I drum my fingers on the desk and try to peek through the tucked away staff door. I'll give them a few more minutes before I ring the bell again.

There is this one particular building I design over and over again. I've landscaped it into a perfect world. It has beautiful windows and a lake and mountain views. I turn and slump against the desk and... funny, I can almost see it being adapted to this hotel. I rub my face and groan. Look at me in a smelly hotel reception area, dreaming.

A throat clears behind me. I squeak and spin around.

"Hi." I wave. "I didn't hear you." Rainwater drips from the sleeve of my jumper and plops onto the floor. Oops.

"It happens all the time." The receptionist, or night manager—whatever his job title—smiles.

He could be between thirty and sixty. His age doesn't show clearly on his face. That isn't unusual in this world. As a witch, I will age the same as a human. Quickly. Witch's lives are fleeting compared to the creatures that live alongside us. Shifters and born vampires are practically immortal. So meeting someone with an unageing face and ancient eyes isn't far from the norm. But my wacky magic is screaming at me that something is off about this guy.

That is disconcerting.

I surreptitiously check his ears for the tell-tale point of an elf. But his ears are rounded. He isn't a shifter and there isn't the distinctive smell of rot that I associate with turned vampires.

But still, he feels off.

Fae? His dark red hair gleams under the lights and the longer I stand there, staring at him like a proper weirdo, the more his dull green eyes brighten. They sparkle with excitement. This isn't him putting on a show and being polite to a customer—no, it is genuine.

Joy.

Maybe that's my problem? I am so used to people not being impressed when they see me. Perhaps his beaming smile is throwing me off completely.

The negative voice in my head that I usually associate with my mum tells me to sleep in the car. But my inner voice, the one that I always stubbornly listen to, purrs with contentment. It's like I have come home.

What the heck is that all about?

"Hi." My hand flaps again in a feeble wave. It's as if my limb has a mind of its own. I pin it to my side and smile sheepishly.

"You're here. Finally," he says with poorly veiled glee. He claps his hands. The guy is practically bouncing on the spot. He is positively glowing. "I can't believe it—"

"Oh no, you must have me confused with someone else," I quickly interrupt. Oh heck, now

I feel bad. I don't want to be the reason that his glowy smile leaves his face. "My car broke down." I point lamely over my shoulder, in the direction of the car park. "Yeah, the power of the car got sucked right out. Even my phone stopped working." I narrow my eyes.

"Oh... well, okay." He scratches his nose. "That explains a lot," he mutters, but then he beams a warm smile at me and claps his hands again. "Let's get you booked in. I presume you're staying and don't want to just use the phone?"

"Yes, please. I'll stay for the night."

"Perfect, that's perfect." He spins and pulls a key from the old-fashioned key hooks hanging on the wall. Twelve rooms. The key from the number one hook is missing, which means there might be another guest. He places the key to room twelve on the desk and then drops to a crouch.

My hand strays to my pocket with the sleeping gun. What is he doing? As I rise on my toes to peer over the desk to see what he is up to, he pops back up with a—I frown—I can only describe it as a tome. It smacks down so hard that the desk vibrates.

What the heck is that?

Has this guy never heard of a computer? No wonder the place is so quiet. Wide-eyed, I stare at the enormous book.

The old spine creaks as he opens it to a blank page, and as he spins it towards me, dust and god knows what sprinkles onto the desk. I wrinkle my nose.

"If you would just pop down your name and sign here." He points to a spot and places a pen next to the book.

I shimmy forward and glance down at where his finger is indicating.

"Here?" I ask with a frown.

I read fiction; I don't read tome or whatever the heck this is. *Should I really be signing my name into an ancient-looking book?* Urm, no.

No, I should not.

Crap. I can feel my whole body ache with disappointment. It seems we will be sleeping in the car. I wish I had a human-sized version of Daisy's travel bubble. I open my mouth to make an excuse and then—

I'm signing the stupid book. What the fuck? What happened? I blink a few times and take the offered key. I blink again and then I am standing in a clean but shabby room. Which thankfully doesn't smell of feet.

What the heck just happened? Was that magic?

The same magic that messed up the car and the phone? I sink to the bed and put my head in my hands. "I've gone and done it now. Signed my life away. Demons. I bet demons are involved." I shudder. "My parents are going to kill me." Ha, the first thing that comes to mind is the inevitable "I told you so" lecture from my parents, not dying horribly. "I am seriously fudged up."

Then there is this feeling, an inner feeling of being safe, of being home.

I've never felt that.

Wow, now that's sad. I've never felt safe or content, no matter how successful I have become professionally. I've always felt something is off, missing, and that I am... in the wrong place. Now everything inside me screams I'm okay. Here is where I am meant to be.

I flop back onto the bed. I know a lot about magic. Even though I am a dud, I'm still a witch. I have felt the worst kind of magic as it trips my tongue and controls my words. My fists clench. Yeah, thanks to my mum, I have had years of a potion working on my mind, so I can tell when I am artificially being controlled. I can feel it. This isn't that. No matter how powerful magic can be, it can't alter what you feel inside. Your inner voice.

I pluck at the covers and my eyes trace the lines of a dark blob on the ceiling. I need to be honest; it wasn't magic that made me sign that book—well, not outside magic anyway—it was something inside me. My face scrunches up. I think it was like, inner me took hold of my body, took me for a joy ride for a few minutes. I shake my head and blow out a breath.

And isn't that freaky?

What I feel about this place is genuine. It must be. But that doesn't mean I am going to be an idiot and walk around blindly. No, it just means I am going to find out what the heck is going on.

Tomorrow.

With a tired groan, I get up. I pull the plastic gun from my pocket and pop it on the bedside table within easy reach.

Even though I feel like crap and my head is swimming with fatigue, I'm also feeling icky from the long car journey, so I run myself a bath. I don't have a bathtub in my flat, so having a long soak is a well-deserved treat.

Before I strip off, I dig out a temporary ward and set it up to protect the entire room. It's a strong one, with both Diane and Jodie's combined magic. At least if anything untoward happens, I will have a warning as the ward will wake me up.

I check the floor for safety, making sure there's nothing hidden that could hurt Daisy, and then I touch her travel bubble and the door opens. Inside, my little dragon is adorably snoring.

When she wakes up, she'll be able to come in and out as she pleases. Though, knowing Daisy, she'll wait till the very last moment to pee, so I set the bubble close to the bathroom and use another tray and remaining shavings for a temporary dragon toilet before also setting up her food and water.

I then fiddle with the phone. Miraculously, it works.

Hi Owen, it's Tuesday. I am safe, but the car died. I think it's an electric issue. I didn't crash it! I'm staying the night at The Sanctuary Hotel. It's about thirty minutes from the safe house. Will you do me a favour and let my coven know?

The phone you gave me also has an issue and it keeps dying. I will use the hotel phone to ring my dad in the morning. Thank you x

I quickly press send before the phone can decide to quit and the message wings its way into the ether.

Ah crap. I wince when I re-read it. The kiss at the end. *A kiss.* I groan and rub the back of my neck. Why did I do that? I added it on without thinking. I nibble on my nail. Of course, it's gone now. *Then* the stupid phone flashes and the screen goes grey. It shuts down. Dead.

Gah. I tap the phone against my thigh as I rub my face. At least he knows where I am, right? In my mind's eye, I see Miss Piggy dramatically blow a kiss to an unimpressed Kermit while saying kissy-kissy-kissy. A kiss on a text is friendly, right? With another wince and a helpless shrug, I stuff the phone away.

I groan at the splash in the steamy bathroom and the echoing flap of wet wings. "Oh, it sounds like it is dragonette bath time," I grumble. "I hope they've given me a lot of towels. We're going to need them."

Before I enter the bath battlefield, I drop to my knees and open the suitcase. I push the knives Forrest has packed for me to the side. Who needs six silver blades and two iron ones, but no underwear? That woman has serious issues.

I pop a knife on the bedside table and empty my pockets of all potions, lining them up for easy throwing, just in case.

A small giggle of disbelief slips from my lips as I grab some fluffy, pink *unicorn* pyjamas. Although they are adorable, I would never in a million years buy them for myself.

Knives and unicorns. Forrest seems really weird.

CHAPTER NINE

I dreamed of a world that I painstakingly pieced together using my architect visions of perfection, from elegant rooms to the minute detail of a single blade of grass. It was glorious.

When I wake up in the cloud-like bed, I feel odd and heavy. As if my conscience has returned to my body. I am so comfortable, I immediately want to go back to sleep. There is a clink next to my ear as if a plate has been carefully set down on the bedside table, the one closest to my head.

That is when I smell the bacon.

I groan and turn my head to where the smell originates. I wiggle like a worm as I unbury myself from underneath the covers. Peeking out, I sniff, and the scent of delicious, crispy bacon flies up my now flaring nostrils.

On the bedside table, placed carefully between potions and the plastic gun, is a toasted bacon butty, and a mug of steaming tea.

I blink.

A bead of tomato ketchup rolls down the crust and plops onto the plate. Oh my, that looks amazing. That has got to be Warburtons Toastie bread.

Where the heck did that come from?

I hold my breath for a second and wait for movement. Empty. No one is here. "Has someone been in my room? I knew this whole place was sketchy." When you freakily sign an ancient tome to stay at a mysterious hotel and later almost have a panic attack 'cause you might have signed your life away, nowhere in that nightmare scenario would I have expected crispy bacon and a cup of tea.

My tummy gurgles as if to say, *mmm bacon.* I blink a few more times and rub away the pool of drool before it reaches my chin. It is then that I notice the room. My drool hand flops onto the bed and my mouth falls open in shock. My head swivels. Instead of it being a rundown nightmare, it is like I am in a six-star hotel or a gazillion pound apartment. My entire face scrunches up with a frown. Well, this is unexpected.

Bloody hell. I fling the covers away and scramble up. But I forget how to use my legs and instead sort of roll out of bed. I slide ungraciously to the floor, the soft spongy carpet cushioning my bottom. Wide-eyed and with my heart pounding, stomach forgotten, I stare at the room.

The room that is mine.

Mine.

More than mine—it's bloody what I made up in my head. What I have dreamed of for years. Outside, through the new floor-to-ceiling windows, are familiar rolling hills, a distant forest and... a lake.

"This is fudged up."

In my sleep, I reshaped a world.

I gasp. Then wheeze.

Woah, I cannot get enough air into my lungs. I rub and slap my palm to my chest. *Breathe, Tuesday, you will not lose your shit.* Black dots appear in my vision, dancing in front of my eyes. I am losing my shit. *Calm down and just think.* I viciously pinch the skin on the top of my hand and wince. Ouch. Yeah, I'm awake. This isn't a dream—no, it's magic.

My whole body shivers.

"It's not like you are being attacked by Power Ranger mercenaries," I reason. I am not in any immediate danger, and no one is breaking down my door. Instead of jumping up and running around the room like a chicken with its head cut off, I take a deep breath, hold it, and slowly breathe out. I concentrate on breathing until my heart rate is back to a regular rhythm and my body has stopped twitching with the need to run. *Panicking only gets you hurt,* I remind myself.

I grab the plate from the side and take a big bite of the breakfast sandwich. Why the heck not? The bacon crunches, and as the greasy taste hits my tongue, I groan. It's made perfectly.

As I chew, I do my best to push away my initial shock. I don't know how I know it, but I do. Now that I can think a little bit clearer, I can *feel* the magic. Somehow, I did this. This is *my magic.*

Bloody hell.

I've gone from a magic dud to being full to the brim. I can't work out if this is a dream come true or my worst nightmare. Magic that I have never had is pounding through my chest, zipping down my arms and legs. The hand not stuffing my face taps my head to make sure my hair isn't standing on end. It is like I have stuffed my finger in a light socket, and I'm being electrocuted. It is as if I am now part of an electric circuit.

I grab the tea and take a big gulp. I think back to what the fae guy said. The elf. *Hello, little lost witch. I am told you're a dud, but you're more than that, aren't you? Your coven has hidden you well.* I pop the last bite of the butty into my mouth. *It's been over a century since I've met one of your kind in the real world. Stupid of you, really.*

"Your coven has hidden you well," I mumble. Well, he got that wrong. My coven—my parents— didn't hide me from this. Oh no, this would be the equivalent of my mum winning a rollover in the National Lottery. "Real world?" I sip the tea and lean back against the bed. As I roll the words around my head—*real world*—I rap my fingernails against the mug and stare down into the tea. The remaining liquid dances to the rhythm of my fingers. Perhaps he wasn't blowing smoke. Perhaps he got something right.

Daisy's claws dig into the soft carpet as she moves toward me, a piece of cucumber gripped between her teeth. It's her favourite snack. A snack that appeared just like my breakfast. She climbs into my lap, joining me in the impromptu picnic on the floor, and noisily crunches.

A world I created. Like... like *a pocket realm.* No.

There is an odd, unpleasant little jump in my chest. No. Whoever made pocket dimensions didn't make them this big. I huff in disbelief. Small rooms and bags to hide equipment. Not... I lean forward and stare out at the forest, at the hills and the bloody lake. Acres and acres of land. Whatever the heck this is, it cannot be that.

Yet, I know every inch of this place. For years, I have been building this in my head. There's no getting away from the fact that I made this.

I rub my face and shake my head. They are a myth.

World walkers, world makers.

Godlike power.

My stomach is suddenly full of butterflies, and I can't help shivering as the small hairs on my body all rise at once.

Everything about them has been conjecture.

Witches—we can make portals, fixed doorways linking places together using the Earth's ley lines. But someone before us made portals to other worlds. That knowledge was said to be lost. Some people said it died with some extinct creature. Others, mainly the witches, said it was a branch of magic that had become extinct.

The only sign of their existence was what they left behind: pocket dimensions. Which are coveted and go for vast sums of money. I stare back outside. To think, as soon as my car rolled down the driveway, I wasn't in Scotland anymore. Goosebumps erupt along my arms. Portals, pocket dimensions, and artificial magic worlds are strange places. If a creature is strong enough and magically tied to it, the dimension can shift and change. But not to this extent. This is so far beyond the small, sad hotel and scrabbly patch of land of last night.

My tummy flips again. I rub my arms, the fluffy pink unicorn pyjamas rise with the movement and my breath catches as— "What now?" I whine.

I stare at my arms. My skin is covered with magical tattoos.

Glowing tattoos.

I gently place the still munching dragon on the carpet and scramble up. I hurry into the bathroom, pull off the unicorn top and peek into the opulent mirror. Glowing silver lines curve complex patterns across my entire body. I cautiously lean into the mirror and trace the delicate dancing swirls on *my face.*

In shock, I stare at myself for several minutes.

Instead of detracting, they highlight my cheekbones and light up my eyes like the best kind of makeup. I don't hate them. *It is like they always should have been there.* No, that is crazy thinking. I back away from the mirror and my naked back hits the cold tiles.

I am frightened but I can't escape the facts. This hotel, this place, this world? Has made *me* magical.

Ha. My mum is going to shit a brick.

CHAPTER TEN

I decide to explore the hotel and get some answers. I have my trusty sleep pistol after all. Which will probably be useless to anyone who can wield magic that can change a world and procure bacon on toast with Heinz tomato ketchup.

Tuesday, it's you. It's your magic. I ignore that pesky inner voice for a moment as I need to hunt for answers, and although this fancy apartment is amazing, I can't stay here and hide. No, I need to get dressed.

Find answers.

The wardrobe has changed from the hotel's basic one to a full walk-in, and it's full to the brim with clothes.

Like the bacon butty, I don't know where these clothes came from. I glance back at the mug and plate I left carelessly on the floor. They've disappeared. The hotel is self-cleaning. Aha. That is perfectly normal.

With wide eyes and slightly hunched shoulders, I turn back, and without going inside, I cautiously poke at the clothes. They sway, and the wooden hangers rattle and screech against the rail.

Has someone, somewhere, found their clothes missing this morning? Do they disappear from individuals? Is this where missing socks go? Or is some poor retail manager going to find that they have missing stock?

It's. Magic.

It's got to be magic. So, that then begs the question: if I wear magic clothing, will it leave me naked in the outside world? What happens if someone slaps me with another null band again? Will the clothes disappear like magic hair colour? Gah, so many questions. I am developing a headache.

I blow out a harsh breath that ruffles a strand of my hair, then push all my questions to the back of my mind. I shuffle into the wardrobe and take a proper gander at the clothes.

I work in a department store that's full of designer gear. I have an eye for quality. I can't help the excited shiver that runs down my spine when I see my favourites. Favourite styles, brands—this is clothing that I could never afford or stuff that I have talked myself out of buying.

I pull out a drawer. It is filled to the brim with expensive underwear.

Within moments, I whip off my unicorn pyjamas. I dress in soft, black trousers and a beautiful, long-sleeved but lightweight top that has a colourful butterfly print. Girly, but also professional, and the trousers are a perfect fit. There is no need for me to dress so smartly; I could put on the jogging bottoms I wore yesterday and a hoodie. But what I am wearing feels right. Power dressing? I shrug. Perhaps.

To finish the look, I grab a pair of black, sparkly trainers. Practical footwear in case I need to run. I think I have already established that I won't be doing any Kung Fu fighting. So getaway shoes are a must. As I stuff my feet in them, I notice they are Gucci. Gucci trainers.

This is nuts.

I leave Daisy to nap. I need her safe in the room. As I close the main door, I double-check the ward. Again, I have no idea how it's still up. What with the room being about six times bigger and all. But it is still there, still working. It will stop any creature from getting inside.

Not for the first time, I fret about leaving her alone. One day soon, I will get my girl a friend.

* * *

I pull the heavy door and step into a very different lobby. My heart makes a quiet leap in my chest. Old and new now mash perfectly together, leaving a breathtakingly beautiful entrance to the hotel. If this magic is all me, I reeeally have outdone myself. Seeing in real life what I have dreamed of for so long is seriously perplexing.

"Where's the guy?" I mumble as I take in the empty reception.

"Larry? He's gone," says a refined voice behind me. I barely refrain from jumping out of my skin and instead, hunch like a tortoise as I try to disappear into a non-existent shell. I spin around.

"Oh," I say when I see the man who is sitting in a chair behind me. Where did he come from? I don't know what to say. I presume this is the guest from room number one. He seems oddly familiar. Short, black hair that matches his black eyes, his skin is almost plastic in its perfection. He looks alien, like he is a walking mannequin.

Pureblood vampire, my frightened inner voice whines.

A born vampire.

I lock my knees so I don't take a step back. *Show no fear, Tuesday. You're his walking, talking version of a bacon butty.* I swallow and try my best to control my breathing. In my mind's eye, I can see myself covered in ketchup and slapped between two slices of bread. I shudder and push the freaky image away.

These past few days have been an eye-opener when it comes to creatures. An elf, a hellhound, and now a pureblood vampire.

I so didn't need to add vampires to the crazy mix.

I have definitely seen him before, but where? TV? Born vampires are rare and most of them are famous. They are the elite, often the top movie stars of our world. *Atticus.* My eyes widen when his name comes to me. What is the head of the vampire council doing here? This guy is super old, super powerful, and way above any experience I have in dealing with all things creature.

I am getting a little freaked out by his cold, expressionless, black eyes as they take me in, his gaze tracing the swirls on my face. I rock slightly from foot to foot and tamp down the urge to hide my face with my hair. Thank goodness I dressed nicely. When he has finished his appraisal, he politely holds his hand out to me.

I automatically shake it. It's warm and silky smooth.

"Atticus," he says with a little bow of his head. I barely stop myself from checking his feet to see if he clapped them together.

He is so formal.

"Tuesday. Tuesday Larson." I cough slightly to clear my throat. My voice is several octaves higher than normal. "You are the head of the vampire council," I point out like a divvy, but I can't stop now as I am on a roll. I decide to wing it even more like I always do. "What are you doing here?"

Has he been lured here too? Or did he do the luring? Crikey, now that's a thought.

"I'm your guest," he purrs. "The Sanctuary is my permanent residence, has been for over a thousand years. With you here, your realm should finally be able to return to the collective of dimensions."

Blood rushes to my head, and I wobble. What? My realm? The collective of dimensions? Crap-on-a-cracker. I have so many questions that I am practically bursting. I guess I need to start small. If I don't, my brain is going to explode.

Should I even trust this man? "It's a pocket dimension?"

"A pocket realm." *Ah, I was close then; one point to Tuesday.* "This is your world, your dimension. It became yours as soon as you arrived and took control. You control the air we breathe, the seasons, and everything we see and hear. There is nothing you can't do."

Atticus moves closer, and I watch, dumbfounded, as he slowly reaches out his hand and gently, with just his fingertips, touches my collar bone. My skin crawls. I barely refrain from slapping his hand away. "The well of power that laps like an immense silver ocean inside of you has been untapped. After a few scant hours of being here, it has come to the surface. A single drop of power while you slept and look what has already happened." He waves his elegant hand in the air. "See what you have achieved without even trying. You are incredible."

This isn't happening. It's not happening. This can't be real, can it?

An incredulous laugh bubbles up in my chest and spills from my lips. I shake my head as I move away from his fingers, and twitch with the urge to wipe away the feeling of his touch. I don't like the strange vampire touching me. His head tilts to the side with a snap and my laughter dies. Friggity-fig, he is scary.

I suddenly wish I was staring into the soft grey eyes of the hellhound, instead of this creature. His black eyes remind me of a shark.

"How is this realm mine? Oh, and have you by any chance got a contact I can speak to about this?" I know I can't quiz a pureblood vampire like I would a random man from the pub. But the desperate words will not stop. "The collective dimensions?" I squeak out with a wince. *Shut up. You are being rude.*

Atticus's black eyes narrow. "I have to say, your cluelessness is endearing." He nods at the tome that still sits on the now fancy reception desk. This one sure appears steadier than the last. "You have a lot of reading to do. When the last host died"—I mouth the word *host*. Huh. Interesting—"the magic allowed me to continue to make The Sanctuary my home. There are other hosts, other worlds, and a guild."

"A guild?"

"The details will be in the book."

I glare at the book. Do I really have to read that thing? It will take me a year. I rub my temple. The heavy tome twitches. I narrow my eyes. What was that? The pages flutter and, with a creak, the ancient-looking thing rattles harder against the wood. Woah. The book wobbles and then, with a flash of blinding white magic, a fancy tablet appears in its place.

I rapidly blink.

The vampire grunts. "Interesting," he mutters. I cringe and give him a hapless shrug. Done with our conversation, he dismisses me with the same nod he greeted me with and prowls away.

I watch him leave with growing panic. "Oh, urm... sir? Urm... Atticus!" I yell. "Do I need to do anything? For you, I mean... I've never run a h-hotel before. Do you need t-towels?"

His head turns and his lips sort of tilt in a semblance of a teeny, tiny smile. "Your magic will meet my needs. Read the—" He shakes his head. "That." He points to the desk and disappears down the hallway.

"Okay, thank you." My hands flap to my sides and I turn to take a hesitant step toward the innocuous-looking tablet. "Ooookay," I grumble.

I shuffle closer to the desk and scoop it up. It is a datapad, a ZS-T, which is the latest model. I turn on the screen and wait impatiently, drumming my fingers on the desk. "Thanks for explaining everything, *Larry.*" My top lip lifts in a snarl. Is this place so bad that he did not want to stick around to tell me what's what? Not even a basic handover. As soon as I got my room key, he must have scarpered. No wonder he looked so happy.

The screen of the datapad remains blank. Did I break it? I press the power button a few more times.

"I broke it," I mutter. What the heck am I going to do now? My heart feels like it drops through my chest. What do I do now?

I'm playing with this magic—unknown, powerful magic. I have no idea what the hell I am doing.

The magic just randomly does shit.

I'm so out of my depth... The datapad brightens and a cursor blinks. My mouth pops open as I watch the letters appear.

It writes: '*Hello, Tuesday. What would you like to know?*' The cursor blinks and my hand hovers, frozen over the screen.

Uh-oh. If that isn't the creepiest thing I have ever seen.

CHAPTER ELEVEN

I stare at the datapad as I nibble my lip. Huh, now that's interesting. I trace my bottom lip with my tongue. It's not sore like it was last night. I frown. When I went to sleep, it was a chapped mess. I must have healed overnight. I rub my chest, puff out my cheeks, and ignore it for now. It's such a small thing when compared to all the magic stuff.

Now back to the tablet that knows my name. What the heck do I type? I huff and strum the desk. "I need to know everything," I mumble.

'You need to be a bit more exact.'

I almost drop the datapad with shock. Wide-eyed, I gently set it down. I can't help the small, manic laugh that spills from my mouth. I poke and pull at my healed lip, squishing it between my thumb and finger. I don't even have to type; the tome slash datapad is listening and has a sense of humour. *Good to know.* Clinging to the reception desk, I shuffle stiffly sideways from the haunted tablet. The cursor on the datapad blinks a little faster.

I clear my throat. "Um, is someone here trying to hurt me?"

'No,' is the curt reply.

I clear my throat again. My mouth is so dry, the salty bacon from breakfast has made me thirsty. I have bacon tongue. The tell-tale clack of a cup and sudden heat next to my hand causes me to drop my eyes to the desk to see a fresh, steaming mug of tea.

Oh boy, they really do pop out of thin air. "Thank you," I say with a nervous squeak. I shrug, pick up the tea, and take a big gulp. Fun fact: I regularly thank inanimate objects. Like cash machines. I've even been known to have entire conversations with a difficult mannequin at work. Unless you've dressed one of those things, you have no idea how awkward the limbs are. So, saying thanks to the magic—magic that works for me for the first time in my life—is the polite thing to do.

Oh! Am I a genie? Is this pocket world like a genie's bottle? If my magic can just make things appear, does that mean hotel guests get three wishes? I huff out a strangled laugh. A genie isn't a creature that exists in this world. I rub my forehead a little too vigorously. Now I know I'm overthinking things. If I am not careful, it won't be long before I'm rocking in a corner and crying.

I clutch the mug and take another mouthful. The tea is delicious.

Oh crap, another thought hits me. I hope I'm talking to the magic, or what was once the book. I don't think I could bear it if Larry, the manager guy from last night, is hidden in a secret room somewhere, watching me and laughing his arse off.

I lean both elbows on the desk. Staying here wouldn't be too horrendous. I'm an introvert at heart. A homebody. I like to be in my own space, doing my own thing. But that still doesn't help the worry in my chest. I have commitments. I mean, what about work? I've been the company superstar since I started at sixteen. I have the lofty accolade of being the youngest general manager in the company's history.

Eight years. Eight bloody years. So much time and effort wasted if I walk away. I huff. I've never even taken a sick day. What are they going to think when I give them zero notice? Oh, this is just awful. Maybe I can somehow take the magic with me? I take another sip of tea.

Yeah, I like being at home but there is a big difference between choosing to stay at home, and not being allowed to leave.

"Am I trapped?"

'No, you are not trapped.'

Okay. So, no one is saying I can't leave, and it's not like I'm stuck in a room on my own. The realm is beautiful. There is an entire world outside the hotel, miles and miles to explore. That's kind of amazing.

Out of the corner of my eye, the damn datapad cursor blinks impatiently.

But... I hate change. I hate the unknown. I hate bloody magic. I hate this entire situation.

"If I leave, what will happen?"

'The realm will go into stasis to wait for another host. Over time, it will slowly crumble until nothing remains.

You will live the life you had before as a mortal witch. The magic that you have inside you will be untouchable on the outside. If you stay, power beyond your wildest dreams, omnipotent magic, and immortality.'

Oh. I blink in time with the cursor. Isn't that how supervillains are made? *Great.* Or superheroes...

'If you leave, so does your new magic.'

If I leave, I return to being the dud witch. Well, that is not something I want to do. Does that make me a bad person? I also don't want to be trapped in a pocket dimension forever. And immortality? That's a scary can of worms.

Maybe I am in a coma, and this isn't real. Maybe it's some wacky, made up dream. I rub the reception desk with my index finger and finish the tea. It feels real.

It feels right.

Leaving all this behind is unfathomable. I tilt my head back and take in the beautiful lobby. I don't need to gaze outside to know this place is perfect. I put myself—my soul—into the fabric of this realm. Even if I didn't know what I was doing at the time.

This is where I'm meant to be. I can run away back to my flat, back to my not-so-perfect life, or I can be brave, explore this strange new magic, and find out who I am.

Grab a hold of my destiny.

I shiver. Wow, I'm not so much a sidekick anymore, am I?

"How does this work? How do we get guests?"

'You help the people who are in search of sanctuary.'

"That simple, huh?" I gripe. "What about bad people? Can my magic handle creatures popping in all willy-nilly?" *It could be millions of people.* I'm twenty-four. I don't think my retail management training covers running an entire world. Nervous sweat trickles down between my shoulder blades.

'It's your dimension, your rules,' it types. The words run together in my mind. The whoosh

and thud-thud of my heart overwhelm my senses. I feel sick. How the hell am I going to do this? A whole bloody world. This magic isn't supposed to exist. I can't do this. I hate magic.

The reality of everything hits me with the force of a double-decker bus. I ignore the magic tablet and push away from the desk.

"Fuck." The swear word echoes around the lobby, and I slam a shaky hand across my lips. What the heck was that? Did I just swear out loud? Crikey, the anti-swear spell my mum had forced upon me must have broken.

My brain must have healed like my lip.

A painful hiccup jolts me. The spell is *broken.* "The spell that's been the bane of my life is gone." I flick my fingers. "Just like that."

It's not the only thing that's broken.

A strangled half laugh, half sob bubbles up my throat along with another blasted hiccup that rattles my chest. "This is wank," I whisper. The naughty word feels alien on my tongue. "Wankity, wank, wank, wank." With each swear word, my voice gets a little louder, shriller, until the last word and I'm screaming. "WANK!" I shove both hands over my mouth to hold the craziness in.

Oh my, I'm going mad.

My legs are so wobbly, I can't take a step. I can't get away. Instead, for the second time today, like a sack of spuds, I sink to the floor. I slam my back against the desk and clutch my knees to my chest.

Why me?

I have learned to live with my lack of magic. I came to terms with my mediocrity years ago. I have finally got a handle on my life, and I am content with the person I am. So what if I don't have a talent? I've never been good at anything, but that's okay. I'm good at my job. I'm a wonderful manager. A nice person.

Now everything has changed again. The goalposts have moved to another bloody dimension.

Why? Everything was going okay. Why did I have to have a sneaky hidden power that comes out of nowhere to ruin my perfectly boring life? Why did I get hit with the weird shit? *I will always be on the outside of the supernatural world. Always the freak.*

I shake my head, and my hair rustles as it rubs against the wood at my back. *Magic.* It will always misbehave and cause me no end of frustration. There is no escape. There has never been an escape. I am doomed.

Most people presume I'm human. I still get the odd, "Oh, you're a witch. What type of magic do you do?" How do you answer that? Say, "Yeah, I am the famous Larson witch who can't do magic, so nothing." It embarrasses them, or worse, the opposite thing happens, and they use that knowledge to belittle me.

In the real world, magic is used for everything. Technology, medicine, silly frivolous things like altering your hair, down to the fit of your clothes. Even as a non-practising witch, my life revolves around it. I cannot avoid it. I must use it in everyday life as it is integrated into the fabric of our society. It's an essential thing, like electricity.

I have learned to grin and bear it. But every time I use someone else's bottled magic, I get this crawling sensation in my gut.

Disgust.

Every time, I hate myself a little bit more. 'Cause the obvious screams at me: *I am not good enough. I never have been good enough.*

It's torture knowing if I had been born a little differently, I'd be capable of creating my own spells. Not buying them—and sure as hell not blowing them up.

I rock a little and rub my forehead on my knee. I thought I'd escaped. I thought I could ignore it. Embrace my beloved outcast role in life. I had that false smile fixed to perfection. "People can only hurt you if you let them" was my mantra. I isolated myself from the witch community, my parents, and my super talented sisters. I put myself in an emotional bubble. All safe.

"I was doing okay. Everything was finally going okay," I whine into my knees. Well, until those damn Power Ranger mercenaries bashed in my front door.

Now here I am, *buzzing with power*.

Buzzing with enough power that I can alter a magic realm with a single thought and make food and drink appear from thin air. Do things that even the strongest witch can't do and would probably kill for. It's a lot to take in.

Instead of being fixed, I am different again. "Is it too much to ask that I be a normal witch?"

With a thud, I smack my head against the desk. I do it again to punish myself. To knock some sense into my stupid broken head.

Why does it have to be me? I swallow down my frustration and the festering pain that sits inside me. I've gone from being the witch who is an embarrassment to this...

A host. A world maker.

How the hell can I do this? I can't. There is no way. Fate chose the wrong person. I'm not strong enough. I'm not brave enough. I've spent my entire life so far running away from magic. Running away from everything. To do this, I will have to embrace everything I hate. The magic I hate. I can't do this. I can't. Not when I can't move from being a frozen pathetic lump on the floor.

Bloody hell, Tuesday, woman the fuck up.

I would but I'm so frightened.

I wipe at the stupid tears that are streaming down my face. I am so bloody frightened.

The mobile Owen gave me rings, and its shrill tone scares me half to death. I almost ignore it. I almost sink into the pity party I'm throwing myself. Almost. I sniff and robotically drop my knees and lift my bum from the floor so I can get my fingers into the tight pocket. I answer, and with a shaky hand, put the phone to my ear.

"Hello?" I croak.

"Where are you, Flash?" His voice is rough. He sounds worried. Listening to him and that silly nickname somehow centres me and smashes through the dark layers of my panic and fear. Without knowing it, he lends me a little bit of strength.

"I'm in a pocket dimension," I rasp.

"A pocket dimens—" He blows into the receiver and the sound rustles. I think he rubs his face. "Wow, you have been busy."

"Yes." I hiccup a sob.

"Okay, do you need help? Do you want me to come and get you? Tell me what you need."

Do you need help? Unless they're being paid, no one has ever asked me that before. *Woah there, don't make it something it's not. Don't forget Dad sent him.* I sniffle. It has been so long since I asked anyone for help. "Please," I say through the lump in my throat.

"Ah shit, Tuesday, you're killing me here. Are you safe?"

"Yes." I think so.

"Can you get out?"

"I don't know... Y-yes, maybe?"

There's a pause as he thinks through what I'm not saying. "Do you want to leave?"

"Things are... complicated."

"We can fix complicated together. So the entrance to this pocket dimension is in Scotland?"

"I think so." *I wish I could wave a magic wand and bring him here.*

My hands and feet tingle, and the swirling patterns I can see etched on my skin begin to move in time with the pounding of my heart. *What?* I have the urge to scratch at my arms and tear the marks off my skin. *I don't like this.* I draw in big, panicky gulps of air, but the oxygen in the room has thickened, and it is almost impossible to breathe. My chest aches and my throat burns. *Something is happening.*

"Tuesday? Tuesday? Flash, talk to me." The phone slips from my hand and clatters to the floor. My ears buzz and whoosh like I am underwater.

Pain shoots across my chest and the magic—my magic—floods out of me. My back bows and my head smacks against the wood. A terrified scream leaves my lips. With frightened tears streaming down my face, I watch as the magic hits a spot in the centre of the room and spreads out.

The area gets darker. It shimmers. Then, like it is made of glass and I have just taken a hammer to it, reality splinters.

The very fabric of the world cracks. The crack widens and a black hole appears. It's round and so dark, it is like I have made a black hole into the universe. A black, endless hole that will suck me inside.

My feet scrabble against the floor, and I press back against the wooden desk. My shoulder blades and spine dig into the ornate surface. *What the fuck is that?* I have never felt this frightened. An ominous feeling of impending doom is screaming through my bones. I feel so bloody helpless. Even when the mercenaries came and the elf attacked me, what I felt was child's play compared to this.

I don't know how I know—perhaps some inbuilt thing inside me recognises the sensation—but the pocket realm adds its magic to the mix until the rippling hole solidifies. The colour changes from black to dark green, and it stabilises. There is movement. A massive shadow appears in the centre of the hole and a person walks through.

"Oh my goodness, this isn't happening. It is not happening," I mutter as I slam my eyes closed. I'm done. I'm not brave enough to look upon my impending death. There is a whisper of movement, and instead of eating my face off, a big warm body smoothly sits on the floor beside me.

"Hey, Flash, you're okay. I'm here." The hellhound tucks me into his side. A warm, solid, enormous arm folds around me, enveloping me in the best kind of hug.

Owen.

It is Owen.

I let out a relieved sob and I sag into his arms. "What? How? I don't understand," I say, mumbling into his very solid chest.

"You sent a portal."

"No... I didn't. That is not possible." I pull away and gape up at him in disbelief. "I sent a portal?"

"Well, I presumed it was you."

"But that is impossible. No one can make portals out of thin air." *No one can make a cup of tea appear from thin air either.* The magic is omnipotent. "So, I opened a portal? I guess it makes sense as I drove here using a magical driveway, so of course, I can open gateways to friends in other worlds without thinking about it." Why not? "Wait... You just hopped into a random portal?"

"You needed me," he says earnestly, looking down at me with those beautiful grey eyes. "You were crying, and you screamed. Of course, I jumped into the portal."

I shake my head in disbelief and hold him a little bit tighter. "Thank you. Don't do that again for me though; that was so dangerous. But thank you so much for coming."

"I never should have left you. I should have driven you my damn self. I'm an idiot. You're not getting away from me again until I know you're safe," he grumbles into my hair.

"It's not your fault. It's mine." It was me. I was super insistent that I could drive myself. The thought of driving hours in the same car as Owen was... Let's just say, after I'd embarrassed myself so fully with the bottom zombie shuffle, I had a huge motivation for me to drive alone. When it comes down to it, at my core, I'm too introverted and awkward.

"What about the elf?" I say into the fabric of his chest.

"Forrest is hunting him as we speak. I'm here for you." It should feel weird that I'm allowing this man, a *hellhound* I've only just met, to manhandle me and offer me comfort. I ignore the voice of my mum that screams impropriety and instead snuggle closer into his warmth. "Don't you know?" His pause makes me lift my chin to peek at him. "We are bottom buddies." His eyes dance with mirth as I groan.

I tuck myself back into his side and let out a horrified laugh. *Bottom buddies.* Oh heck. I can't believe he made me laugh.

How can I not fall instantly in love with this man?

CHAPTER TWELVE

Love, I scoff at my silly thoughts. What would the hellhound want with me? I don't know him. I lean against him anyway, and we sit quietly. There is no give in Owen. No softness in his body. It is all hard muscle and bones, wrapped in a harsh, predatory strength. I have never felt so safe.

Tuesday, he is an unattainable dream. How can I expect anybody else to love me when the people who should love me unconditionally don't? They don't even like me. I am an embarrassment. I don't even make a good friend. All I want to do is stay at home, play games on my computer, watch TV, and read. I'm boring. My tummy flips and I move away from Owen's heat.

I'm a throwaway person.

I've been picked up and put down so many times that I now expect it; I expect to be thrown away. So, when I see this powerful, handsome man, my life experience up to now tells me he is so far out of my league that there is no point in even trying.

Yet, each moment I'm with him, he cradles my fears in his gigantic hands and he smothers me with genuine kindness. I've never met anyone like him. He is special. That is why I know when he gets a full look at the person I am... he'll be appalled. He will no doubt walk away like everyone else.

What would he want with me?

I have come a long way from the little girl who used to steal spells.

Sure, I have days when I wobble, when my heart hurts so much it's hard to get out of bed. The days when I'm starved for affection, and even when I am surrounded by people—I am alone. It's always been easier to hold myself back, to keep part of myself tightly wrapped, hidden away, so when the time comes, there will always be a small part of me left that will pick up the pieces and be there to stick the broken bits back together.

The only person who is going to be with me day in, day out, is me. So, I will temporarily borrow his strength, and when he leaves, which he will, I will be okay.

I will keep plodding on.

I roll my eyes. Bloody hell, I am annoying myself now. Boohoo, no one loves me. Other people have it way worse. I peek up at him through my loose hair. The silence has become awkward. I need to say something. "The datapad," I blurt out. My hand points to the tablet still on the desk above us. "It said if I stay here, I will be immortal."

"Oh. Well, you shouldn't believe everything you read."

"I know. It just freaked me out. This whole situation is scary. When I got here, this was a rundown hotel." I wave my hands wildly. "Does it look like that to you? Rundown?"

"No."

"I did this, Owen. I changed the pocket dimension somehow and now I don't know what to do. I'm a freak, a powerful freak, and perhaps immortal. Will I have to watch everyone die?" I bite my tongue to stop any more frantic words from spilling out of my mouth.

"Tuesday, everyone dies. There is no such thing as true immortality." I wince and blink at him through my scratchy and undoubtedly red eyes. That means a lot coming from a shifter.

Everyone dies. I guess being immortal is a subject he is aware of. Shifters are one of the so-called immortal races. But everyone knows shifters are a predominantly violent race.

"You are ancient, aren't you?"

The hellhound smiles down at me and shrugs. "I wouldn't say ancient. I've not hit a thousand yet, but I'm close."

"Wow." It's hard to get your head around that. I am so out of my depth with this guy, it's not even funny. Young shifters struggle to survive adolescence. To live to a hundred is an achievement, to be almost a thousand... Well, that means Owen is a very dangerous man.

I scramble up. I suddenly feel uncomfortable

and a little silly to be sitting on the floor. I grab my phone and without discussing it, we both move away from the reception area and into the lounge. I sink into one of the comfortable chairs.

I watch as the hellhound circles the room, peeking through windows and checking behind doors for threats. If I relax my eyes to the point of my peripheral vision being hazy, I can see the hellhound's power as it wafts about the room. A shiver runs down my spine. I've never been able to do that before.

Finally, Owen chooses the vacated chair that the vampire sat in. I guess it gives him a perfect view of the room and all the doors.

"If you need help and I'm not around"—he takes the phone still clutched in my hand and inputs a number—"ring Forrest. She's the only one I trust to keep you safe. Even though she comes across as..." Owen sighs and rubs his eyebrow. "She's an amazing person and she'll die to keep you safe."

My eyes drift to the ceiling as I picture the just in case arsenal of knives next to the bed. The ones she packed in my bugout luggage along with the toy gun. Calling scary Forrest would be a last resort; I hope I'm never in such a dire situation to need her help. "Thank you. I'm sure I will be fine. I'm already feeling better. I am so sorry you had to see me like this. I don't normally..." I fake smile and shrug. "It's a lot to deal with."

Owen nods with understanding. He sits forward in the chair and his kind grey eyes trace the glowing tattoos on my face. "Are you going to explain?"

I nod and wiggle in the chair. My mouth is dry as a bone, probably more from nerves rather than the bacon. I don't know where to start.

Will he believe me?

There's a clack and a cup of tea and a mug almost overflowing with whipped cream and little marshmallows appear on the table in front of us. I frown at the unusual choice.

Owen picks up the froufrou drink. A pink marshmallow escapes the mountain of cream and rolls off the edge of the mug. His hand whips out and he snaps it from the air and pops it into his mouth. He grins at me and my insides twist. I have never had such a visceral response to another person. It is terrifying. He settles back in the chair, and as the hellhound takes in my incredulous expression, he sheepishly smiles.

"Thank you. That is one handy trick. Hot chocolate is my favourite drink." I blink at him. "Forrest's fault," he mumbles in explanation.

With the steam drifting from the cup warming my face, I animatedly tell him about what has happened so far. I finish with a flop of my hand. It's not even ten in the morning and I'm exhausted.

"The book you signed was the one you turned into a datapad?" Owen asks as he runs his hand through his short hair.

"Yes."

He nods. "I don't like this. But sometimes magic can't be explained logically, as you know." The hellhound leans towards me. "I don't need to tell you to be cautious." His warm breath breezes over my face and I am enveloped in his scent of cinnamon, vanilla, and the taste of chocolate on his breath.

He smells like the best cinnamon bun ever. Weirdly, my tummy rumbles and—clack. Mortified, I stare at the plate that appears. A huge, square cinnamon bun with lashings of white icing and a sprinkle of chocolate sits on the table between us. I have no doubt my face is bright red.

I shove the pastry into my mouth with a mumbled "thank you" to the magic. Yeah, thanks soooo much.

The hellhound watches in amusement. "Do you want one?" I ask after I swallow the mouthful. He shakes his head and laughs as he leans forward to pluck a piece of bun from my top.

Oh wow, did he just do that?

I huff out a small, mortified laugh. I can't believe I missed my mouth. With a whoosh, my entire face glows with an embarrassed heat. I wiggle and surreptitiously scan my top for any other surprises.

"You are adorable."

While I finish the pastry as quickly as possible, more cat than wolf, the hellhound slumps back in his chair. Each muscle is deceptively relaxed. Owen rubs his bottom lip with his thumb as he thinks. I avert my eyes as my stomach does a weird flip flop. Gosh, he is sexy.

And now I'm blushing again. My entire face is on fire. He is only here to keep me sane and to deal with this nightmare. It's not an opportunity to pant after him. I need to drag my mind out of the gutter. Be professional. I take a deep breath and ignore the fact that all I can smell is him.

I'm annoying myself.

I plant my elbow on the chair's arm and rest my warm cheek in my palm as I wrangle through the magic problem.

First, it's bloody day one of this freakfest. I need to stop being so hard on myself. I've always been an overachiever. I ignore the nasty voice in the back of my head that wants to point out that my so-called overachieving attitude never helped me with magic. I mentally give it the middle finger. The voice that still sounds distinctly like my mother can bog off. Now, I know for sure, I never was a normal witch. No matter how much I tried, I'd have never been able to achieve anything in the real world.

This whole thing is like starting a new job. I don't know anything, so I can't be cocky. I slump back in my chair, mirroring Owen's relaxed pose. Instead of looking at what I don't know, I need to change my thought process and focus on the things I do.

I nibble my lip. I don't feel trapped—it's like I'm at home in this pocket realm. My eyes drift to the phone in my lap. "It's cowboy time," I mutter. I narrow my eyes with a stray thought that makes my heart race. "Was the time the same when you left?"

"Ten to ten. Cowboy time." Owen barks out a laugh, and his grey eyes sparkle as he puts his empty mug onto the table. "I haven't heard that in years," he adds with a grin that would melt the knickers off a nun. I feel my cheeks heat again. "Yes, the time here is the same as home."

I give him a thankful nod. Phew. "Okay, so no time changes." That is a good thing. I've heard of some pocket dimensions where time is faster or slower and no one wants that.

What else? Okay, I also know my magic here is as easy as breathing. I can practically do whatever I want. I mean, I made a portal door out of nothing just to get Owen here. Not that it was easy—I thought I was going to die. Portals are supposed to be attached to ley lines, but I produced one out of thin air and stabilised it with my magic. That is unheard of crazy, and sort of ticks the box on omnipotent power.

Now that I've opened a portal, something tells me it will be easier to open one again. I tap my thigh. I guess I'll have to practise these new freaky powers.

Yay. Great. Something to look forward to.

Without warning, Owen's nostrils flare and his hand shoots out towards my face. The empty cup in my hand slips from my grip, but before it hits the floor, it disappears. I let out an *eep* sound in terror and, wide-eyed, I jerk away from his massive limb.

"What the heck?" Did I say something wrong?

CHAPTER THIRTEEN

Behind me, there's a panicked squeak and I turn my head to find a man wiggling in Owen's grip. "Larry?" It's the guy that checked me in, the missing staff member.

Owen's muscles are tense as he drags Larry around the back of my chair. The smaller man's hands claw desperately at the hellhound's wrist. His shoes squeak on the floor as he tries to scrabble away, and his eyes roll in his head like a frightened rabbit.

My hands shake uncontrollably from the adrenaline rushing through me. I wobble to my feet. Sitting makes me feel vulnerable. For a moment, I thought my new friend was going to hurt me.

Crikey, my heart is having palpitations. He scared the shit out of me.

"Tuesday, I'm sorry," Larry wails as our eyes meet. "I thought you'd be mad, so I used the tablet you made to talk to you. It was me." I knew it! Was he laughing at me too? "My job is to help you. But I don't know you and I didn't want you to kill me. Tuesday, please don't kill me."

"Tuesday kill you? I'm the one with my hand wrapped around your throat, dickhead," Owen says with a growl as he gives Larry a rough shake in emphasis. "He's not what he pretends to be," he grumbles. "I don't know what this thing is. He doesn't make a sound, and he doesn't have a scent. He was invisible until I grabbed him."

Larry's face is getting redder and redder.

"Don't pretend you need to breathe. She is not doing it to save you." The carefully hidden hellhound power ramps up and hits me square in my chest as Owen's other hand lights up with a blue flame. I gulp.

Apart from the scuffle in the hotel room when I was struggling with the effects of the null band, I haven't witnessed the full effects of his power. Not really. I haven't seen Owen's grrr side. Not like this. The violence is shocking. The fire magic is shocking. The hellhound has been nothing but kind to me. But going from his sleepy, relaxed state to aggressive in the blink of an eye, even when it's not directed at me, makes my heart race crazy fast. The alien magic inside of me flares and my pounding heart misses a beat.

Oh God.

My magic doesn't like it. No, not mine. The realm's magic doesn't like this confrontation. The word *sanctuary* screams inside of me over and over. It echoes till the word is running through my blood and stamped on my very bones.

Okay, I get it. I grit my teeth and slam my eyes closed. The magic is like a living thing. I mentally grapple with it and it rushes out of my useless grip like a waterfall. No, like a tsunami. It hurts as it smashes inside me, wanting to get out and wreak havoc.

None of that, I growl in my head. *Settle the fuck down.*

I can't do this, a small part of me whispers. This is way too much. I can't do this.

A whimper slips from my lips. Oh no, I can't do this. I am not going to be able to stop it. My hair is moved to the side and a warm hand wraps around my neck and massages it gently. "You are okay, Flash. I'm sorry I scared you. Just breathe." His voice sends a soft rumble through me. With his touch, goosebumps rise all over my skin, and I can't help the shiver that racks me.

The hellhound is lending me his strength.

I swallow and then take a single deep, shuddering breath. Then another. His hot, heavy hand on my neck grounds me, and with an aggressive prod from me, the magic of the realm dissipates—no, it retreats and allows my magic to settle back into a pool in the middle of my chest.

I cautiously open my eyes and I nudge Owen with my elbow. "You are hurting him. The realm doesn't like it. It doesn't like the violence." The big hellhound immediately lets go of Larry and he stumbles a few steps away.

Larry stands there, wide-eyed and shaking as he rubs his neck.

"The truth," Owen spits out.

Larry swallows and his Adam's apple bobs. His face screws up as he tries to think of an answer that will satisfy the growling, terrifying hellhound. "I was created by the first host." His eyes implore me, and he presses his hands together as if in prayer. "Please don't kill me, Tuesday. I didn't mean to desert you. I was frightened. I thought you'd be mad that I lured you here. Then when you started crying..." He throws his hands up in the air and his lower lip wobbles. "I felt so bad. Then the big guy came and tried to strangle me." Larry plucks at his fingers, his green eyes wide with fear. "Only the host of the realm can destroy me. I was only made to be temporary, but I've been here for over a thousand years, looking after the hotel. I feel pain." He scowls at Owen and rubs his neck. "I'm as real as anybody. Please, I can help."

"You're a magical construct?"

"Yes. Yes." Larry points at me as if he's a teacher and I answered a question correctly in class. He even gives me a double thumbs up. His eyes crinkle with relief and he nods his head so fast, I worry it's going to pop off. "I direct the magic to where it's needed. I was made to keep the world functioning until a new host could be found. But the host never came and as Sanctuary slowly crumbled, I got worried. In desperation, I put feelers out into all the worlds. I was so sure I could find a new host. I found you." He grins.

A realisation pokes my brain as I make a connection. "Ah, it was you. You stopped the car." I narrow my eyes.

Larry's happy face creases with worry. He nods and twists his hands. "And the phone. I didn't want you to call for help until after you'd entered Sanctuary. I knew that once you got here, you'd find your home. You need this pocket realm, just like we need you."

I stare at him. I should be so mad. I should be raging mad. But... I'm not. I guess he has a point. As soon as I stepped inside the hotel, my non-existent magic took over my body and got to work. I lift my eyes to take in the beautiful lobby. I did this.

I just wish I had a way of knowing he was telling the truth.

"Alright, magic man, say we believe you. Which I don't. What about Tuesday signing the book? What was that all about?" Owen drops his voice to a threatening growl. "What did you do?"

Larry takes another step back and holds his hands up in front of his chest as if to ward off an attack by the angry hellhound. "Wow, he really doesn't like me, does he?" he mumbles. Owen takes a menacing stride toward him. Larry frantically waves his hands. "Everyone, every guest, has to sign in," he squeaks. "It is a normal procedure. She didn't sign her life away. I did nothing but get her here. I swear, I wouldn't hurt her. I would never hurt you, Tuesday."

My magic oddly chimes inside me with some sort of creepy magical confirmation, as if agreeing with his words. Crap-on-a-cracker, what now? What the heck was that? A weird magic lie detector? I shake my head and blink rapidly. That was freaky. It felt like my brain was tickled.

"He isn't lying to us," I mumble as I rub the side of my head.

Owen takes a deliberate sniff, perhaps smelling for a lie. Can shifters do that? He grunts in acknowledgement.

"Okay?" I whisper.

"Okay." The hellhound agrees while giving Larry the stink eye.

Larry grins and claps his hands together. It is like the sun has come out from the gleeful expression on his face. Then his smile disappears, and he slants his head to the side. In a monotone voice, he says, "They know you're here and request an audience."

"Who?" I ask at the same time as Owen grumbles.

"Oh, for fuck's sake. What now..." He washes his hand across his face. "Who?"

"The collective of dimensions."

Oh. Now this sounds like a whole new level of fun.

Arrrah.

"Do I have to meet them in person?" I whine as I brush my hands down my black trousers.

"Not in person. None of you will meet in person. Hosts, as a general rule, don't leave their pocket dimensions. Here, you are at your strongest, and the longer you stay, the less inclined you are to leave," he says with blatant honesty. "The conference call will start in ten minutes. Come, let me show you to your office."

Oh heck, talk about short notice. What a bunch of twats. Don't they know how to schedule meetings properly? They're doing it on purpose to throw me off my game. Well, we'll see about that. The idiots probably don't realise I'm already floundering. What's one more thing to add to the overflowing bag of crap my life has become?

CHAPTER FOURTEEN

Owen gives a low whistle of appreciation. Yeah, the office is better than I imagined. While the reception area came from the five minutes or so of dreaming while I was waiting to be checked in to the hotel, the office nestled behind and to the left of the reception took me years to lovingly construct in my head.

My office at the department store is tiny, stuffed in a corner within the main stock room with its puke green paint. It's only big enough for a desk and two chairs. With one wall full of CCTV monitors and the other walls plastered with schedules and planners. I do my best to avoid the cramped space and try to be anywhere else in the store.

So, it stands to reason I've dreamed of something a little fancier over the years. It is the amalgamation of an office and a library. An ultra-modern space with white walls and glass shelves. Huge floor-to-ceiling bi-fold doors look out onto a patio area overlooking the lake. Huh. Technically, the view of the lake shouldn't be possible.

"With the position of this room within the building, these doors should have a partial view of the car park," Owen says, pulling the words right out of my head. He slides the door open and steps out. I lean against the glass and watch him prowl to the side of the building. With each stride, he runs his hand against the wall, perhaps searching for illusions, or an obvious explanation.

I hope he can tell me. I take a moment to breathe in the sweet air of a perfect spring day. Which is strange in itself as... isn't it supposed to be winter?

"We are in a pocket world and Tuesday can bend reality to her every whim," Larry scoffs an explanation. "Of course she wants a pretty view from her office. Come now, stop messing about. My mistress needs to get settled in the conference room."

I shudder. "Oh no, please don't call me *mistress*." I follow him to a door that wasn't in my original design. Larry pushes the door open and the familiar smell of feet wafts into the air. I wrinkle my nose. He smacks at the wall a few times and there is a click. The pale glow of the ceiling's single bare bulb highlights a sad and drab room.

The conference table has seen better days. No windows. The cream paint on the ceiling is coming off in strips and the corners have clumps of black mould. Debris from the peeling paint and plaster litters the table.

Owen, like a shadow, follows me inside. His boots crunch as he circles the table. "Nice."

"I didn't make this," I mutter.

"I can tell," he says as he flicks at a piece of blown plaster. It immediately breaks off and crumbles to the floor.

"The room only opens when a council session has been called. If you try, you should be able to fix it before the meeting." Larry bounces from foot to foot and twists his hands. He wants me to do just that.

I shake my head, vetoing the idea of making the room pretty. Until I can see for myself who is friend or foe, I will give them nothing. I will not paint an irresistible, bright, shiny target on my head. I don't want them to realise my strength, and nothing brings out the worst in people than someone else's weakness.

Not that I have any strength... I don't know what the hell I'm doing. But I am going to go with my gut. As an obvious underdog, it will show their true colours faster. These people are—if Larry can be believed—immortal, and immortals have all the time in the worlds. A hundred years to them is probably a day to a witch. I can't be arsed playing a long game. Either they will help me or attack me. I might as well get it out of the way sooner rather than later. At least while I can hide behind the hellhound's bulk.

Fun times.

"Will they know how much this world has changed overnight?" I ask Larry as I pull out a chair.

He shakes his head. "No, they won't, and they'll never come here. They can't. Hosts don't go to each other's dimensions. It imbalances the realms and confuses the magic."

So that means the possibility that they will send in spies, so my ruse will not last for long.

I might be wrong, and these people might be lovely and helpful. But I've learned over the years to expect the worst. Most creatures are selfish and predictable.

So, if I'm playing the role of the underdog, I need to dress the part. I glance down at the pretty butterfly top with its delicate colours and flowy sleeves. It's not the ideal outfit... I need to show them what they expect.

A frightened mess.

A hair bobble appears in my hand. *Thank you.* I scrape my hair into a sloppy ponytail. Since I woke up this morning, my hair has been like silk, it's so smooth and shiny and it seems longer, the length now hitting my waist. My skin is the same. If I ignore the swirling magic for a second, I can feel the difference as it glows with health. Even my nails are harder and appear as if I've had an expensive manicure.

The plastic gun clacks onto the table as I pull it out of my pocket. The hellhound does this sexy enquiring thing with his eyebrow. "Forrest," I murmur in explanation. He grunts. I haven't got time to run upstairs and change, so I close my eyes and think of the clothes that I arrived in. The fabric on my skin changes. It goes from the light, floaty fabric to the heaviness of cotton. When I crack my eyes open, almost unwilling to look, I see a black oversized hoodie and jogging bottoms. I puff out my cheeks with relief. Perfect. I silently thank the magic yet again.

The sleeves slide over my hands, and I pull the hood up, shadowing the glowing marks on my face, and I shove the gun back into my pocket.

As I sit in the chair, it creaks underneath my weight and lists slightly to the right. Whoops. I push a little bit more of my weight into my left bum cheek to keep the chair level. I hope this meeting doesn't drag on.

Across the room, beautiful grey eyes watch me. The hellhound gives me a nod. He knows what I'm doing without me having to say. Smart wolf.

I place my phone on the table and raise an eyebrow. "Larry?" He gazes back at me blankly. It takes everything in me not to headbutt the table with exasperation. "What do I do now? Are we video conferencing?" I wave my hand to incorporate the entire room. "There is no technology. Do I use the phone?" Larry opens and closes his mouth, while Owen growls. This time, the growl is deeper and rumbles from his chest.

I shouldn't find his growls and grunts so fascinating, but I do.

"What? Oh yes, sorry, the magic will bring them. It'll beam them into the room. Well, um, not them exactly. But a magical version. So, you can, you know, speak." He flashes his teeth in a too-white smile.

I sigh and close my eyes. I understood that completely. Not. This is beyond my comprehension, and for my sanity, I should run away as fast as I can and go home.

Owen mutters something under his breath as he prowls around the room and settles behind me. Everything in me is hyperaware of him as he stands at my back. His shifter power, along with the heat of his hellhound magic, makes shivers randomly zip up and down my spine. *Instead of frightening, his hellhound power is...* Nope. I yank on that thought. *Hellhounds aren't yummy.*

The room buzzes and the little hairs on my arms rise as the sudden change in room pressure makes my ears pop. My guests shimmer into existence. Oh-uh, here we go.

Showtime.

CHAPTER FIFTEEN

Four creatures—two men and two women—sit across the table. It's the oddest thing to see them magically projected. I have to blink a few times to get my eyes to focus. *"Help me, Obi-Wan Kenobi. You're my only hope."* Princess Leia's voice from Star Wars pipes up in my head, and I smirk.

I'm glad they can't see my expression. Smirking wouldn't make the best first impression. I might appear to be a sullen teenager with my hood pulled up and my face hidden within its shadows, but I instinctively know I did the right thing as I notice another obvious thing about my guests.

Their fancy, glowy markings.

While my face is covered with pretty swirls, the creatures opposite me have a swirl here and there. The marks must indicate power, and I am covered head to toe.

It's not something I need to be highlighting to a bunch of unknowns.

Thank goodness I hid my face.

Underneath the hood, I give them a sweeping glance, my eyes trail from left to right. The first man has white hair that's cropped close to his scalp. He is painfully thin and everything about him is white, from his lips to his skin tone. Even his eyes lack pigment.

Next to him is a woman. Her skin and long hair have a slight green tinge. She has a single, prominent swirl across her sharp cheekbone. The second woman is the most human-looking of the four. She has a round face, brown hair, and hazel eyes that shine with intelligence. The last man, a male version of the woman sitting next to him, has this sneer on his handsome face—a sneer that he's aiming at me.

Oh, and they all have the familiar tell-tale pointed ears of the *aes sídh.*

Elves.

Huh. I frown and shift slightly, and the dodgy chair creaks. I don't know what I was expecting. Aliens perhaps, not the fae. Something inside me chimes a reminder, and a memory flashes of the elf who attacked me. He also had short hair. Perhaps he wasn't an elf from Earth?

Great.

"How delightful. A hellhound bodyguard." The green skinned lady purrs as she runs a finger against the swirl on her collarbone, highlighting her impressive chest. She smiles at Owen like a crocodile.

Whoa, the woman has waaayy too many teeth.

"Maybe after this meeting you can guard me." She licks her lips.

Eww.

I wrinkle my nose and can't help myself, I swivel, being extra careful not to unbalance or break the already wobbly chair, so I can see Owen's face. The hellhound has taken up a guard position behind me. He stands with his legs wide apart, and his hands rest almost casually at his sides.

Ever the professional, he doesn't react to her words. Though his soft grey eyes have hardened like flint. *The dead eyes of a killer.* I take in a shuddering breath. *Stop it, Tuesday. That's unkind. All Owen has done is try to protect you. That's his game face.* I'm lucky to have his help. It's not like I'll be able to fight off four alien elves when I couldn't handle one. Thank the stars they aren't actually here.

The poor guy promised to protect me, yet we don't know from what. Thanks to this strange world, and now this impromptu meeting, we've both been dropped right in it. I feel sorry for him.

In good conscience, I can't allow this to continue. He's a hellhound, for spell's sake. He's the best of the best, the ultimate soldier, and instead of going out and rescuing people, he's here, playing bodyguard for me. It's a joke. I need to tell him he is free of his promise, as it's not his job to stand with me. This isn't his fight. It must be a helluva favour he owes my dad.

I'm not worth his time.

I do my best to give him a small, reassuring smile. His left hand clenches. Yeah, after this meeting, I'll send the poor guy on his way.

Reluctantly, I turn my attention back to the

creatures across the table. The elves—no they aren't elves, are they? They are hosts, and thinking back to first impressions, a sexual proposition doesn't make a good one. It seems like I'm in for a fun meeting. The hellhound isn't the only one who needs a game face.

"Poor little lost host, you must have been so lonely in a world that doesn't understand you. Earth, isn't it? Peeking out of that hood, you appear human." Crocodile lady smiles at me and I shudder. I can't help but count my teeth with my tongue. Yeah, crocodile lady has at least double the gnashes in her wide mouth. Freaky.

"You are earthborn?" The man on the right sniffs with distaste. "Earth is full of scavengers. It's a backwards world. For many centuries, it has not been advantageous for us to trade with the snivelling, vile creatures that roam that planet. The last time I checked, they treated humans like slaves and hosts like witches. Can you believe that? Witches? We are gods."

Next, he'll be pounding his chest. I blink as he continues to rant, and he waves his hands in the air. *Some god,* I mentally scoff. I use that title very loosely—his words. Witches on Earth can't be so bad if at one point in history some host dipped their DNA into the gene pool.

I must have a recessive gene.

Should I tell him? Nah. I keep my gob firmly closed and allow his rude comments to fly over my head. What does it matter to me? Who cares what these aliens think? I'm not an ambassador for Earth. I'm also numb to this type of game, thanks to my mum. No one can play it better than her. I still rub my hand down my leg in a self-soothing motion. I've trained for this. This exact moment. Dealing with my mum, my coven, and dealing with nightmare customers and colleagues has led up to this.

"Little human host," crocodile lady continues with a toothy smile, "is there something wrong with your face?" She drops her voice to a creepy whisper. "We don't mind scars."

Gah. It takes everything in me not to roll my eyes. Now they are calling me out. I have no choice. I must drop the hood, as I need to show my face.

"My apologies," I say in a fake timid whisper as I reach for the hood with a trembling hand. "I didn't think, and the room is cold." As the fabric slips away from my head, my heart jumps. I duck my head and screw my eyes tight as I ask the magic for its help. A push of power answers my call, making the skin on my face tingle. As the heavy fabric slaps against my back and loose hair from my ponytail settles around my face, I feel all but one mark fade, like a mask. They disappear underneath a layer of magic.

Phew. It'll do. I lift my chin.

The crocodile lady smiles with satisfaction as her eyes scan my face. They all appraise me and take in the lack of markings.

"Are you sure she's even a host? Just look at her. A single measly marking. She isn't powerful. The human blood has ruined her," says the brown-haired fake god with a dismissive sniff.

Witch. The words *witch blood, not human,* scream in my head. I lift my chin higher and keep my mouth firmly closed. They are pissing me off.

"Look at this room. She can't even do a basic change. She's not one of us. Thank the rivers I can't smell this place. It's disgusting. She's disgusting," crocodile lady pipes up.

Nice.

It takes everything in me to hold in a sigh and a nostril flare. Losing my temper now would be a huge mistake. This is something I'm used to. At least she's direct and saying it to my face. Meh, her words won't trigger the Mum gene. I've heard worse.

I smile.

"Look at that." Crocodile points at my face. "She doesn't even know she's being insulted. What a waste. She is such a pretty little thing to look at, those big violet eyes... she'd make beautiful babies. Tendris, you always said you were waiting for a host mate." She elbows the white-haired elf, and he grunts with dismissal.

A low growl sounds behind me. Owen's boots creek against the wooden floor as he shifts his weight. I wave my hand frantically below the table and the growl cuts off. I don't think they heard him as they've continued to talk about me as if I'm not in the room. I've seen what I wanted. My eye twitches and I give it a rub. Sorry, but the hosts are a bunch of pricks.

I haven't even had a chance to explore the realm yet, as these creatures demanded an immediate meeting. Without asking. What is it about my face that gets everybody up in arms? They go from nought to sixty with insults. Even when I haven't said anything to warrant it. Not yet anyway.

I loudly clear my throat. "Excuse me," I say as I tap on the table to get their attention. "I'm sorry. I thought you could help me, advise me. Now I see that's not the case. If you'd excuse me, I have things to do." I rise from my chair. As I stand, I tuck a strand of hair behind my ear and deliberately allow the baggy sleeve to roll down to my elbow, flashing the silver swirls on my arm.

"Oh Jupiter, her arms," the brown-haired lady squeaks. "Please, please don't leave." Something in her tone makes me pause. I groan as I see the genuine panic in her brown eyes. What's one more minute? I tug the chair back and go to sit, but the poor chair has had enough, and it crumbles into pieces. I stare at the sad chunk of wood in my hand and puff out my cheeks. Without thinking, I drop the wood and wash my magic across the room. The power hits the room in a wave and from one breath to the next, everything changes.

Whoa. Seeing it happen in front of my eyes is a trip. It's like I've gone full on Disney.

The conference room now mirrors the office next door with white walls and floor-to-ceiling windows that also overlook the lake. A fancy glass wall now separates the two rooms, letting in lots of light. That's much better. I nod my head and the protective mask of magic peels away from my face as I casually pull out the now solid, elegant chair to take a seat.

The hosts' mouths are open.

"My name is Tuesday Larson. The hellhound gentleman behind me is Owen, and Larry here is the previous host's magical construct. Gosh, look at that"—I narrow my eyes—"I have manners. Not bad, I guess, for a vapid Earth savage."

For a few moments, the only response I get is silence.

Wow, awkward.

So much for keeping your gob shut. Yay, nice one, Tuesday.

"She is feral." Crocodile lady recovers first. She snaps her teeth and takes a deep breath, to prepare for what will be an epic rant. "She doesn't understand the rules. You can't just—"

"No. She's magnificent. I take everything I said about Earth and the humans back. She doesn't know the rules, so she isn't confined to them. Her magic is wild." The brown-haired guy leans forward and points his finger at crocodile's face. "Don't you dare ruin that." He's a brave man. I wouldn't point a precious digit anywhere near those teeth.

Crocodile lady proves me right when she tries to take a chomp out of it.

Yikes.

Their images combine for a split second, and he smirks. Oh yeah, they're not really here. He leans back with a smug smile on his face.

Thinking about what he said, I'm happy for once that the host magic is a complete unknown to me. It's refreshing I don't have to conform to someone else's version of perfection. I can listen to what my magic is telling me and do it on the fly. I have to bite my lip to stop myself from grinning like a loon. I like the idea of being wild.

The lady with the brown hair clears her throat. Her cheeks are flush with embarrassment. "I think we need to apologise to Miss Larson. I'm sorry that we didn't introduce ourselves. It's a little overwhelming finding a new host. My name is Nyssa. This is my brother, Nestern. The lovely lady next to me is Zaina, and last but not least, the gentleman at the end is Tendris."

I huff. It's a little bit too late for polite introductions.

"You deliberately mislead us," Tendris says with a white-eyed scowl.

"Yes," I reply with a sharp nod. His eyes widen, and I shrug. What? I'm not going to lie. Well, not entirely anyway. I neglect to tell them I hid my markings 'cause I was shitting myself.

"It was a test," he says as he rubs his face.

"Yes."

"A test we failed," Nyssa says in a mournful tone. I shrug again. I need to wrap this meeting up.

The way Zaina, aka crocodile alien host, is now glaring at me is making me feel uncomfortable. If looks could kill, I'd be dead and buried with a pretty headstone. She pointedly brushes a chunky gold ring on her right ring finger with creepy reverence and then glances at my empty ringless finger and smirks.

I notice each of my visitors has one. Nope, I'm not in the ring club. The rings must be powerful artefacts. I guess I will add that to the list of things I have yet to find out. Zaina is now smiling at me.

Some psycho part of me wishes she was corporal. I stroke the toy gun in my pocket. I'd love to shoot a foam sleeping bullet into the middle of her green forehead. I duck my head and grin at the thought. Shame it would pass straight through her. *Look at me, a plastic gun in my pocket and I've turned into a right rebel.*

Okay, back to getting answers. "So, you are the council for hosts?" What did Atticus call them? "The collective of dimensions?" My eyebrows rise with my question, and I plaster what I hope is an encouraging expression on my face.

"Council—" Nyssa lets out a strangled laugh and turns to her brother for help, finding something interesting on his hand. Did I say something wrong?

Nyssa abandons her chair. On the way to the window, she walks through the table. The magical projection of her flickers so much it makes me want to vomit. She takes in the view and her hand hovers against the glass. "Beautiful view," she murmurs. "I can see for miles." The other hosts quieten their bickering as they also take in the view.

Zaina grinds her teeth and snarls. "You're powerful then. So what?"

"And you've learned quickly," Tendris says in a low voice. His white eyes remain focused on the lake.

"If you would like, I can teach you, help you with your magic. I can give you the tools to keep yourself safe," Nyssa offers.

"Thank you."

"Well, I won't. Her power will bring out the sealgairí and I'm not killing myself to protect a baby host. She will be a magnet for trouble," Zaina snarls.

"Who are the sealgairí?" I try to pronounce the word the way crocodile lady did, but I make a mess of it.

"Just keep out of my way, Wednesday."

I roll my eyes. As if I haven't heard that one before. "No, my name is Tuesday," I say with a sad shake of my head. "Wednesday is my sister."

"What?" Her green face scrunches up with confusion.

"Boy, it doesn't take much, does it?" I mumble.

"Your sister's name is Wednesday?" she splutters with incredulity.

I snort. "No. But you should have seen your face." I grin. All three of my sisters have lovely, normal names. It's only me who has a wacky one. Talk about tempting fate. I think my mum was so sure that I was a boy she didn't even think about picking an alternative, so when it was revealed that I was a bouncing baby girl, she let my dad name me. I was born on a Tuesday. Yes, really. *Thanks, Dad.*

"We are the hosts," Nestern says in a low voice.

"Pardon?" I rapidly blink. Oh, he is answering my question that upset Nyssa before about them being part of the council. I don't think I quite understand. Did they not send the council? The guild?

"There are four of us, well, five of us now." Nyssa returns to her seat, waves at the others and smiles warmly. "That is the reason we arranged this meeting so quickly." She leans forward with enthusiasm, but her smile doesn't reach her sad, hazel eyes. "Miss Larson, you are in danger. The hosts have been hunted to extinction. We are the last."

Five of us? "Oh." Well crap.

CHAPTER SIXTEEN

After I arrange a training session for the following morning with Nyssa, I cut the magic to the room. It is so easy to do, like flicking a switch. *Bam* and they are gone.

"Extinction. Bloody hell." *Gah, Tuesday, why did you show them your magic so quickly? Why am I so impatient?* I flop my head down on the table and groan. My quiet life as an outcast was preferable to being hunted. "I don't want to be an alien elf," I whine.

"You're not an alien elf," Owen says with gruff amusement. "You are still a witch, but with host magic." I let out an unladylike grunt. I'm far from being a witch. My sweaty forehead squeaks against the table as I attempt to press my pounding head into the wood.

"Was that wise, to show your markings and magic like that?" Larry asks, voicing a polite version of my own scattered thoughts.

"You tell me, Larry," I grumble. "Probably not." I sit up and rub my face. Great. Even the magical construct thinks my move was a bit pre-emptive. *Nah, it was worth it just to see their faces.*

I get up, and with wobbly knees, I leave the conference room. The two men follow silently behind. Not thinking, I trundle through to reception. Aw heck, I should have kept this conversation private. Before I can turn and retrace our steps to the office, a sound bubble pops up around us. It's similar to a Don't Hear Me Now spell. Wow, that is kind of neat. Freaky, but a cool piece of magic.

Larry prods the bubble with an approving nod. I shrug. It's not like I did it on purpose. This magic stuff is nuts. I'm throwing magic around without a chant or spell in sight. "I needed to do something," I continue. "They were walking all over me. Did you hear what they said? What a bunch of d-dicks," I stutter. For some reason, perhaps because I'm tired and I'm a little jittery, the word *dick* is heavy on my tongue. My brain misfires slightly at the odd sensation of finally being able to say out loud whatever is in my head. I rub my leg. I don't think I will ever get used to it.

My head goes back to the big reveal. I have thrown all my cards down. I hope I made myself look stronger than I am. This all feels like fate is pushing me aggressively forward. I still don't know if this is going to blow up in my face. I hate not knowing if I am doing the right thing. Although I think the hosts are frightened and have more problems on their plates than my existence, my gut says any future ordeals I have will unlikely come from them.

"No, I had to reveal myself. I had to claw that meeting back and now they think I'm an evil genius," I add with heavy sarcasm. The lie detector inside me pings. The thing even works on me. Oh shit, I hope there is some way to turn the damn thing off. I white lie to myself frequently. At least it's good to know that during that meeting I had lie detector backup. They didn't lie. "When you're as weak as me, you learn how to bluff," I finish lamely.

"The sealgairí. Have you heard of them?" I ask Owen with a wince as I know I am again butchering the pronunciation.

"No. But the word means *hunters* in Irish. I will ask my contacts."

"Host hunters." I shake my head. "Thank you. I'd appreciate that." A wave of dizziness hits me, so I lean as casually as I can against the desk. No one needs to know that it's holding me up. If I ignore it, it'll go away. I sigh and rub my temple.

I blink away another rush of dizziness and meet Owen's concerned gaze. He hasn't been fooled by my casual lean. "I'm sorry she was rude to you. I should have said something."

"No," the hellhound replies gruffly. "You did the right thing."

"No, I didn't. I should have called her out. She was being inappropriate. I'm sorry you had to listen to that." I'm ashamed of myself. I reach over and squeeze his warm hand. Then I turn my attention back to Larry. "Larry, one thing I wanted to ask: why did you get a notice of the meeting, and I didn't? Are you, like, a magical personal assistant?"

"You just need to let the magic know."

"Great. Is there anything else I must let the magic know about?"

"Yes." I tilt my head to the side and wave my hand in a "get on with it" gesture. *Come on Larry.* "Oh, there's so much to tell you, it would take me weeks and weeks."

"Right." I narrow my eyes. Larry rocks from foot to foot. "You know you don't have to keep things from me. I will not kick you out or, heaven forbid, kill you. Just be honest, yeah? I need your help. I need a friend."

"A friend?" Larry blinks at me.

"Well, yeah..." Embarrassed, I casually pull the phone out of my pocket and tap it on my hand. I turn the phone back on and it works perfectly. "I always need more friends," I whisper.

"I am your friend!" Larry giggles with childlike glee. I lift my eyes, and he beams a smile at me and bounces on his toes. "I've never had a friend before. That's amazing."

"Friends." I smile at his antics and hold my hand out. He bounces towards me and gently shakes it.

"You just have to open your senses and the magic will tell you everything you need to know."

I nod and try it. To focus, I close my eyes. He is right. It is so weird, like I am touching a phantom part of my consciousness. I can feel everything in this pocket realm if I only reach out with my senses.

With a mental nudge, against the blackness of my eyelids, a map appears. "A map of the realm!" I gasp. *That is nuts.* I push my surprise away, wrinkle my nose, and keep my eyes firmly closed. "I guess it's not *everything* I need to know, but it's a start." Owen grunts an acknowledgement. Somehow, everyone in the realm shows up like coloured blobs on the map. And if I poke the black blob, I just know the vampire is quietly working away in the library. Gold. Daisy is playing with some friends. My entire face scrunches up, and what I am doing grinds to a halt... Woah. What? Friends? Um, that is new. I know she's safe and content, so I will refrain from charging off and going all mama bear.

Thinking of mama bears, I open my eyes and squeeze the phone in my hand. No time like the present to knock something off my horrendously long to-do list. With a deep breath and my stomach flipping with nerves, my thumb hovers on the keypad, ready to dial my dad, which will no doubt entail a conversation with Mum as well. I swallow.

Nah, I think I'll leave that fun call for another day. I should check on Daisy and her *friends*. Uh-oh. My eyes widen. I have no idea what a dragonette will conjure up with the realm magic listening to her every need. "I need to check on Daisy." I move and then stagger to the side. A strong hand grips me underneath my elbow. "Oh, thanks," I mumble. "What the heck is wrong with me?"

"You've just used a shit load of magic. Magic that you have never used before last night. Of course, you are wobbling around like Bambi. When did you last eat?" The hellhound gazes down at me with a frown.

"The cinnamon bun?" Owen scowls. "Oh, and I had a bacon butty this morning."

"So, a magically made pastry and a breakfast sandwich? It might feed your future guests, but do you know if it's nutritious for you?"

I groan, shaking my head and barely refrain from slapping myself on the forehead. *Oh,*

Tuesday, why do you not think things through? The man is going to think I am a complete moron. "I've no idea."

"Okay, so you need to eat some proper food before you do anything."

"Yeah, okay, sounds like a plan. But... urm... I don't know if I made a kitchen. I'm guessing there's no actual food here." We both turn and stare at Larry, who shakes his head. That's a no to the food idea then.

Owen growls. Larry waves his hands out in front of himself as if to ward off an attack. I roll my eyes and the hellhound drags his hand across his face. "There is no need to panic," Larry squeaks, continuing his dramatics. "The food here will sustain Tuesday." He turns to me, his green eyes pleading. "It doesn't come from your magical source. The pocket realm can fulfil your every need. Owen is right; you have used a lot of magic. You just need to eat more."

A nutty protein bar appears in the palm of Owen's hand. "I could get used to this; the magic is incredible." The wrapper rustles as he opens it. "When you're feeling better, perhaps we should open a portal and get some fresh food delivered, just in case." He glares at Larry and hands the bar to me.

I nod as I stuff it in my mouth. "Have you been to a pocket dimension before?" I ask when I finally finish chewing.

"Yes, several. None this big. I can't wait to explore."

"Me too." After I've eaten two more protein bars, I already feel better. "Oh, I really need to check on Daisy. She's up to something." With my energy levels restored, I hurry for my room. Owen follows silently behind me. It's strange having such a huge but silent man following me around. The shifter sure pumps out some heat. No wonder Daisy likes him.

His warm breath tickles my ear. I close my eyes in exasperation and suck in a shaky breath before shuffling faster away from him. "Where are you going?" I grumble.

"With you."

I spin around to face him. I have to tilt my head way back to meet his eyes. Heck, I still cannot get over how big he is. With a huff, I put my hands on my hips, ready to argue. I can't have him following me around all day.

He already makes me feel awkward, and the crush I have needs to be squished before I shame myself any further.

"I'm safe. You don't need to do the whole guarding thing. No one is going to get in here without me knowing about it."

"Really?" he says, raising an eyebrow and folding his muscly forearms across his chest. "You know that for a fact, do you?"

I groan and rub my face. "No," I mumble underneath my hand.

"Well, you let me know when you know everything about your magic in this world. Then I will leave you alone."

I blink.

The hellhound grunts.

Ahh, we are at a stalemate.

Gah, the hard-headed hellhound. Nothing I say will convince him. "Fine. I just think an elite hellhound's time could be better spent than babysitting me." He grunts. I huff and spin on my toes. Now stomping my feet, I continue walking. I am sure he needs a break. I know I do.

I open the door to my snazzy room and wander inside. The whole place is about three times the size of my flat back home. It has three extra bedrooms. I rub my face and groan for what feels like the millionth time today. That's another thing I need to do—cancel my flat's lease. Every minute I stay here, it looks less likely I am ever going to go home. I bet my landlord will be thrilled to see the back of me, what with the Power Ranger mercenaries smashing apart his expensive building ward.

"Daisy?" I say in a cutesy voice. I search the entire apartment and when I have to look a second time, panic bubbles inside of me. She isn't here. Why isn't she here? "Daisy Duco? Oh, no, oh my goodness, did the magic take my dragonette?" If this bloody pocket realm hurt my Daisy...

Owen opens a door and I want to shout at him that Daisy couldn't possibly be in there, behind a closed door. She hasn't got thumbs. But his rumbling voice stops me. "Tuesday, you need to see this. I think she's here, and she's... got friends?"

The friends. I rush to him and take in the world beyond the door. I thought I'd seen everything but this—this is nuts.

"Dragonette utopia," I mutter in shock.

Did I wish for Daisy to have friends? I think I did this morning at some point when I was leaving. Oh heck. But I also remember her eating a cucumber snack, so she might have done this herself.

The room isn't a room, but a lava field. The rocky area has lava pools interspaced with volcanic hot springs. The eggy odour of sulphur fills the air. There is a tree in the centre that must be fifty feet tall. A deep-looking hole within the root of the tree hints at a cave underneath. When Larry said the magic could bend physics, he wasn't kidding.

But what has my mouth flapping open is all the dragonettes.

It's dragonville.

A bright blue dragonette takes a big bite of volcanic rock and noisily crunches it. "Oh no, what has she eaten? She must have gorged herself silly. Daisy is going to have a tummy ache." I rub my abdomen in sympathy. "I'm normally so careful with what I feed her." Daisy is only young, and we've focused on a special dragonette mix diet, with the perfect number of rocks to help her digestion.

We stand and stare at all the dragonettes running, flying, and playing. My heart breaks a little, to think Daisy has been lonely. It makes me feel like I've been selfish. Keeping her all to myself.

Daisy scrambles around the tree and dashes towards me. I drop, ignoring the bite of uneven ground on my knees and can't help but smile as she charges into my arms. "Are you having fun? I hope there aren't any boys."

As I stroke her golden scales, her excited heart flutters underneath my fingers. Instinctively, I let a sliver of my magic trickle its way through her. I don't know what the heck I'm doing, but for my sanity, I need to check that she's physically okay. After only a few seconds, my magic dissipates happily. I sigh with relief. Daisy is perfectly healthy. Her tummy is fine, she's just exhausted from playing and overdue a nap.

"They don't smell real," Owen says in a low voice. "They smell like Larry." Oh. I nod. That makes sense. Fake dragonettes are safe dragonettes.

Done with my fussing and using my knee as a springboard, the little gold dragon springs away from me. With her wings flapping, to add an extra oomph to her run, she scampers off towards a hot pool. It will be a few more years until the bones in her wings are strong enough for her to fly.

I stand, wiping dirt and stones off my jogging bottoms.

"Hey." Owen nudges me. "You okay?" I swallow a few times and twist my hands together. I don't think I can answer as my emotions are all over the place, so I nod and then shake my head almost at the same time.

I'm not okay.

His heavy arm settles around my shoulders, and he pulls me against his side. I melt against him. After ten silent minutes of watching the dragonettes play, his big hand cups my chin and his grey eyes find me. I expect him to say something poignant. "Best pocket dimension ever." He grins. His smile involves his eyes, and he practically lights up.

Wow. My heart misses a beat.

"Do you want to go for a walk?" I rasp out. Staying inside is making me anxious. I need to get out of the hotel and get some fresh air. Not that I know if the air is fresh. I know nothing about this strange realm. It's scary.

Owen grunts a confirmation, and I shuffle along beside him as we head down to the ground floor. I'm sad. It's that feeling that you get when your best friend has a group of new pals, and you don't fit in. I know it's daft. Most people would say Daisy is only a dragonette. But for the few months that I have had her in my life, she's become important to me. I love her.

Now it appears I've been cruel, selfishly keeping her to myself. I rapidly blink so I don't cry. I've never seen her so happy.

It's a good thing and I shouldn't be feeling sad. What an ass I am. I should be happy for my little dragon.

CHAPTER SEVENTEEN

We leave through the main door. The path that was cracked and bumpy last night is smooth at our feet. I can't believe that was only last night. So many things have already happened. No wonder my head feels like it's going to explode.

Owen takes one step for every three of mine. I try to widen my stride, but I slip and almost pull a muscle. Out of the corner of my eye, I catch the hellhound's lips twitch as he represses a laugh. Thankfully, the big oaf slows down.

As I walk normally, each step I take is lighter. The air smells sharp and crisp, a far cry from the pollution in the real world. If I relax my eyes, tiny floating filaments spark and crackle with magic. Full of energy. This pocket realm is more real to me than the world I come from. Everything around me buzzes with magic. The feeling of being home thrums through me. It builds up through my legs and zings into my chest.

Home.

"Do you feel welcomed, as if you have come home?" I ask him.

"Peaceful. There's a level of safety here that I haven't felt before. Welcomed, yeah, but not like I've come home. Is that what you're feeling?"

"Yeah, it's weird." I rub my chest. "I've never felt it before."

"But—" He stops his words and rubs the back of his neck.

"What?"

"Well, you are from a big coven. Don't you feel like that when you go to your Mum's?"

I laugh. It sounds bitter to my ears, and I shake my head. Without thinking, I overshare. "I'm the coven's embarrassment. The lack of my power rubbed my parents the wrong way." I inwardly groan. I've said too much. The hellhound is practically a stranger, and worse, my dad sent him to help me.

It's my turn to awkwardly rub the back of my neck. He must think I'm a proper cow. "It was my fault. I was... urm... a troublesome child." I shrug and fake a smile.

The hellhound narrows his eyes. I trust Owen, and I have a huge crush on him, but he's friends with my well-respected dad. I don't even want to go near who he'd believe if I told him the truth.

Nah, even I wouldn't believe it. Reputations are broken in moments, and with a little digging, he'd find mine is way past the dust age. Broken and ground so fine, it's just sand. I am seen as beyond nothing. A day of being a fantastical host doesn't change any of that.

I will always be the defective witch.

A small sigh of pain slips from my lips and I pull at a piece of rock that's embedded itself into the fabric of my jogging bottoms. I'm a nice person—unless I am channelling my mother— and if there's one thing creatures don't understand, it's niceness. It freaks them right out.

But it doesn't matter if you are a nice person when your entire coven thinks you are a waste of space. That is why I am terrified for him to get a full look at the person I am. He will be appalled and will no doubt walk away like everyone else. I thought I got over this. I know better than to live in the past. Now there's an awkward silence between us.

The path changes to a crunchy golden stone. It's the real fancy stuff I admired at a country estate. My eyes drift across the empty car park. It seems bigger than it did last night and there's a signpost that wasn't there yesterday, directing people to a leisure centre, to the swimming pool and gym. Crikey, there is also a sign for the stables. Heh, I can't remember that one.

Something nags at me, something is missing... My eyes scan the empty car park. Oh. Hang on a minute. The car is missing! "The hire car is gone," I squeak. "I was thinking about sending it back... Did I?" *Oh heck, what did I do with the car?* I bounce from foot to foot. Goodness gracious, if that happened, this place is even more dangerous than I thought.

Owen frowns and fishes out his phone. It appears tiny in his hand. I don't know how he doesn't press all the buttons at once, his fingers are so big.

I can't even bloody think without the magic doing something wacky.

Stop doing that, I internally whisper. The breeze playfully tugs at my hair, and I stare at the crunchy stone underneath my trainers. If it's listening to my thoughts, then it can listen to this. *If I need your help, I will ask, but you need to stop reacting to my every thought. It's creepy. I may not be talking to you, so double check first, yeah? Thank you for being so smart and helping me, but just ask or wait until I'm more direct. Okay? It's freaky. You are freaking me the hell out.*

And now, now I'm going crazy.

"The car is back at the hire company. It appeared out of nowhere with the keys in the ignition." Owen lifts his sparkling eyes from the phone and raises an eyebrow.

"Oh." My hands flop about in a "what can I do?" gesture.

"Handy, eh?" he says with a grin and a friendly nudge that makes my silly heart flutter.

"Very," I mumble.

I tuck a strand of hair behind my ear as I desperately search for a change of subject. "Urm, do you like being a hellhound?" I blurt out. Yeah, hit him with a nice simple question. I roll my eyes. I guess I want to know more about this man. He has this whole masculine energy thing going on, yet his kindness seeps through. It is a heady combination.

Owen tips his head to the side in contemplation and we continue walking. "Yes, I enjoy stopping the bad guys and helping people. It's not a nine-to-five job, and a time or two, things have got so hairy, I didn't think I'd make it. I miss being out in the field with the lads. I've been watching Forrest's back in Ireland and that girl..." He smiles. My heart squeezes in disappointment that the smile isn't for me. "She can get herself into a hell of a lot of trouble."

Forrest again. Not only do they work together and have a relationship where he can guarantee her help without having to ask, but he also drinks what I'm guessing is her favourite drink. No way I can compete with a friendship like that. My heart sinks and I force my face into a normal expression. Jealousy doesn't suit me. *I have lost the plot.* The sooner this guy leaves, the better.

"I've never been so busy. I don't regret what I am, what I've done. It's in my blood. The only thing I regret is not getting to a bad situation quicker, being too slow to save an innocent. That can eat you up if you let it. When you see the worst in people over and over again, it gets old. It gets old real fast. I guess I have always been destined to be a soldier."

It's his calling. I can appreciate that. His honesty floors me. I was lucky to have lived a privileged life for as long as I have. I might have been an outcast, but at least I was safe. The horrible things Owen must have seen, had to do. Yet, he'd do it all again to keep people safe. The hellhound is a hero. I reach over and rub his forearm, and he smiles at me.

With an *oof* of surprise spilling from my lips, Owen pulls me to his side and wraps his heavy arm around me. I dip my head to hide my smile. *Only friends,* my inner voice screams. *He is out of your league.* With that single thought, the smile is wiped from my lips. I can do friends. I can push my feelings away and be friends with this man. It's not his fault that I am hopelessly in love with him. When we come to a turn in the path, I take the chance to slip from underneath his arm. It is the right thing to do.

It isn't until we walk for a while that I realise something else is making me uneasy, and I take a few minutes to pinpoint exactly what it is. There aren't any birds or insects. No signs of life. There is only the sun and the breeze.

The tickle of wind and the squeak of the branches from the trees above us, along with our footsteps, are the only sounds. Wow, it's freaky. Now I recognise it, the environment around us is so fake, and unsettling.

Like we are strolling through virtual reality.

I close my eyes and ask the magic to fix that. I don't want this place to feel odd. There is already the fake sun and weather. I open my eyes to see a fat bumblebee buzz pass my nose and a monarch butterfly settles on a patch of bluebells underneath the trees. I don't know if they would be about this time of year, but they aren't real, and it's not like I'm going to create a hard frost and kill them.

They are perfect. A giggle escapes me as a bluebottle smacks against Owen's cheek. He frowns. "Your handiwork, I take it?"

"Yes."

"I like it." He rubs his face. "Perhaps not the kamikaze bluebottles, but I like the signs of life."

When we turn the corner, and the trees fall away, the path slopes down towards the lake. I stand and take in the view. The lake is huge, and it is so much bigger than what it appears to be from the hotel. There are a dozen or so ducks, noisily quacking. I smile as we get closer and I watch a duck bob upside down in the water, his bum bobbing up and down as he snatches at some duck delicacy below.

"Do you want to go out on the lake?" Owen asks.

"Huh?" I eloquently reply. My full attention is now on a male mallard duck who is chasing the females around and getting nowhere. They are so lifelike. It's kind of like I ate the red pill and I've joined the Matrix.

"The boat," Owen says, giving me a gentle nudge. His big hand points to a pale blue rowboat that's moored to the side of a quaint wooden dock.

"Oh, I'd love to. I've never been in a rowboat before." I clap my hands and bounce on my toes. I'm excited to explore the lake that spreads endlessly before us.

Owen grins as he holds the wooden boat steady and with a hand, he helps me in. The boat doesn't dare move an inch with the big hellhound gripping it. Once I am sitting, Owen gets in, showing for a big guy he has the balance of a fighter. He settles on the bench seat opposite me and unties the rope, flinging it onto the dock so it doesn't get wet. He then picks up the wooden oars. I nod with encouragement as he digs them into the water.

That's when things get a little confusing, a little bit strange. The boat bounces forward and then lists to the side. It circles back to the dock and bumps into it.

Wood grinds against wood and the oars splash. They splash a lot.

Owen swears under his breath. *Don't you dare laugh.* I suck both of my lips into my mouth and bite down as we continue to go around in a weird circle. *Don't you dare laugh.* I rest my elbows on my knees and politely pretend to watch the ducks. The poor guy doesn't need me staring at him as he increasingly gets more and more frustrated. I casually slap my hand across my mouth to hold in the laughter that is trying to bubble out.

After about five minutes of him rowing and a pool of lake water at my feet, I must ask him. "Owen, have you ever rowed before?" I mumble the burning question through my hands.

Don't you dare laugh.

He must have, right? Owen's ancient. He is from a time long before modern technology. Perhaps he has forgotten?

Owen growls down at the oars. He tightens his grip, the muscles in his forearms tense, and the wood creeks. I think any normal oar would have shattered with the pressure he is exerting. He sighs and lifts his head. He gazes back at me, his grey eyes earnest.

"Well, um... I've used the rowing machine in the gym."

That's it. I lose it. Laughter rips out of me, and I'm howling.

The man is adorable.

"I thought it would be easy."

Tears stream down my face, and the boat rocks violently as Owen's laughter joins mine. "Y-you've used the rower at the gym!" I gasp out. Laughing so hard, I have to hold my abdomen as it's hurting. "Oh, Owen," I say when I can. I wipe my eyes. "I needed that. Thank you." I beam a smile at him, so big my cheeks hurt. He blinks at me with a stunned expression.

"I like it when you are happy," he says gruffly.

CHAPTER EIGHTEEN

When we get out of the boat, I'm still grinning like a loon. I secure the boat before Owen can and laugh at his growl.

"You need to eat a proper lunch," Owen insists. "Let's have a picnic." As soon as the words leave his mouth, a picnic blanket appears on the grass and then one by one, plates, glasses, a basket of food, and a bottle of what appears to be freshly squeezed lemonade appear.

You can say a lot about the host magic, but it's incredibly handy. I have a feeling it's going to make me lazy.

I secretly smile and we settle on the grass. I've never had a picnic before. Owen loads up a plate for me. I blush and mumble my thanks.

As I nibble at the beetroot and feta cheese salad, the sun filters through the trees. It's warm on my skin but not burning. I guess if I can control the weather and the sun isn't real, I can probably also sit outside all day and never burn. I tilt my head up and smile as a welcome breeze flutters across my face.

"Back home, I bet it's freezing," Owen rumbles. I nod and stab at the salad to get another forkful. "I like that your favourite season is spring. The weather here is lovely."

"Huh. I didn't even realise I loved spring so much. Everything I do seems instinctive. I guess I need to think about the weather more if people are going to stay. Maybe it needs to mirror the outside world. Perhaps something I can try later? When I've got more of a grip on the magic. Not that I'm going to go crazy with the rain or anything." I do a full-body shiver and stuff the salad in my mouth.

"You don't have to do that. Like the fae lands, the different courts have the same weather all year round."

"That's a good point."

"I think what you are doing so far is impressive. I've never seen anything like it before." I drop my eyes and poke at the salad. *He thinks my magic is impressive.* My heart sings.

Owen's mobile rings and I wave away his look of worry with a smile and a nod. "It's fine," I mouth. "Answer the phone." Smoothly he gets to his feet and prowls away.

I turn away to give him some privacy.

After a few minutes, he returns but doesn't sit down. A sad yet determined look takes over his handsome face. "That was Forrest. She needs my help."

Oh.

He looks worried, torn between helping me and his duty. I can't have that. Lives are probably at stake. So, like I did when I drove off in the hire car, I again decide to convince him I'm happy to be alone. This isn't his fight, and it's unfair of me to manipulate his time.

"Look at where we are; nothing is going to happen. I will be perfectly fine. Do you need to go now? Where would you like me to send you?" I don't want to do the entire Exorcist opening the portal malarkey that I did to get him here. But I somehow think if it's my idea, using my magic without being forced by the realm, it should be easier… I should be able to do it, easy-peasy. It will be a piece of cake. I hope I will be able to send him to where he needs to go. *Gosh, I instantly feel sick.*

"Yes, please, if you don't mind. Back to where I originally came through will be fine. Flash, I'm sorry I have to leave you. I know you're dealing with a load of—"

"It's fine," I interrupt as I snap open a portal behind him. *Wow, I did it.* "I understand. I didn't expect you to be here long anyway. You have a very important job to do. Thank you so much for helping me. I appreciate it." I drop my eyes from him as my stupid heart hurts. I'm being ridiculous. I fix my gaze on the picnic blanket and thread a tassel between my fingers. "Please be careful."

"I'll be back. I shouldn't be long," he says gruffly.

My magic pings with his lie.

"Sure." My lips pull up to show the fakest smile he's probably ever seen.

I don't need magic to tell me I'm also lying out of my ass.

Everything inside me screams, "Don't go! Please don't leave me!" But I have my pride, and those words would never leave my lips. I cannot be that selfish. My problems are minuscule compared to others. Creatures need him, and Owen does not owe me anything. He has already done so much. He doesn't need to do anything more or be involved with any more of my shit.

"Make sure you eat. You've got to aim to eat at least double what you normally do."

I roll my eyes. "Yes, Dad." I wave my hand towards the portal. "Go. Be careful and I'll see you soon." Owen nods and steps into the portal, then with a final look back at me, he is gone.

Everybody leaves. I am, after all, a throwaway person.

A sad sounding whine comes from my throat and I slam my hand across my mouth to absorb the sound.

It's okay. I'm okay. I am just being a bit daft.

I force a forkful of salad into my mouth. It tastes like ash on my tongue, but I finish every bite. Once I finish the desert, I roll my shoulders, and with a wave of my hand, everything is gone. As I crawl up from the ground, I look at my hands. I don't think I need the hand gestures. The entire waving my hands about is kind of weird. If I'm ever in a situation where I do not want to show my intent, I need to stop doing the weird wave. Otherwise, I might as well get a fake wand and glitter.

I turn to walk back to the hotel, and cold encompasses my limbs. The sensation is eerily odd. The magic tingles a warning and then my entire existence folds around me. Sunlight, starlight, the magic explodes, and everything that I am is violently ripped away.

Oh no!

CHAPTER NINETEEN

I hold in a terrified scream as I'm swept along like I'm caught in a rip current. As the dizzying world settles around me, I attempt to school my face into a serene expression. A group of strangers is staring. I so meant to do that... Did I *Step?*

I bloody teleported. Unbelievable. I think I left my stomach back at the lake. I'm in reception and at least a dozen dryads are standing before me, the remnants of a portal fading behind them.

"Gracious host," a lady says, stepping forward from the group. She drops into the most incredibly low curtsey. I blink a few times and my mouth flops open. What the heck? How do I react to that? I internally groan when all the dryads follow her lead. Fourteen of them, my magic helpfully supplies.

I wave my hands in the air and a "Hi" squeaks out.

My frantic waving encourages them to return to normal, and the lead lady continues what must be a readymade speech. "We are here for sanctuary—our trees are in peril. The humans and the dwarfs demand progress, so they have been ripping out our forests and ignoring the environmental protection orders the fae council put in place. No one will help us, and we are dying." The willowy lady leans towards me, her pale blue eyes glimmer with tears. I swallow and have to pin my arms to my sides so I don't fidget.

"I'm sorry to hear that."

"With your permission, mistress host, we would like to bring our trees to be rooted in your pocket world. We will lend you our strength, and you will allow us to live without fear so all branches can flourish, and leaves can nurture the ground."

Ah, that sounds completely ceremonial, and I have no idea what to say. My eyes flick about nervously like I'm a cartoon villain. I need Larry. "Well, okay." *Nice one, Tuesday. Real eloquent.* I give myself a sarcastic mental thumbs up.

The surrounding dryads all seem to breathe a sigh of relief at my words. Encouraged, I try again, hoping for the best. "You are all more than welcome." Better. This is all a bit of a shock. What more can I say? The poor dryads are dying. I can't have that on my conscience. And who doesn't love trees?

"Thank you, mistress." I inwardly cringe. The whole *mistress* thing is weird. It's something that we can work on once they've settled in. The other dryads join in with their thanks as I frantically look around for Larry. Where did he go? It's not like he needs a toilet break.

"Here is our sacrifice."

The—what now? Sacrifice?

The dryads part and a girl is unceremoniously dragged between them. Her dirty clothes hang off her painfully thin frame. When the dryads let go, I see the skin on her forearms is cracking. I look closer and see it's not just her arms. Like the bark of a tree, her skin sloughs off from her face and neck.

I worry even a slight touch will make it crumble. She needs urgent medical help. My heart ricochets off my ribs as they roughly push her towards me. The momentum of the push is too much. Her left leg drags behind her, and her right leg can't keep her weight. She flops to the floor in a tangle of limbs at my feet.

I silently yelp, my eyes widen with horror, and I drop to my knees. Without thinking, I reach out my hand and she flinches away.

Of course, she does. She's a sacrifice.

Her eyes roll about like a frightened horse and, with the last of her strength, she drags herself away from me. My heart flips. It cracks in my chest.

"You'll take her remaining life force as payment for our relocation?" the dryad asks.

A strange gurgling sound leaves my throat. My tongue is numb, frozen, and I don't know how to respond. *"You'll take her remaining life force as payment for our relocation?"* The leader's voice keeps echoing in my head. This whole situation is beyond me and my life experience. I mash my lips together. Oh no, I'm going to puke. I dry heave into my fist.

Maybe I should try to make my face into a villainous snarl, try to convince them I'm an evil creature. The threat that they undoubtedly imagine I am. *This is all too much.*

Everything around me instantaneously drifts away. Dimly I realise I'm in shock. For a few moments, I can't see or hear anything and it's like my brain shuts down and reboots. What happens if I am sick or I give in to the floundering panic that lies in wait beneath the shock. If these creatures are willing to sacrifice one of their own, what will they do to me if I act like prey?

Where the heck is bloody Larry when I need him?

As if answering a summons, the redheaded construct pops into existence. He takes in my wide-eyed form on the floor with the girl and casually steps over us.

"Welcome to The Sanctuary," he says in his friendly, jolly tone. I scowl. Can't he see everything is going to shit? "If you will all sign our terms and conditions, I can get you settled." He grabs the check-in datapad. "Are you okay to sign on behalf of your party? Excellent. If you just sign here and here. I see you brought a sacrifice. Lovely."

Lovely?

I realise the fae creatures are politely ignoring us. It's as if a family member and a friend isn't rasping with pain and fear on the floor at their feet. Like a piece of rubbish, they ignore her. Acting as if I'm going to suck the remaining life out of her while they check in.

What the hell is wrong with these people?

"Wonderful. Now, are we relocating your trees?" Larry herds the dryads away and they make their way outside.

Leaving the girl to her fate.

Anger ignites and the magic in my chest bubbles with the violent emotion. This is supposed to be a sanctuary. Sanctuary shouldn't require sacrifice. I need to get away from these parasites before I do something I'll regret. With a single thought, this time controlled, the magic twists around us and, with another gentler wave, sucks us into the ether.

* * *

We are at the top of the hill, at the edge of the forest. The lake is far below us and we are sheltered from any wind. The dryad pants next to me, on the verge of hyperventilation. Her breath wheezes through her cracked lips and rattles her chest.

The girl rolls into a ball. "Please, make it quick. Don't let it hurt," she whispers.

I brush away the loose forage and then sit down next to her. I hug my knees. "What's your name?" Whoa, my throat is so damn tight. The girl's rapid breathing pauses. I can see her confusion at what she must think is an odd question. Murderers don't ask people their names, right?

"E-Erin."

"Well, Erin, my name is Tuesday. I know what you've been told, but it isn't true... Well, it isn't true of me. I will not hurt you. In fact, I'm going to try my best to help you." I rock slightly and nibble on my lip. "I'm thinking that you're struggling because of your tree?" Erin moves, so I take that as a nod. "Okay, so I'm going to—somehow—fix you both."

Erin lifts her head. Hazel eyes blink at me with utter, desolate confusion. "Is this some kind of joke?"

"No." I've never been more serious in my life.

"You're not gonna kill me?"

"No, but I need your help. You see, I've been a host for a day, and I've never done this before." Unless I count sending my magic through Daisy.

"A day? And you're willing to try to save us— me and my tree?"

"I want to try."

A tear dribbles down the side of her face and another follows.

Oh.

Erin buries her head in her hands and sobs. I wiggle on the ground and my hands uselessly flutter. I want to comfort her, but I don't know if I can. A minute ago, she thought I was going to suck the life out of her. It isn't every day that your friends and family attempt to sacrifice you to a *monster.*

I'm the monster.

I tuck my hands underneath my knees and rock a little as she cries. The dryad's pain is infectious, I want to ugly cry too. But I hold it in. I desperately hold off my thoughts. I can't dissect all this now. Erin is too important; she is the priority. So, I force myself into a blank state, a professional numbness.

When I think about this later, or if I dare to tell anyone, I will probably rage. But now, with the dryad crying, beyond the forced numbness... I feel so sad.

I hope Owen comes back soon. I need a hug.

When Erin's sobs are but a whisper, I clear my throat. "Are you ready for me to try?"

"Yes, please," comes the muffled reply.

"Okay, I need to urm... touch you." I cringe. "Can I please hold your hand?"

I can't even imagine how brave Erin must be as she takes in a shuddering breath, unfolds herself, sits up, and places a delicate hand in mine. Even though her hand feels like I'm holding a piece of wood, and slivers of bark-like skin sprinkle into my palm, I give it a gentle and what I hope is a reassuring squeeze.

"Okay." I take my own shuddering breath and close my eyes. I don't have to call my magic; it's there.

The tattoos glow bright white, painting patterns on the trees behind us as they swirl and dance on my skin. I can imagine I look a little like a disco ball.

The magic knows what I want, I guess 'cause it's a part of me. Like my heart, the beat pushing blood around my body. The magic is the same. It's a part of me. How quickly things have changed from visceral hate of magic to comparing it to an organ. Never in my wildest nightmares would I believe that could happen.

The silver magic flows into the dryad. Oh. Oooh, I can feel the rot. The pain of her tree, the agony from the very top of its branches down to its roots. Something heavy has crashed into it, and the tree has been ripped carelessly from the earth.

They are connected. Symbiant. And both are dying. Through that connection, my magic enters the real world. It crawls through the earth. With pinpoint precision, I free the crushed branches from the ground and gently unwind the roots that are buried in the mud. I ease the tree's pain as I call it to me. I pull it through a portal.

The portal opens behind us, and I pick the perfect spot. Where the soil is full of nutrients, sheltered from the elements, but where the light from my sun will hit the tree perfectly.

The ground gently parts, pulling the tree into its warmth. Each root is unravelled and repaired. The magic creeps in a spiral around the trunk, healing all wounds, spreading out inch by inch across the branches and encouraging new spring growth.

My forest is already full of magic and as connected as I am; I can hear the hum of the wood's joy at having such a beautiful fae tree join its company. Erin's tree sings back. No longer in pain. When it can do no more, my magic gently and reluctantly swirls away.

Erin groans and my concentration wanes. I blink and sweat rolls in my eyes, making them sting. I screw my eyes shut and dig deep into myself. I'm only half-finished. Now comes the scary bit: healing Erin.

I can do this. I must.

My magic gently creeps inside of her and immediately starts repairing her cells. It heals to the point where her body can then take over.

I can almost see the red and white blood cells rush into each area. My magic collects the toxins and the rot as it goes, repairing and syphoning. My breath becomes laboured as Erin's breathing stabilises, but I push on. I just need a few more minutes.

There, it's done.

I slump to the forest floor and Erin rests against me.

"You did it. You saved us. Oh, Tuesday, thank you. Thank you so much... Oh, are you okay?"

"I'm fine," I slur. The two paltry words get stuck in my throat. *It is not safe to lie here*, warns my inner voice. I force myself to roll onto my side and I blink up at Erin. I don't have to force my smile. "Hey, you look great." My eyes swivel to her tree. "You both look great." Erin's short brown hair is glossy, and her skin has returned to a soft, healthy shade.

My head is a little floaty, like I have low blood pressure as I sit up. I can't look at Erin for this next bit. I trace the soil with my finger. "The other dryads, urm, they're on the other side of the forest." I can feel them. "I didn't know if you wanted to be closer. If you can give me a few days, I can mov—"

"No," Erin quickly interrupts. "If it's okay, I'd like to stay here. This spot is beautiful. If it's okay with you, I don't want to see them. Not for a while. Not ever, if I can help it." A fat tear runs down the side of her nose.

"Take all the time you need. Do you need somewhere to stay? I'm tapped out, but you can stay at the hotel overnight. I could build you a cabin? You don't have to see them."

"I will stay with my tree. Do you mind?" Her hazel eyes shine with unshed tears. "I'd like to sleep now."

"Oh, of course," I squeak out. I do an undignified roll onto my knees and somehow, with pure will alone, I scramble to my feet.

"Thank you. Thank you so much, Tuesday. You saved my life. I can't quite believe it." With each word, Erin steps back towards her tree. When they touch, her human form fades, and she becomes part of the trunk.

"You are welcome," I rasp.

CHAPTER TWENTY

After the overwhelming trauma of the day and with horrible thoughts bouncing around in my head, I thought I would never sleep soundly again. But I slept like a log. As soon as my head hit the pillow, I was out. I can only attribute it to using all that magic. My brain might still be actively freaking out, but my body was done. I slept so hard that when I woke up, I almost felt hungover.

Daisy stayed with her dragonette friends, which made me kind of miserable. Then I had to deal with my conscience, telling me I was being unbelievably selfish. I need to be happy for Daisy and be here if or when she needs me.

I'm up bright and early. I have already stuffed my face with breakfast. Taking Owen's advice to heart, I ate more than usual. I dress carefully in a high-neck, cap sleeved, navy cashmere midi dress and knee-high boots.

I've left my hair down, and it swishes against my waist as I make my way to my office. I need to have it cut, but I know if I do, I will hate the shorter length. So, I will refrain until it really needs it. Although, with the new magic sloshing through me, that might be some time.

I'm startled when I see Atticus sitting in the lounge area of reception, casually drinking a mug of something. I presume coffee.

Not blood. Gag.

He assesses me with those black eyes of his, and once I've passed some vampiric test, he greets me with a silent nod.

"Morning," I say, returning his nod.

"Good morning. I see we have more guests, the tree fae."

"Yes. I hope they won't disturb you. Your privacy and comfort are important."

"Not at all. I like the changes you have put in place. It makes for more of a pleasant stay. Don't worry, I won't eat any of them." He flashes his fangs.

I roll my eyes at his theatrics. He's not the first vampire that I've dealt with, even if he is the first pureblood. But the guy is super old, and he has a reputation to maintain.

"That's good to know. Although I should warn you, my magic will not allow you to harm another guest. Please let me or Larry know if we can help to make your stay more pleasant, or if you need anything."

"I will. Thank you, good lady."

"If you'll excuse me." Atticus nods and I spin away. I head to the back of reception and my office. But a stray thought stops me in my tracks. Burning curiosity. I turn back to the vampire and the nosy question spills from my mouth. "What are you doing here?" I wince. Yeah, I said that so beautifully. "You can tell me it's none of my business, but you are..."—I point to his immaculate suit and the whole 'grrrr I am a pureblood vampire' thing he has going on—"and this is..." I wave my hands at reception and bug my eyes meaningfully. "The hotel was not a nice place to stay before I arrived."

Atticus tilts his head to the side, and his black eyes take me in again. I'm almost positive he's going to tell me to get lost. "I loved a woman once. She went missing and all I could find led me here. To this hotel."

"Oh," I say eloquently. Well, that's deep. I wasn't expecting that. I shuffle from foot to foot but maintain eye contact. I've inadvertently asked a painful question and now I must see it through. The least I can do is look him in the eyes. "I'm sorry."

"I will stay until I can find what happened to her."

Oh. My stomach twists when he allows me to see the pain in his eyes. It is like a real-life tragic love story. My lower lip wobbles in sympathy. "She must be a very special person." I can't imagine being loved that much or loving someone so much that I can't move on. My eyes nervously flick about reception. "There is something not right about this place."

The vampire's black eyes narrow. I take that scary look as confirmation. I think little of what goes on here will get past him. I'd love to pick his brains. I'm sure, in talking to him, I'd get the nitty-gritty of this pocket realm.

But you have to give a little to get something back. Build trust.

So I aim for honesty, hoping sometime soon, the vampire will help me.

I nervously lick my lips and plough on. I need to trust my instincts. "When the dryads arrived, they brought a sacrifice. They wanted me to drain a girl of her power. Her life force. Erin... She's nice... She's alive," I squeak out as I wave my hands in the air. "I didn't, you know, urm, drain her. I'd never hurt an innocent." I shrug and scratch the back of my head. I drop my voice. I should have put a privacy bubble in place, but my magic tells me there is no one else around. "Look, it's only day two, but no matter how long it takes, I'm going to get to the bottom of everything. If I can, you know, find answers about your lady friend... Help..." My words come to a stumbling halt when he scowls.

His anger rents the air around us. My heart jumps a beat and my stomach flips. Shit, this creature is scary.

He takes a deep breath in, and it's like a mask falls into place. "Your kind words mean nothing. I've given up hope. I know she is dead." He taps his chest, and his voice drops darkly. "I just can't seem to move on. That's what happens with old things. Change is hard."

"Not just when you're older. I hate change." I wrinkle my nose and scratch my wrist. "It gives me hives." Atticus's top lip moves in an awful semblance of a smile, and with a dismissive nod, he takes his mug of *coffee* and prowls away.

I sigh with relief and wipe my sweaty palms on my dress. That wasn't a conversation I thought I'd be having with the vampire council leader. I think he is the European leader, actually, not just Britain.

I shiver and scamper to my office. Let's hope the knowledge of his lost love doesn't bite me on the bum and he kills me. I puff out my cheeks and la-la in my head for a few seconds.

I have a meeting with Nyssa, the nicer host. Hopefully, I'll find some answers. I don't know this lady. I know I can't blindly trust her. I can't blindly trust anyone. So even though she was nice to me when we first met—well, nicer than the other hosts—I must remind myself she is not a friend.

I debate on where to take the meeting. I don't need to be showing her any more than I already have. So I decide to use the conference room again. Larry said the conference room only opens for council meetings, but I find no issue.

I take the same seat and strum my fingers against the glass table as I wait. The time ticks. I'm early. In the end, I don't have to wait long. The meeting magic pulses in my chest, in the rhythm of a telephone. When I acknowledge the weird sensation, the air in front of me shimmers and there she sits.

"Hello, Tuesday." She greets me with a warm smile that I instantly don't trust. I've seen the same look reflected on my face.

"Nyssa, thank you for meeting me." I smile back with my own professional but fake warmth.

"I am happy to. Now, you must be bursting with questions. Let's start with you asking me everything you need to know."

Wow. That is blunt. I have the almost overwhelming urge to word vomit everything that is going on in my head. I smack the eager words back down my throat and prioritise what I want to discuss. What is the most important?

My mouth is dry. "Thank you. That's a kind offer." I swallow and a mug of tea appears on the table. I mentally thank the magic and wrap both hands around it. Nyssa watches the whole thing, a flash of greed in her eyes. Interesting. Can her pocket dimension do that? Or is it unique to mine?

It's not important. I need to come to grips with this entire power sucking thing because if I don't, it's going to drive me crazy. "Do they pay? If you have a hotel in your dimension, do they pay to stay as a guest?" What I'm getting at is, do they pay with people? I still can't get over the whole situation with the dryads. It is sinister. The entire host thing is so snide.

"Well, there's only ever been one hotel in our history, and that's yours. No one else has strangers coming into their dimension. The security risk is immense. I would never put myself in that situation. My pocket dimension is small, with no outside space. I use my magic to build magical spaces—trinkets like bags, storerooms, nothing too elaborate. My clients love the fact that they can buy a magical bag. It weighs next to nothing, yet inside it holds their entire wardrobe." She leans forward in her chair as her eyes assess me. "The host that created your dimension wanted to help people. Can you believe that?" She titters into her hand. "He was the first to die. He wanted a world that could be a sanctuary." She wrinkles her nose. "But he didn't have the power. It was in a time when communication with the other worlds was difficult, not like it is now. I'm sure with your connection to Earth you'll be able to get enough guests. To answer your question, people do pay, and not all ways are monetary. To maintain the bonkers idea of keeping a sanctuary, you'd have to leech off your guests' power."

Stealing people's power seems to be a common theme.

I hunch in the chair and hug my arms around myself. I'm uncomfortable. It looks like my disgust in the dryads was unwarranted. They were so desperate, and they thought they were offering the right thing.

No wonder hosts have been hunted down, the snarky voice pipes up. This time I must agree; it doesn't look good.

Nyssa continues, seemingly not aware of how uncomfortable I am. "I guess you can charge money. Many a host has become exceedingly wealthy from our gift. That's what I do. But in running a pocket realm, energy matters. If you ignore the risks, the whole hotel idea has merit. Say you have guests—their essence adds to the magic. It's different with every host and every dimension. A small dimension like a storeroom can be powered for a thousand years with a few seconds of someone's life force—a drop of blood. A realm the size of yours"—she looks out of the window—"with the way it has grown, you might require years."

I'm unable to cover my horrified expression. I blink rapidly. Is she for real? I've given up my career in retail management for a hotel, a realm, that will cannibalise its guests.

Oh my goodness, what have I done?

No, there's no way I'm allowing it to do that. What about Owen? Has this bloody hotel been eating him? I think I'm going to be sick.

"Look at your face. You don't have to do that, Tuesday," Nyssa says, her eyes bright with understanding. She waves her hand across my arm, like an air kiss. "Close the hotel if the idea is so terrible. Keep your magic to yourself. You don't have to worry if you think about yourself. Why would you waste your magic on helping others anyway? No one else cares we hosts are dying. Take the power back, shrink the world to a manageable level and live your life." Nyssa narrows her eyes. "You want to help people?" She smirks at the idea and at what she sees on my face. "But you hate the idea of a power exchange. Think about it another way. You're from Earth?"

I do an odd little shrug of acknowledgement. My shoulders and neck are so tight.

"You spend, say, eight hours of your life a day working to earn wages to live. Your time in exchange to pay your bills. Yes?" She stares at me meaningfully and I nod. "Staying in your pocket realm, your sanctuary"—her nose wrinkles and she snarls the word with disgust— "the guests pay in power rather than money." She leans back in her chair and does a little stretch. She rotates her wrists in a way that, if I was with her in person, I'm sure I'd hear the click of her joints. "Both ways suck a little on the soul. At least this way, the hypothetical guest doesn't get sore feet and the hours in the day are their own.

"The balance is up to you." She holds her hand out and tips it like a scale. "Which way the needle falls. Too much and you hurt people. Not enough, and the pocket dimension disintegrates around you." She wiggles her fingers. "This balance doesn't make you evil. It is just a different payment system than the one you're used to. You wouldn't get much power from a pixie, barely a drop. But you could take a sizeable chunk from an immortal, like your hellhound. He wouldn't even notice the exchange."

Her explanation makes me breathe a little easier. It makes sense in a freaky, horrific way. Not that I'd touch any of Owen's power. Or anyone's power without permission. It's not something I could ever condone 'cause I'm not a psychopath.

This conversation highlights the difference between the hosts and me. I'm never going to belong, and you know what? I'm happy with that. I don't want to.

I think what hurt me about Erin's entire situation was that I could see myself in her shoes. I've always been seen as the weak person in a group. I do not doubt that in a reverse of fate that involved witches, it would have been me up for the role of sacrifice.

"I could pay the cost," I mutter.

"No, that's not possible, and it's completely unrealistic. The magic doesn't work that way. As I said, magic requires balance. But you don't have to keep The Sanctuary open. You don't have to have a hotel. You can just close your doors and pretend this has all been a bad dream." She smiles with satisfaction, happy with her advice.

Huh. Maybe a little bit too happy.

CHAPTER TWENTY-ONE

I get a warning tingle that a portal is about to open and then Larry's frantic voice comes from reception. "Tuesday, come quick."

"What now," I groan. I slam my hands on the desk and spring up, abandoning my business plan to see what all the fuss is about. I guess I need a break.

I stride into reception. The hotel is in chaos.

Everything slows down. It's like I am on the set of a film as smoke billows from the portal and heart-stopping moans rent the air.

The cloying smell of sweat, burned hair, and blood permeates the hotel and makes me gag. I cover my mouth and sway as my feet root me to the wooden floor. All I can do is stare in shock at the frantic activity before me.

A huge portal is open. It almost spans the entire room, and messed up looking creatures are getting spit out onto my floor. Dressed in tattered black uniforms and overspilling with weapons, the creatures' oversized eyes, pointed ears, and long hair announce these new *guests* are elven.

Not just elves, as I see the tell-tale black warrior markings peeking between the ripped fabric on their arms. Aes sídh warriors, to be exact, not normal fae. Two of them look to be seriously injured and they stay where they've landed, although one is rolling about and groaning, so he can't be that bad.

"I am not trained to deal with this shit," I mutter. It's like I have woken up into a lucid nightmare. An average, if not strange, day has inexplicably changed to this. What the heck am I supposed to do? *I am a soon-to-be ex-retail manager, now a reluctant hotelier. I can adapt.* I square my shoulders, lift my chin, and calmly track my unexpected guests.

The elves are setting up defensive positions.

In *my* reception.

That will not do.

When one of them shunts a sofa away from the window and goes to break the pane of glass with the hilt of his knife, my brain goes into instant emergency manager mode. I need to get control of this clusterfuck. Now.

"STAND DOWN! THIS IS A SANCTUARY, NOT A BATTLEFIELD!" I bark.

The elves stop what they're doing for a second and eye me like I'm nuts, then continue as if I haven't spoken. At least the elf that was going to break the window refrains. "Naughty elf," I magically growl in his ear as I shove the sofa back to its rightful place. He jumps, rubs his ear, and looks about wildly.

An episode of a medical drama comes to mind and the theory behind basic triage. "ANYONE WITH CUTS AND BRUISES BUT WHO DOES NOT NEED IMMEDIATE MEDICAL CARE, PLEASE WAIT OVER THERE!" I yell, pointing to the left of the room. "EVERYBODY ELSE GO WAIT IN THE LOUNGE AREA!"

I puff out my cheeks and rub my temple. When I ran from my home, I brought at least four vials of Jodie's healing potion with me. Forrest also stuffed in another six bottles. I am not prepared for war... but the aftermath of a skirmish? Yeah, that I can do.

Larry scurries to my side. "Larry, please, can you make sure they have everything they need?" With a tug of magic, I pull the potions from my room and shove them at him. "Start handing out healing potions."

"Of course."

"Thank you."

Larry clutches the potions to his chest and rushes away. I rapidly move through the elves towards the quiet one I had seen on the floor. The elves ignore me. "NOW PEOPLE! GET MOVING!" I clap my hands and shove them with my magic. "THE MORE TIME YOU STAND ABOUT STARING AT ME, THE LESS TIME I HAVE TO HELP YOUR FRIENDS!" They grumble and hobble to their allocated sides of the room.

Better.

A few of them flick their long hair behind them as if they are fashion models. I roll my eyes. Now all but the seriously injured elf remains in the centre of the room.

Oh, and his scary-looking friend. Yay. Her dark hair, which is as long as mine but decorated in intricate plaits, glares at me. Her big, brown eyes are full of hate. Gee, it wasn't me who kicked her arse and hurt her friend. She needs to reign all that hatred in. I stare her down. I am pissed. The anger, combined with fear, makes me brave.

"Move," I tell her.

"I don't know you," she snarls.

I shrug. "Yeah? I don't know you either, but it didn't stop you and your fellow warriors from crashing into my hotel lobby, did it? You came to me, so move out of my way so I can help him." For a second, I think she's going to throw down and start stabbing me with the wicked-looking knife she is clutching. But she must think better of it. Not getting up, she shifts on her knees, allowing me barely enough room to see what I'm working with.

The unconscious elf is at least alive and bleeding profusely from a stab wound in his abdomen. I place both hands on his wound, and his hot blue blood squishes between my fingers. I wrinkle my nose. Gah, I should have thought about gloves.

This is gross. I am not trained for this shit.

At least the healing magic will deal with any cross contamination. He won't get ill because of my hands.

No, I am more at risk from the unfriendly elves.

If this is an entire court of warrior elves, popping through the portal, I'm in serious trouble. This is supposed to be a hotel, not a hospital. Why on earth did they decide to come here? I've got no idea.

I hunch and brace my hands so they don't shake. *Gosh, I feel vulnerable.* With that thought, I erect a barrier around reception. Not only to stop any of the dryads or Atticus from stumbling into this nightmare but to stop the elves from wandering. I don't want them to cause any trouble while I'm busy and my back is turned.

The realm's magic shudders, and more people come through the still open portal. In my peripheral vision, the portal spits out another bloody mess. Then, with energy that makes my hair flutter and stick to my sweaty face, the portal snaps closed. Thank goodness for that. I didn't want to close it in case I trapped anyone.

I blow at the hair stuck to my cheek and focus. I haven't got time for finesse. I need to heal him quickly. Sinking into the magic, his life force flutters. It is barely hanging on. I throw my magic into his body, using what I learned from healing Erin. Was that only yesterday?

My patient groans. I wince, and the female elf's hand drifts to the hilt of her knife. My eyes narrow on her fingers, and I grind my teeth. *What a cheek. I don't have to help her friend. These guests are taking the piss.*

With a mental snap of my magic, her weapons disappear. All the weapons in the room disappear. I should have done that as soon as they arrived tooled up to finish a war. That was a mistake I won't be repeating.

I wonder if I can make it so the portals won't allow weapons to come through? That might be a superb idea. Most creatures are, in themselves, walking weapons, but at least it limits the risk of being stabbed.

The noise in the room intensifies as my *guests* notice the missing weapons. Their shouts grow in outrage and the angry energy in the room peaks. "YOU WILL GET YOUR STUFF BACK WHEN YOU LEAVE!" I yell. I lift my eyes and glare at the woman. "That was your fault," I mumble churlishly.

"I don't need a blade to kill you," she spits.

I roll my eyes. "Good to know. Neither do I. If you twitch a finger towards me, I'll send your arse back to where you came from. M-kay?" She narrows her eyes at me and nods. "Wonderful." I grin manically, showing too many teeth.

Owen would be proud.

More magic and the elf's gnarly wound closes. I pat him on the chest. "There you go, Mr Elf, as good as new." Feeling exhausted, my hands drop to my sides, and I sag back onto my heels. My leather boots dig uncomfortably into my knees.

"I apologise. Tensions are high from the battle. Thank you," the female elf says, surprising me. The old fairy tale about the fae and their thanks is unfortunately exaggerated. Some say if you thank the fae, you gain a life debt, and vice versa. That isn't the case. But I appreciate the apology.

"No problem. Glad I could help." She pulls her now semi-conscious friend to his feet and guides him to the lounge area where the others are chugging down water. I drag myself to my feet and stumble to my next patient.

Gosh, I am drained.

A humongous black wolf lies in the middle of the floor and a petite girl with a mass of pink hair holds his shaggy head in her lap.

Shifters can heal from anything. Their cells regenerate every time they shift. That's why they don't age once they've hit their biological age of majority. Well, unless they encounter silver, which halts the shifting process completely, then all bets are off. After all they need to be alive to shift. Silver. That's what's happened to this big fella. He is riddled with silver and is bleeding out.

I drop to my knees next to them. "A silver bomb," the petite girl rasps and then violently coughs. "The dust... It's in our lungs. He knocked me out of the way and took the brunt of the shrapnel. You bloody idiot, Nanny Hound. Why did you do that? I would have been fine." Her voice is so raspy, it's like she has smoked two packs of cigarettes a day. I'd have put it down to silver damage, but I've heard her voice before. I recognise it instantly.

Forrest.

"You will help him?" she begs, lifting her eyes to implore me.

Her eyes hold a deep, haunted sadness with an edge. They whisper of death. My heart bounces and nerves twist my insides. One eye is yellow, and the other is too but with a hint of green pooling at the bottom. It makes her wild gaze difficult to hold.

I knew Owen's friend would be fierce, and also pretty, but I did not expect her to be so tiny and innocent-looking.

So bloody powerful.

She's a shifter. A formidable one. I tilt my head; her magic is weird. It bites at mine. Not with aggression, I don't think, but almost playfully. I ignore it and the goosebumps that spring up.

A female shifter in my hotel, covered in blood.

Oh heck. If anything happens to her... it doesn't even bear thinking about.

Female shifters are super rare. There are about ten in Europe. Ten. Wars are fought over them. They are coveted and squirrelled away like precious jewels, and yet, I have one covered in blood, kneeling next to me as she coughs out silver particles. *I should heal her first.*

But if I do, the black wolf will die. While I know she will not die anytime soon, the indecision wears on me. A niggle in the back of my head tells me I know this wolf, but I push the painful thought away. It can't be him. Surely fate wouldn't be that cruel? I sit back on my heels and try to steady my hands, which tremble with fatigue and nerves. *You're spiralling. Snap out of it.* I need to think of triage.

"Please try to heal him," she rasps.

This is a little more than repairing an open wound. "I will do my best. Come on, wolf, let's get you better." I don't know anyone who could fix this. I mentally roll up my sleeves, take a deep breath, and get to work.

With my heart still hammering, I thread my fingers through the wolf's beautiful, densely packed fur. His outer layer is coarse, and the downy undercoat super soft. I gently probe his wounds. He has chunks of silver sticking out of him. Like a furry pin cushion. I know if I don't get the silver out, and he doesn't bleed to death first, the metal will poison him and cause necrosis.

I can do this. Yes, it is a complicated procedure, but I can heal him. I'm the only one here who can.

This time, I close my eyes. I need all my concentration as I reach out with my magic. Cautiously, I touch the shifter's energy with the intention of not disturbing it. I imagine the pad of my finger brushing a pool of water so softly the tension breaks and the water ripples out. My magic is the ripple.

Gently, oh so gently, I follow the ripples through the tissues of his body, hunting out even the minuscule amount of silver nanoparticles. Destroying any trace of the dangerous silver oxide while also repairing his cells. Each cell vibrates at a slightly different frequency. I must match it.

On and on my magic travels, destroying and repairing until... there is nothing left.

Everything inside of him is normal.

"I did it," I whisper. I gently stroke him and then turn my attention to Forrest. "Okay. Now you."

"You are exhausted. I can wait."

"No, you can't. Please?" I hold my hand out, and with a scowl, she places her dainty, pale hand in mine. I do the same thing. This time it is much faster as the silver has settled only in the places where she has breathed it in. Her nasal passages, trachea, and the delicate bronchial tree of the lungs. "There," I say with a satisfied smile.

"Thank you."

"You are welcome."

"This is your fault. If you hadn't encouraged him to work for the fae, this would have never happened," an angry voice snarls. I sigh and lift my head.

"Arsehole, can't you just, you know, like, not be a prick for five minutes?" Forrest growls at the tall, fierce-looking blond man standing above us.

Another shifter.

"Forrest," he growls back, his green eyes flashing.

"Fuck you." She flips him off with both middle fingers and turns away. When she catches my eye, she smiles sheepishly. "Sorry about my brother. He's a dick."

I give a small chin lift in acknowledgement and duck my head back down to assess the black wolf. He still hasn't woken up, and I am worried I have done something wrong.

Forrest's brother prowls around us, and in response to his aggressive body language, she gently lowers the wolf's head to the floor and stands. Using her tiny frame to block her brother from getting any closer, she herds him away from us. With each step, she pokes him in the middle of his chest. My lips twitch. I like her style.

"Yeah, 'cause he isn't in any danger while working with you," she scoffs. "What a load of crap." Poke, poke. "Next time, use your own guys and leave my friends alone. The fae don't need your kind of help, arsehole."

"No fighting at The Sanctuary," I mutter. I ignore them as they continue to bicker. With growing panic, my magic washes over the wolf. Again, I check him, his blood, his cells, and I can't find any trace of silver in his system. I scrape my messy hair back as I think. He should wake up... any second now. It is then I notice that I'm still stroking the wolf's beautiful fur. I am too tired to blush. What a strange thing to do.

I reluctantly pull my hand away. As soon as my fingers leave him, the gorgeous black wolf shifts. It's a blink-and-you'll-miss-it transformation as he changes shape.

Beautiful, rich dark skin and a naked, muscular torso greets my suddenly wide-awake eyes. I've never seen anyone this well-proportioned in useful muscle—ever. I almost swallow my tongue. Mesmerised, I follow the rise and fall of his chest with each of his shallow breaths. I force my eyes up his torso instead of down... The wolf's grey eyes find me. He grins.

Wow. My heart misses a beat. Thank the stars he is okay.

"Hi, Flash."

CHAPTER TWENTY-TWO

"Owen. You're okay!" Forrest drops to her knees beside us, her brother long forgotten. My gorgeous hellhound beams a smile at her like she hung the moon. My raging libido screeches to a halt and my addled heart hurts. My soul cracks a little.

He loves her. I can see it.

With a delicate hand, she pats his chest and I can't help but grind my teeth as my eyes fixate on the motion. *Get off him.* Everything inside me cries. My magic whips out with fury. Forrest doesn't even blink when the naked hellhound she is petting is suddenly dressed from head to toe in his normal black combat gear. *Better.*

"You had me worried there for a second, Nanny Hound. Never pull a stunt like that again. If you had died, I would have gone after you and dragged you from death, just to beat the crap out of you." She huffs and then grumbles, "I'm glad you're okay." Then she hugs him. She loves him too.

Warm grey eyes catch mine over her head and he shrugs as if to say, *what can I do?* My face contorts into a brittle smile and, with determination and a total lack of finesse, I scramble to my feet. "I need to organise this mess. Please excuse me." I turn on my heel and wobble away. "See Larry if you need anything," I say over my shoulder.

Owen is just someone my dad paid to help me. There is no need for me to be upset and I am not the girl who will go after another girl's man. That is the worst thing to do to another person and now that I have seen Forrest in person, felt her power, it would be immoral, and frankly suicidal, to step on her toes. *They love each other.*

My stupid heart is eviscerated.

Instead of running away, like I want to, I reaffirm that I have a job to do. I need to focus on what's happening around me. Owen must have opened the portal here for the warrior elves while he and Forrest tackled some big bad who uses illegal silver bombs. I hope this wasn't anything to do with the elf they were hunting, the one who tried to kidnap me.

As I stomp towards Larry, with each step, I feel more and more like hammered shit. I am quite sure nobody can tell. I'm sure I am pulling off the hundred-percent-in-control-of-the-situation-vibe. I have my manager face plastered on. Crikey, using all that magic in such a short span of time has drained my energy dry.

If this is going to be a typical day in my life as a host, I'm probably going to be dead before the end of the week. I shake off the macabre thought as a high energy protein bar is slapped in my hand.

"Oh. Thanks, Larry."

"No problem. The way you wobbled across the room, I thought you needed it." Well, there goes the idea that I'd nailed my getaway. I scowl and, with trembling hands, carefully unwrap the bar and stuff my face. *I should wash my hands. They are still kind of gooey from the first elf.*

As I chew, another man swaggers over to chat with Larry. He is a shifter, with light hair. He is also dressed in black. Huh. The shifters must work closely with the elves. Which is strange. From my history lessons, working nicely together is unprecedented. Shifters and elves have a nasty intense history of hating each other, and if I remember correctly, shifters may not set foot in Ireland.

It appears things have changed. I shrug. As long as there isn't a ruckus at the hotel and they aren't trying to kill each other, it has nothing to do with me.

On our walk, I remember Owen saying he and Forrest were working in Ireland. I guess I was too busy drooling at Owen to put all that together.

"We will be out of your hair in an hour," he tells Larry in a soft, lilting Irish accent. "I didn't even know this hotel existed. This is a pocket realm, right? With the power buzzing around the room and the fact nobody can wander off as there is an impenetrable force field in place, all evidence points to the fact you must be a legendary host." He slaps Larry on the shoulder. "That's incredible."

My eyes flick between them, and as I chew, my jaw aches. Why are these extra nutty protein bars like chomping on concrete?

"I've never met anyone alive with your branch of magic before. My boss would be interested in working with you."

"Me? Working with me?" Larry splutters. His bright green eyes widen. "Oh, no, sir. You must have me confused. I am but a lowly servant of my mistress." Larry presents me with a flourish of his hand and a click of his heels.

Cute.

"Hi," I say, as I cover my mouth to hide my chomping. As my mouth is still full, the word comes out garbled. The empty wrapper crackles in my grip as I give the shifter a tired wave. The shifter stares at me as if I've got two heads.

"You? You're the host?" he scoffs. "But you are just a girl."

Dick.

I ignore his faux pas. Frankly I can't be arsed.

On the plus side, at least I've finished the protein bar without getting any blood on it. Go me. Larry hands me another. "Thank you. So an hour?" I ask, waving the protein bar as if trying to hurry the shifter along. I have important things to do. Like... cry. "You said you will all be leaving within the hour?"

As I unwrap the new bar, my hands no longer tremble. My energy levels have already increased. My lip curls at the state of my hands and in response magic washes across me, cleaning my navy dress and skin of any residual sweat, goo, and blood.

Handy.

I bite down on the new bar as the shifter chokes on his own spit. Oh dear, I have unintentionally shocked him with my quick clean up. I refrain from offering to pat him on the back. Perhaps Larry should, as they are so chummy.

"Yes, um... mistress?" the shifter mutters, his tone full of disbelief.

The word *mistress* coming from him hits a little bit below the belt. I wince and shake my head. "Oh no, none of that. Ignore Larry, please call me Tuesday."

"Tuesday?" His hard brown eyes narrow. I can almost see his mind churning as he rolls my name around in his head. "Don't I know you? Aren't you Matthew Larson's daughter? The younger one?" He raises an eyebrow.

Oh no, he knows my dad. Can this day get any worse?

"The dud." He nods sagely. "Your lack of magic has been truly exaggerated."

"Can't fool you, can I?" I fake titter. *I need to get out of here.* "Yes, I'm Tuesday Larson, and yes, I have host magic. You are? I know we've never met." I drop the fake smile and narrow my eyes.

"Mac. Pleased to meet you, Tuesday." He holds out his hand. After transferring my snack into my left hand, I reluctantly shake it. "No, we haven't met, but I've seen a photograph of you in your father's office."

Oh. I nod wisely. Insinuating I know about the photo. I didn't know Dad had a photo of me. It must be a group one. I clear my throat.

"So this is *your* pocket realm?"

"Yes."

"Impressive."

I back away from the shifter. "Well, I will just—"

"Our weapons?" Mac taps his thigh and narrows his eyes.

"Will be returned once you've entered the portal."

"Thank you for your help," he says reluctantly. "We wouldn't have survived if it wasn't for your timely portal and assistance. Please give your father my regards."

"I will. Well, thank you for visiting The Sanctuary Hotel. I hope you visit us again, under less exciting circumstances. Larry will help if you need anything. If you will excuse me." I don't wait for confirmation and instead spin on my heel and hurry away.

I fixate my eyes on the door behind reception, not trusting myself to search out a certain hellhound. As I beat a hasty retreat, I catch the raspy voice of Forrest as she tears into Mac. "Sexist much? You'd think being my friend you would have learned not to be a dick."

CHAPTER TWENTY-THREE

Lightning flashes across the sky as thunder booms so loud it rattles the glass. It becomes so dark outside as angry grey clouds roll in and a torrent of rain smashes against the floor-to-ceiling windows.

I made it rain.

Without conscious thought, my mood has affected the weather. I refused to cry, so the realm does it for me. I stare at the sheets of rain, matching what I feel inside, and my guilty thoughts go to Erin and the other dryads. I'm sure the trees will welcome a drink unless I flood the bloody place. I push the clouds apart and release the odd energy in the atmosphere.

What I need to do is work. It's what I am good at. I drag the datapad towards me and click back to my business plan. I studiously make a note that I need to improve the residential suites. It will take me a while to gather the power needed, those damn fae warriors and their power sucking visit. I absentmindedly brush my magic against the realms. *I can't...* my thought trails off.

It should be almost empty from the giant portals and everything, but it is full to bursting. That is not right.

What has it done? Have I accidentally hurt someone?

Oh no, no-no-no.

My overwhelming panic makes me shake like a leaf. I feel sick. *I knew. I knew I should not have trusted this cursed place.* With a pulse of power that I will no doubt regret, as it makes my head spin and my heart pound in my ears. I close my eyes and spread my magic out as I would when healing a body.

Against the blackness of my eyelids, the realm's map appears. As each guest pops up, I urgently do a mental check on them. I start with the elves and the shifters in reception and work slowly outward to the fae in the woods. My entire body sags against the desk as I discover each person is safe and accounted for. Thank the stars.

The realm has not stolen a smidgen of power. In fact, all my guests are glowing a little more with each second that passes. Huh. While my magic is still doing its thing, I tap into the realm's magic a little harder.

I need to know more. I discover an immense bubbling pool of power at its centre. It was not there before. I frown. As tentatively as I can, and with the same creeping delicate fingers of magic I used with Owen, I explore the edges of the deep well. I see where the trickles of power and rivers of magic are coming from.

A relieved laugh spills out of me as I realise what I am seeing: the dimensional realm does not need to steal power. The power, kind of like the formation of clouds, happens naturally. The invisible energy that radiates off every living creature sheds naturally into the air. I can somehow see it. Under normal circumstances,

I would only feel the power when someone like Forrest is scarily powerful. But on my mental map, I see it. I see Forrest glowing like the sun and all my other guests moving stars around her. Their power saturates the air, condenses, and forms into invisible droplets. Which then pool into the realm's well of power.

The varied creature presence alone is enough to replenish the magic. The magic then meets the guests' needs, including my own.

Magical symbiosis.

It never needed to take any power by force. The entire revolting sacrifice saga was a complete farce. Did the other hosts know? Gosh, this changes everything.

Unless... I open my eyes and blink as they re-adjust to the bright light of my office. Unless the magic is fooling me. My stomach dips, and I groan. I sink my head on the desk. Perhaps I need some time out in the real world to get my head on straight. I need to think without any interference, as it's obvious the magic wants me here.

I don't know what is real.

I don't know if I am being manipulated.

I can't trust myself.

Of course, I can't trust myself—I convinced myself that I was in love with a complete stranger, and all the while he was in love with another girl. I turn my head and my cheek presses into the frigid glass of the desk. First, I need to eat to replenish my energy, then wait for the elves and shifters to leave. Then spend a few hours away from this crazy place.

There is a rustle in the hallway, of scales rubbing together, then a scrape of claws on the wood. With a grin, I leap from the chair and fling open the door. Daisy scampers in.

"Hey, pretty princess, this is a pleasant surprise," I say in a singsong voice. "How did you get down here with the magic blocking reception?" I firmly close the door behind her and sit back down. I wouldn't put it past her to Step. I hold out my hands and wiggle my fingers. Daisy jumps, her wings flap, and she gains enough height to land on my lap. "Perfect landing. You are getting so good," I praise.

With a deep contented purr rumbling in the back of her throat, she tucks in her wings and curls into a ball. I gently stroke along her spine and sniff. This is nice. Normal. I blink a few times. I am not crying.

* * *

A mug of hot tea is balanced on my tummy. I grab the individually wrapped piece of Terry's Chocolate Orange. The chocolate normally comes in a bar or in a fancy orange shaped ball that you have to tap on a hard surface to unleash the orange milk chocolate segments. But this packet is special. It has all different flavours of chocolate mixed with the famous orange.

I narrow my eyes and my mouth waters as I fiddle with the wrapper one-handed as my other hand precariously balances the cup. This one is white chocolate. Daisy, who is now sitting on my desk, watches my antics with interest. She juts out her head and with her left nostril, sniffs at the chocolate. She wrinkles her muzzle, completely unimpressed. "No? Good. Chocolate isn't for dragonettes," I tell her wisely.

The plastic wrapper rustles and the piece of white chocolate jumps. A sound of dismay leaves my lips as, with only the one hand, already encumbered with the wrapper, I'm unable to catch the runaway treat in time. The chocolate falls. "Noooo," I groan, horrified as it falls the wrong way, plopping into the cup with a splash.

My poor tea.

I like my tea super-hot, so I can't just stick my fingers in and fish it out. Jodie, my sister, says I have an asbestos mouth, that no tea can be too hot for me to drink. I shrug and strum the porcelain. What can I do?

I stare down at my cup mournfully. I tip it, but I'm unable to see past its brown watery depths. Never mind. I was going to dip it in anyway. I guess now I will have to wait to eat it.

I take a sip. Like a tea connoisseur, I tilt my head to the side and smack my lips. *Huh, the tea tastes the same.* I wiggle my fingers over the bag, and with a dramatic flourish, I close my eyes and reach inside. I crack my left eye open. Oooh, this one is dark chocolate. This time, I unwrap it well away from the cup.

Once I take the last sip of my brew, I grin when I spy the white blob nestled at the bottom. I tip the cup to my mouth and give it a shake. "Come to me, my sweet," I mumble. The white mass doesn't want to move, so I bang the cup on my bottom lip to encourage it. I watch in cross-eyed fascination as the blob oozes towards my mouth.

Slowly, oh so slowly.

"Gah, come on." I stick my tongue into the cup to give it a prod of encouragement. I grin when the melted goo hits my taste buds.

Yum.

I'll have to remind myself to do this again. I could become a superfan of tea-melted chocolate goo.

When my tongue can't reach the remaining chocolate, I stuff my entire hand into the cup. I hum as I use my index finger to scoop up the chocolate trail. Once collected and the evidence from the chocolate mishap erased, I lick my finger clean.

Still humming around the finger in my mouth, I lift my eyes. The hellhound is leaning against the wall. Staring at me. My finger comes out of my mouth with a pop.

I wince.

His grey eyes dance with amusement. "Here you are."

"Here I am," I say as I duck my head and play with the empty cup. I ignore Daisy's happy yip as she greets the hellhound. The traitor. My fingers trace the handle, and my eyes fixate on the movement. I can't look at him.

"Why did you run off?" he asks gruffly.

Owen isn't wearing his normal combat gear. Instead, the hellhound has on grey suit trousers and a black shirt and tie. He looks gorgeous. My stomach flips as if I have got a load of fairies bouncing about in there. Bouncing around drunk.

His big body moves, and he prowls across the room. He stands next to the chair. The heat and the masculine smell of him fills my senses. My mind flashes back to his nakedness and I feel my cheeks go instantly red.

Ah shit.

"I..." *Tell him the truth.* My heart hammers in my chest and my stomach feels as if those stupid drunk fairies go *crazy* inside me. I lick my lips. "I wanted to give you and your girl privacy."

"My girl?" Owen's voice rumbles. "What? Who? Do you mean Forrest?" He laughs.

It's not bloody funny. I can feel the red from my cheeks spreading down my neck and onto my chest. Anger bubbles inside me. Women should build each other up, not tear each other down. Yet, this hellhound thinks the entire thing is hilarious. I will not mess with another girl's man.

My hand tightens on the cup, and I hunch into myself. I must seem so pathetic.

"Hey. Hey, Tuesday, look at me."

I shake my head. His big hand cups my chin and he tilts my head so I meet his eyes. "I haven't got a girl. Forrest is like my adorable, crazy, annoying little sister. I love her; she is pack." I freeze and my breath sticks in my throat. "I'm single, Flash."

He. Is. Single.

The magic doesn't ping. He isn't lying, not that I think he would, but... Oh my, he isn't with Forrest.

"You are? You are single?" I whisper.

"I am. What about you?" His dexterous fingers of his other hand knead the area behind Daisy's horns, and she wraps her tail around his wrist.

"Urm... single. Very, urm, single," I squeak out as I do a bizarre movement with my hands.

Owen chuckles. "Are you now?" He moves so close that I can see little blue flecks dancing in his eyes. I gasp and breathe in his warm, minty breath and the fresh scent of soap. He's had a shower.

"Yes," I croak.

"That is good to know." My heart almost stops at his breath-taking smile. "But you won't be single for long. Not if I have any say in it. I am gonna make you mine, Flash." My mouth pops open, and Owen brushes his thumb across my bottom lip. The taste of him fills my mouth.

"You are?" I rasp against his thumb. "Me?"

Oh.

My entire body is on fire. He is so close I can feel the whisper of his breath on my lips. I squirm in my seat as he closes the scant inches between us. I go cross-eyed as I watch him. He kisses the tip of my nose. And then the left side of my mouth. Then the right. Not quite a kiss. I have the sudden desire to feel that full mouth on mine.

"Can I kiss you?" he whispers roughly.

"Oh, thank—" Before I can say more, Owen swoops in and wraps his arms around me. He lifts me from the chair and into his body. He growls. The sound is so deep, it rumbles in his chest. My heart skips a beat. Dumbfounded and so turned on, I think I'm going to explode. I close the gap between our lips.

I'm kissing him! I am kissing him! And he's kissing me back!

Bumper cars, my addled brain whispers strangely. Wow, the hellhound has fried my brain. It's like an impact of pillowy bumper cars. His lips are firm, but also so soft. Owen tilts my chin to get a better angle to pillage my mouth. His tongue nudges against my lips and I open. Oh my goodness. Our tongues twirl together.

This is an epic kiss.

Way too soon, he pulls away from my mouth, and I follow his lips with a tiny, disappointed moan. "Your dad gave me a heads up—he had an interesting conversation with our friend, Mac. Your coven will arrive any minute."

Dazed, I blink at him and rub my lips together. They are tingling in the best way. "Okay..." I say dreamily. "Can we... at some point... urm, do that again?" My voice comes out breathless, as if I've run a mile.

"Abso-fucking-lutely."

CHAPTER TWENTY-FOUR

I collapse back in the chair in bliss, then my kiss-addled brain starts firing, and the words, *"Your dad gave me a heads up; he had an interesting conversation with our friend, Mac. Your coven will arrive any minute,"* finally sink in and echo around my brain.

Oh no.

No-no-no. My eyes widen. I bend forward and wrap my arms around myself as dread fills me. My mum and dad are coming. They are coming and my time to get a grip on this situation has run out.

Bloody Mac. That damn shifter has gone and dobbed me in to my dad.

My mum is going to flip out. She is going to be a thing of nightmares. I sink back into the chair and my hands shake as I imagine her face when she found out about my new, shiny magic. Not from me, oh no, but from one of my dad's associates. I cringe. She's had time to work herself up into a frenzy, and now they are coming to visit.

Yay.

"What is wrong?"

"Nothing," I whisper.

"Tell me what you are thinking that has such a sad, frightened look on your face."

"They are my thoughts," I grumble in a petulant tone.

What is it about our parents that can reduce us from perfectly normal functioning adults back to little kids?

"I am fine."

Owen chuckles, making me feel even more silly. His grey eyes narrow, and he places his hands on my desk and leans toward me. Our faces are so close, my eyes cannot help but drop to stare at his beautiful full lips.

Crikey, the man is beautiful.

"You are a terrible liar." He taps his nose. "The fear wafting from you burns."

"Oh." *Oh crap.* I look down at my hands and cringe. "I'm sorry." I don't want his sensitive shifter nose to have to deal with my stink.

I try to roll the chair away, but the frustrating hellhound just follows me, concern and determination written all over his face. He grabs hold of the chair and wheels me back towards him as he sinks to his knees. *He is trying to make himself smaller.* My tummy flips.

I take in a deep breath and blow out a series of short breaths to gain control. My knee bounces.

Somehow, I know he will respect my privacy and let this go. But he's earned an explanation. Am I brave enough to be honest? I've never told anyone. He is going to see my coven in action for himself. There will be no hiding it.

Forewarned is forearmed, I guess.

But then... she's always so lovely around strangers, and even with my coven, she hides her nastiness so well. They see me as the bad penny. I'm her scapegoat. If I tell him and she acts all loving, then he's going to think I'm a liar. I don't want to see the distrust or distaste in his eyes. It would break me further. This is why I don't let anyone close.

I chomp on my lip, and then the words blurt out. "I'm worried about what she will say, what with the whole host thing..." My voice trails off and Owen's eyes soften. I drop my voice to a bare whisper. "She can be a bit much, my mum." I twist the cashmere fabric of my dress and thread it through my fingers. "It's stupid, but she can be scary. I-I didn't ring her when I should have and now Mac—"

"Hey. Hey, Flash, I got you." His humungous hand comes up and his thumb brushes away the stupid tears that are trickling down my face. *No, he doesn't.*

"You are only here 'cause my dad asked you."

"Is that what you think? I'm not staying 'cause your dad asked me. Tuesday Larson, you intrigue me. I have an overwhelming urge to be around you." The hellhound smiles down at me. I lean into his hand and close my eyes for a second. "I am on your side. I will always be on your side. If you want me to, I can meet them and send them back on their way. You don't have to do anything you don't want to do. I've got big shoulders; I can deal with your mum. I can be your rock, your shield."

Wow.

No. One. Has. Ever.

"Or if you don't want me as a shield, I'll be here to pick you up, dust you off if you ever fall."

Oof, my heart just doubled in size, then exploded. I am done for.

"T-thank you," I rasp. The hellhound kisses my forehead, and I turn my head and kiss his hand that was holding my face.

I am so in love with this man. I don't care if it's only been a few days. Soul-deep, I feel overwhelming love. He is *mine.* I might not be his, but I don't care, even if it makes me a fool. He is worth it.

"What you need is to stick with people who pull the magic out of you, not the madness." I blink at him and sniffle.

"I hate magic," I whine.

Owen chuffs. "It is a quote, and I meant it figuratively. You need to be around people that bring out the best in you, not people who drive you crazy or frighten you."

"She is my mum."

"Doesn't matter," he says gruffly. "You hate your magic? Huh. Really? From what I can see, you were made for this. Your use of magic is effortless. For you, it is as easy as breathing. Do you think the other hosts find it so easy? Do you think I've seen anyone do what you do? Forrest told me how you dealt with the warriors. How you bossed them all about." His eyes twinkle. "How you saved Sebastian and healed me. You are so incredible, unique, and so damn brave. Stop doubting yourself. I believe in you."

I sniff again, and my lips curl up into a tiny smile. Owen is super old. He must know what he's talking about, right?

"Are you going to be okay?"

I nod. "I think I am."

"Good. Okay, I am gonna go have a little chat with Mac," he growls.

The hellhound kisses my forehead and prowls out of my office to go deal with his friend who Owen thinks is still loitering in reception. I think, from his expression, he is also planning to put

Mac in a headlock and punch him a few times in the face. Ha. I want to put Mac in a headlock and see if I can punch him in his face. I'm so mad at him. I knew the shifter was a dick. I didn't know the extent of his dickishness. If I had, well, I would have charged him for the use of the hotel. I huff and get up from my chair.

I rub my arms. I need to think of a way to get Owen the hell out of here, at least for a few hours. I don't want the man I love being brought into my coven shit. We have this special thing going on. We've had our first kiss and now... Now my mum, my dad, and whoever else from my coven are coming to ruin everything.

Ah shit.

My hands flutter as I firmly tug and then smooth out the fabric of my dress. From what I can see, it looks immaculate. I tuck a loose strand of violet hair behind my ear and sigh up at the ceiling. *I'm a horrible person.* I know it's not Mac's fault, and he isn't a dick. I shouldn't blame him for my mistake.

It's my fault. I should have told my coven before anyone else had the opportunity. This is on me.

I'm glad then that Mac has already left the dimension with the last of the elves, including Forrest, and her brother.

"Come on Daisy Duco, our pain in the arse coven is coming." Daisy gets up from the desk with a stretch and an enormous yawn. She waves her wing at me, her way of asking me to carry her. I roll my shoulders, scoop her off the desk, and shuffle into reception. With a flick of magic, I drop the barrier around the front of the hotel and—

Gosh, everything inside me wants me to lock the portals down and run.

I love my coven, but I don't want them here. This entire situation is going to end up being an embarrassing mess. Different versions of this moment have played out before. It always ends with me the loser.

Owen's phone rings. "Hello. Yes, sir. I will ask her." He puts the phone to his chest. "It's your dad. He asked for you to send the portal. He has tried asking for sanctuary without success."

No, they don't need sanctuary; they never have. It's me that has needed it from them. *Get a grip, Tuesday,* I mentally snarl. *Other people have it worse and your witch girl problems aren't even that bad.* I need to count my blessings.

I picture my dad in my mind and visualise opening the portal at his location. With a snap of magic that crackles the air and makes the little strands of hair on my nape raise, there's the familiar warning tingle, and then, with swirling green magic, the portal rips open into my realm.

CHAPTER TWENTY-FIVE

Great, my panic is making me sweaty. My heart thuds and I fidget. The first to come through the portal is Dad, followed swiftly by the rest of my coven. Cool as a cucumber, Dad strolls into the middle of the room, his hands behind his back as he takes everything in with a raised eyebrow.

I also glance about and try to see the hotel from his perspective. It is exquisitely beautiful. I am so proud of the changes I've made.

In the exact spot my dad is now standing, an elf was bleeding all over the floor. Now, the entire lobby is immaculate. You could not guess a massive group of elves and shifters had stomped their way through here only a few short hours ago. For someone who doesn't like to clean and who has, in the past, given her dust bunnies names, a self-cleaning hotel is epic. Like a mega jackpot lottery win.

I take a deep breath, move my neck from side to side, and shake out my hands. My poor fingers are cramping as they have been balled so tightly into fists. A light breeze ruffles my hair and cools my sweaty cheeks. In my next breath, vanilla and cinnamon invade my lungs. The hotel somehow smells of comfort, like I have burned a dozen cinnamon and vanilla candles for their visit.

It smells of Owen.

I huff out a surprised sound. Whoa, it does. I sniff again. It smells just like the hellhound. How strange. It is like the hotel is trying to calm me down.

Thank you. I hope the realm's magic knows I'm grateful. It is also a reminder that if this all goes tits up, I can always stuff them back in a portal and send them home. For the first time in my life, I have the power here.

Daisy flaps a wing and I wince as her long claws dig into my shoulder and arm. My dragonette nuzzles me, the scales of her muzzle brushing against my cheek. I cluck her underneath her chin and kiss the extra soft skin between her nostrils.

"Hi, sweetheart," my dad says to me, then nods politely at Owen, who is standing directly behind us like a sentry.

"Hi, Dad. Thanks for coming," I mumble awkwardly.

My mum doesn't say hello. She doesn't say a word. At first, I think she is giving me the cold shoulder as I watch her sashay across the room to the seating area. Her heels click ominously on the wooden floor. Each clicking step she takes tries to drag me back to my childhood, and the helplessness I felt makes me cringe. When Mum gets to the window, she pokes at the curtains, flipping the fabric between her fingers as if to check the thread count. She then looks out at the lake with a satisfied sigh.

Oh no, she's not mad at me. She is proud. It took me a moment 'cause I didn't recognise the contented expression on her face.

"Hi, Auntie Tuesday. Hi, Daisy. Hellooo, hot bodyguard," my fifteen-year-old niece Heather says as she barely glances up from her phone. She manages a half-hearted wave as she bounces towards my favourite chair.

"Heather!" Ava squawks.

Heather's curly blonde hair flutters around her shoulders as she collapses into the chair. "Great. You have fast Wi-Fi," she mutters, ignoring her mum as her thumbs rapidly move across the screen.

"I am so sorry, Owen. She's at that age. Thank you for looking after Tuesday. It is nice to see you again," Ava says.

My mum is fluffing up all the loose cushions. She is practically buzzing, overflowing with joy.

My other two sisters break out of their shocked trances and, as a unit, turn and rush towards me. Jodie gets to me first, and I'm engulfed in her strong perfume as she hugs me. Daisy sneezes and then lets out a hiss when Jodie doesn't immediately let go. Daisy's tail whips about like a cat. She dislikes the intrusion into her body space.

"Hush, mini monster. I am allowed to hug my sister," Jodie chides. "Little sister, I've been so worried." Within the hug, she shakes me. Daisy wraps her tail around my arm and grumble-growls her disapproval in my ear. "When you didn't get to the safe house, I thought something awful had happened to you."

It had.

"I am sorry. As you can see, I'm okay." I hold my arms out for a visual inspection, but Jodie hugs me tighter. "I'm sorry I worried you."

Jodie, out of the four of us, is the spitting image of Dad, just a tiny female version. I have to look away from those brown eyes when she finally lets up her hug-fest and meets my gaze. They radiate with equal parts hurt and concern. "You have a lot of making up to do." Jodie lowers her voice. "I understand why you didn't message me. It just makes me sad you avoid us because of her."

My dragonette is done with another angry grunt as if she is highlighting just how much Jodie has ruined her day. She pushes off my shoulder and jumps. She is airborne for a few seconds until she smacks into the centre of Owen's chest.

The hellhound lets out a surprised grunt and then allows the golden dragonette to snuggle into the crook of his arm.

"Oh. Well, now that is interesting," Jodie says as she eyes the pair.

I can feel the redness heat my cheeks as I see her brain working overtime. Daisy hates everybody—everybody but me, and now Owen. "Afternoon, Owen," Jodie says with a huge grin.

"Hey, Owen," Diane says as she unceremoniously shoves Jodie out of the way. Then it is our older sister's turn to pull me into an embrace.

"Ladies."

Diane is five years older than Ava, six years older than Jodie, and that makes her fourteen years older than me. She's the spitting image of our mum, with her dark blonde hair and violet eyes. When I see her, my heart always does this silly little jump, and I can't help but be cautious around her, which is entirely unfair, as she is nothing like our mum.

Diane is incredibly sweet, unlike her creepy boyfriend. I can't believe he is here. Andy, the boyfriend, loiters behind her like an unpleasant smell. He pulls his hands from his pockets and scratches the back of his neck. His dark hair is all over the place. It's only been a few minutes, and he already appears to be bored with our coven reunion.

"What have you been up to?" Diane whispers as she hugs me fiercely. Squished against my sister, out of the corner of my eye, I frown as I watch Andy trundle over to the nearest wall and tap it with his knuckle.

What a weirdo.

I don't know if he thinks that's a manly thing to do or thinks the walls are made of paper.

Everything is real, dickhead. You'd think as a shifter, he'd know a little about magic. I do my best to ignore him as his dirty trainers squeak-stomp across the floor. But then the cheeky sod attempts to go behind reception! Before I can say anything, Owen is suddenly there, in his way. My hellhound narrows his eyes in discouragement. Daisy adorably snaps her razor-sharp teeth, providing backup.

Andy puffs up his chest, scowls, and stomps back to my sister's side. He mutters under his breath about elitist shifters and something about fire extinguishers.

"You've had some big changes," Jodie says as Diane finally lets go of me with a sniff.

"I can't believe you didn't ring and ask for help. How on earth have you dealt with all this on your own?" Diane says almost at the same time. She crosses her arms and shakes her head.

It is not as if I can say, "Oh, you know, it's me against the world," so I shrug and mumble, "I didn't want to bother anybody."

"She's not been on her own," Jodie says with an eyebrow wiggle and salacious grin. She drops her voice into a sexy cadence. "The hot hellhound has been guarding her body."

Diane snorts.

Crap, I hope he hasn't heard her. Uhm. Owen's silent amusement dances in his eyes and he coughs suspiciously.

I clear my throat, my damn face going red. The blood rushing to my cheeks is practically vibrating. "As you can see, I am okay."

"Okay," Diane tuts. "You are more than okay. The magic is off the charts strong. I can't believe you sent us a portal! A portal! Out of nowhere. Do you know what level of magic that is? No, of course you don't. Witches would kill for that level of skill, and you do it without a spell or a potion in sight. I can't believe how much you've blossomed, Tuesday. I am so proud of you."

"Oh, urm... thanks."

"What the heck is the magic on your face?" Jodie asks in a way that only a sister can.

I shrug. "It's a host thing."

"It's pretty," Diane says, her eyes tracing the swirls across my skin.

"Thank you, though you should have heard me scream when I first noticed them and the light show started. They freaked me out."

"I bet. Beautiful, but scary, huh?"

"You've had a hell of a long weekend." They continue talking over each other and I can feel the start of a headache.

"I wonder if you'll be able to make small pocket dimensions. Those things are crazy expensive. It would be great practice for your new magic and fantastic revenue for the shop," Jodie says.

"I guess I can give it go."

"Wow. You have your own pocket dimension." Diane lets out a squeal and spins in a circle. "This is so cool."

"It's a pocket realm," Ava says.

I smile at her and nod. "Yes, it is."

Ava has our mum's violet eyes and our dad's dark hair, which is a striking combination. She is a tech witch—the proper term is technomancy. Her magic is so unique. She can combine magic with technology with breath-taking results. She is more at home with computers than people, so she doesn't hug me, which I appreciate. But I get her thousand-yard stare in reprimand.

I groan. "Again, I am sorry. I have only been here a few days, and you cannot believe what a nightmare it has been. It's been a lot to deal with."

"Yeah, we heard about everything," Jodie replies. "We just didn't know it was *you* until a few hours ago."

"What?" My entire face scrunches up with a frown. "But how could you have—"

"Heather!" Mum snarls at my niece. "Stop sulking and get off your phone. This is a coven meeting, not time to talk to your friends. You need to step up, child. We have only just risen from the shame of having the worst witch in Europe."

"Mum, don't speak to Heather like that. She is nothing like Tuesday," Ava says, blocking her daughter from our mum's sight. Ava's wide eyes meet mine when she realises what she just said out loud. "Oh, Tuesday. I didn't mean... I'm sorry."

My magic pings with her lie.

I rub my chest and drum up my best fake smile. "No, it's fine," I rasp. I duck my head, but I am not quick enough as Ava sees the hurt in my eyes. She moves towards me. I am quick to hold up a hand to keep her at bay. "Honestly, it's fine." My bottom lip wobbles.

Talk about putting me on a pedestal and then kicking it away. Yeah, wow. It's always a guarantee my coven will keep me humble.

"We heard about the elves," Ava says quietly.

"And the dryads," Jodie says.

"The entire UK is talking about you," Diane adds.

"What?" Horror fills me. "No. No. It's supposed to be a secret."

I am not ready.

"It was Mum," Jodie mumbles.

"I informed everyone I could," Mum says as she clicks back across the room towards us. She snatches the phone out of Heather's hand and drops it into the bag that is nestled in the crook of her elbow. Heather whimpers.

My sisters unconsciously move out of her way and Ava grumbles under her breath. Heather looks a little lost as she stares at her empty hand.

"You told people?" How could she have in such a short timeframe? "You told others what I am? Mum, how could you? You don't understand. There are these hunters—"

"Of course, I did. I made a magical announcement."

I sag in defeat. A magical announcement is a huge expensive spell, mostly used in wartime to send out a message to *every witch* in the United Kingdom.

Yay...

"Your power should be celebrated. Your magic will make the history books..." she continues, crowing on about how elevated the coven has become. I rub my forehead as I silently freak out.

How could she do that without speaking to me? I knew keeping my identity secret would be impossible, but I thought I had a little bit of time. Time to perfect my magic, time to learn to protect myself, protect the coven, and now I've got no bloody time at all.

Oh, bloody hell.

I can't think, what with the metaphysical knife that is sticking out of my back, biting against my shoulder blades. I swallow down what feels like a lump of lead in my throat and for a few seconds, my vision goes hazy and my head spins.

I feel the warmth of the hellhound, a trickle of awareness as he moves closer behind me like a rock turning the tide of an ocean. "Breathe," Owen murmurs, the spearmint of his breath caressing my cheek. His soft lips brush the shell of my ear. His hot hand slides down my body to rest on my hip, and he gives me a small reassuring squeeze. Lightning rushes up the back of my legs and, all at once, my knees are weak. My arm slides against his hand and his thumb traces the soft skin on the inside of my wrist. Ha, goosebumps are traitors.

I take a shuddering breath, and I lift my chin. For the first time in my life, I know what it is like for someone to have my back against my mum.

"You shouldn't have told anyone, Mum, it's way too dangerous." My voice is firm. I become the woman who competently scaled the career ladder at work. The woman who dealt with a massive group of warrior elves. "Do you realise you've put the entire coven in danger?"

"Danger?" my mum scoffs. "I've put the coven on the map more like it. Oh, my darling girl, you do not understand our world as you've been squirrelled away for years with the humans in your shame. You don't have to do that anymore." When I continue to stare at her, she tuts. "Honestly, Tuesday, you are so dramatic."

She turns her head to bring Dad into the conversation. He is eyeing Owen's hand, which is still resting on my hip. "Matthew, you agree, don't you? We needed to get ahead of the situation. What with the fae in Ireland going on and on about the great dryad rescue."

The great dryad rescue? What on earth?

"We had to make sure everyone knew the return of a legendary host was, in fact, a witch. A

Larson." She nods her head at Dad, and he noncommittally shrugs back. "Wonderful. Oh, Matthew, you should have seen Patricia Cordell's face. I've waited years to put her in her place."

"Dad, are you listening to her? You have got to understand—"

"Don't you try to manipulate your father," my mum spits. Her hand whips out and she points a jabby finger at me. My heart jumps and I can't help the minuscule flinch.

There you are.

Her *oh darling girl* charade didn't last very long. Her mask just keeps on slipping. A boom with a flaming sound effect chimes in my head. *Burn.*

In response, Owen's hand on my waist gets a little heavier. His chest rumbles behind me with a barely repressed growl.

"I'm your mother and I know what is best for you. If you had listened to me in the first place, we would have figured out this whole host magic thing years ago. What did I do to get such a disrespectful and stubborn daughter?" Mum's tone implies me being stubborn is the worst possible trait one can possess.

Mum, I learned it from you. It's a coven trait.

She throws her hands up in the air and turns her attention to my sisters. "I brought you girls all up the same, so I don't understand why Tuesday is so... Anyway, let's get back on track. As soon as I found out the news, I announced it to the community. I have already had two marriage offers." Mum claps her hands with glee. "Two!"

What?

I've never seen her look so excited. It's freaking me out. More so when she beams a smile at me.

CHAPTER TWENTY-SIX

Confused, I shuffle my feet. I tilt my head and peak up at Owen. His lips are pinched, and his jaw is tight. Nestled in his arm, Daisy lazily blinks at me. One of her wings is flopped, daggling across his muscled forearm, the other against his chest. She is lying belly up with legs akimbo, toes pointed as the hellhound tickles her tummy. *I'm glad one of us is having an enjoyable time.*

I rub my temple in an attempt to relieve the huge stress headache that is building. He must have worked out what's going on. I wish he would fill me in, as I haven't got a scooby. Why is my mum talking about marriage proposals?

"Margaret Harris's son, Peter, who is only a few years younger than you. Twenty-two. The best witch in his class." She nods smugly. "The other man is fifteen years your senior. It's all very sad his wife died during the riots. He has two little girls and has been holding out for a powerful new wife."

Is she... talking to me?

My mum grabs hold of my wrist and tugs me away from Owen to deftly manoeuvre me around my sisters. She snaps her fingers at Dad, and he obediently places a datapad in her hand. She waves it in my face.

I look at Owen in alarm. It might be the light tricking me, but his shoulders look even broader, and *blue flames* flash within his eyes.

Whoa. Flame on.

"This one is Peter." I wince as Mum pinches the inside of my arm to pull my attention from Owen as she points at the image of a nice-looking guy. She flicks the page to a *long* list of the stranger's attributes. Of their own accord, as my eyes drift down the page, they seem to cling

306

to a highlighted section and a notation about his sperm. I squeak and wave my hands in the air; my panicked flailing makes her drop her hold on my arm. Mum scowls and tries to make another grab, but I skilfully avoid her and rapidly back away.

"That guy? You want *me* to marry him? Are you kidding?"

"No? Oh, well, the older one—"

"Neither. No way." I wildly point at Jodie. "Jodie would make an amazing wife."

"Oh, thanks. Shove me under the bus instead," she mumbles.

Uh. "Sorry," I mouth.

Witches, like many humans, marry. But I never knew that there was a weird underground arranged marriage thing going on in the background of our society. Male witches are super rare, but we don't need male witches of our kind to procreate. Heather's dad is fae. The magical gene is incredibly strong, and it seems to produce powerful witches, no matter the bloodline. Strong, full-blooded witch parents don't necessarily make a strong child. Look at me.

Before this mess all started, everyone thought I was a dud, or I had magiclexia. In the scheme of things, fate and a creature's DNA does what it wants. Again, look at me. Where the heck did the host magic come from? Magic is weird.

Unless you are from a coven with super old-fashioned rules and a fanatical need to keep their bloodlines *pure,* I presumed no one else in the community cared.

I guess from the manic glow in my mother's eyes, landing a rare male witch as a husband is considered a great honour.

"Don't you think I've tried?" Mum whines and throws her hands up in the air. "I've been working away for years to get one of you girls a decent match. Years. Now, out of everyone in this coven, it's you. And *you* have the gall to say no? I don't think so, young lady. It is a great honour. Don't you dare ruin this for me. You will do as you are told."

A great honour out of my nightmares.

I am in love with a hellhound. As if I'd say okay to marrying some random guy. Even if my soft heart did not belong to Owen, I can only imagine having another coven as in-laws. Gosh, more random witches sticking their oars into my life. I'd have permanent hives.

"Mum, I will not marry a stranger. Why would you ever think I would?"

"I neither have the time or the crayons to explain how important this is," my mum snarls. Wow. I'll have to remember that insult, as it was a good one. Even after all these years, she still has the ability to hurt me. Never underestimate the power of words. "YOU WILL DO AS YOU ARE TOLD!" she screams.

My ears ring. I am so angry, for a second, I lose my good girl filter. "This is bullshit."

"LANGUAGE!" Mum yells.

Jodie's mouth pops open and then she grins with understanding.

"Wow, Tuesday. I haven't heard you swear since you were a kid," Diane says with narrowed eyes as she blinks her long lashes at me.

"You can swear?" Mum gasps.

Yes, Mum, the nasty anti-swearing spell you made me take is finally broken. Ta-da. Go me. "Yeah, well, it's hard to swear when your mother puts a gag spell on you," I blurt out bitterly.

The silence is deafening.

Shit. Did I say that out loud?

"A what?" Diane squeaks. "No... You wouldn't." She laughs awkwardly and looks around. "Mum, she is kidding, right? Mum?" When Mum says nothing to contradict my statement, Diane narrows her eyes. "That is abuse."

"Mum?" Ava says.

"It was a strong, illegal potion," Jodie says as she looks down at her feet and toes the floor.

"Jodie, you knew?" Diane elbows her in the side. "You bloody did. Why didn't you tell me? Mum, I don't understand why you would do something so awful." Diane's hurt but angry stare is laser focused on Mum.

Mum shrugs and looks at Dad for help.

He remains silent.

"When? Mum, when did you put... a what?" Diane tilts her head to the side and her violet eyes flash. "An anti-swearing spell? When did you put an anti-swearing spell on my little sister?" My feisty blonde sister steps in front of me while holding her arms out wide, almost as if she can protect me from something that happened years ago. "When did you do that?"

"I was sixteen," I say helpfully. I shuffle forward and place my hand on her shoulder and squeeze it. "It's okay. It is in the past. Jodie only knows 'cause she tried to help me a few years ago."

"Why didn't you ask me?" Diane spins around, pointing at her chest. "You know potions are my speciality. I could hav—wait. What? Back up at sec. You were sixteen? Sixteen," she whispers.

"Mum," Ava snarls.

I can't believe that my sisters are sticking up for me. Perhaps it is Owen's presence that is motivating them? Or maybe I've never given my sisters enough credit.

Wow, they love me.

"You always said she had a stick up her arse." Andy chortles and slaps his leg.

Hilarious.

"Andrew, now isn't the time," Diane chides. She turns back to me and grips the top of my arms. "Look, I did say that. I said it a lot, but I didn't understand. You hid it so well. I used to think you not swearing was ridiculous. I used to think it was an adorable, weird quirk." Her voice drops and her eyes fill with tears. "I used to laugh at you, Tuesday. All this time I thought because you couldn't do magic, you were bitter, twisted... jealous." She swallows.

"But you weren't jealous, were you? You were just trying to protect yourself from her." An angry tear runs down her face, and she wipes it away. "From our mum." She spins, blocking me again from our parents. "Mum, how could you? What else have you done?"

"I did what I had to do." My mum lifts her chin stubbornly and glares back at my sister. "And don't use that tone with me. I'm still your mother. When you have children Diane, you will understand—"

"I have a daughter and I don't understand, Mum," Ava interrupts.

"It worked out in the end, didn't it? I was right. Tuesday just had to learn to apply herself. Look at this place. It must be worth a fortune. Once we get a grip on her magic, there's no telling what she can do."

"You won't be going anywhere near Tuesday and her magic," says a menacing voice.

Owen.

CHAPTER TWENTY-SEVEN

Owen is watching me. His eyes glisten as they stare, and I see about a million questions hiding in his beautiful grey eyes. *What is he thinking?* I unwillingly stare at the way his muscles seem to ripple with his every movement as he prowls toward me.

He'll be the death of me.

He reaches across and takes my hand in his. My skin throbs with the contact. Tiny sparks pass where we touch, and they careen up my arm until the silver marks dance like a disco ball.

Whoa.

The awareness of his body from mine is like a living thing inside me.

"What? Who are you?" *Knock it off, Mum. No one believes you didn't notice the seven-foot hellhound.* "Why are you even here, pawing my daughter? Keep your hands to yourself. She. Is. Taken. This is coven business, shifter. So why don't you"—she flicks her fingers at him—"hurry along. Matthew, get rid of him. He shouldn't be here for coven business."

My dad hunches and makes a sad sounding sigh. Dad learned a long time ago not to interfere with the women of our coven. His words, not mine. I think he thought it was best, as he was—and again, I quote him—outnumbered. For a man who is always professional and in control of his work life, he's really under the thumb when it comes to his wife.

"Hellhound," Owen corrects. "And I hunt people who break our laws," he says in a dark warning.

Mum makes an unimpressed humph sound. You have to hand it to her. She really doesn't give a monkey's.

I don't know what Owen will do if she roots around in her bag for a nasty potion.

"No, he is staying. He is with me," I tell her. "But don't, you know, kill off my mum," I mutter out of the side of my mouth.

Owen squeezes my hand in reassurance.

Mum glares at me in a way that screams, "Wait until I get you alone." "I can make him forget if needed," she says with a malevolent smile.

"Mum! Don't you dare." My breath seizes up in my throat. There is a hallow silence that raises the hair on my arms. The hellhound is preternaturally still, and his face is carefully blank. Is she trying to get herself killed? His hellhound power floods the room, battering my mum's weaker magical signature out of the way like a battering ram.

"Wow, you are racking up illegal magic use, Mum," Diane mumbles.

"Power hungry bitch," Ava says under a breath.

The hellhound's power has nothing on mine. I drop Owen's warm hand and move. I glare at my mother, and with each stride I take toward her, the livid magic inside me floods the space. "You will not touch him. You will have to go through me first and I'm not a little girl anymore," I snarl.

The room goes dark, and outside, thunder cracks. Heather screams in fright at the lightning strike that follows. It hits the roof of the hotel and travels down through the building, dancing and crackling against the windows. The sweet, pungent aroma of ozone and magic fills the air.

Owen's tree-trunk sized arm wraps around my waist and he boldly lifts me. He moves me away from my coven, away from my crazy mother. He puts me gently on the floor. *Is it time for them to go home yet?* I willingly shuffle behind him, and I rest my cheek against his back.

Crikey, Tuesday, that was a little bit dramatic.

It has been a long day; that is my excuse. I glance at the clock on the wall and groan. *Is it only two o'clock?* I yawn so big my jaw pops. It has been a crazy day, and I need to keep my wits about me, but soon, I will need sticks to hold my eyes open. I could sleep for a week.

I push the clouds away and take a deep, cleansing breath to settle my magic. I breathe deep until all I can smell is his scent. Oxygen has vanished, replaced by cinnamon. "Sorry," I murmur.

With flaring nostrils, Daisy peeks over Owen's shoulder. She chirps and a little puff of smoke spirals from her nose. With cat-like agility, her claws stab into Owen's shoulder and back as she scrambles down to me. Owen grunts. "Gentle," I reprimand. I then smile when her scaly little body wiggles into my waiting hands.

I move to stand next to Owen as Daisy clambers up my arm and then balances between my shoulders, her back legs on either side of my neck. Her front claws dig into my head, pulling out wisps of hair. Her tail whips from side to side and her wings flutter for balance. I don't bat an eye, used to her antics.

Luckily, at the moment, she's all smoke, but I have it in the back of my mind. I could always use a hair potion to fix any accidents if my cute little beast set my hair alight. Owen's hand drops to envelop mine and we thread our fingers together.

"Don't make a choice just yet." Mum's pointy finger is back, and she draws an imaginary circle in the air around us as she moves forward, seemly unaffected by my outburst or the quietly livid shifter.

"I see where this is all going. A hellhound? Really, Tuesday?" Her eyes take us in with pity, and she shakes her head in disappointment. "You will change your mind when you get bored with his muscles."

She looks at Dad and narrows her eyes. "Thinking about it..." She taps her bottom lip. "The longer we take to decide on the lucky husband, the better and the more offers we might get. "If we rush in and pick a witch, others might think we are too keen. It makes sense to wait. I can make them work for it." My mum beams a creepy, satisfied smile.

I am glad Owen is here to grab a hold of me, otherwise, I'd be going with my urge to knock my head against the reception desk, while wailing, *why me, why me?* Why won't she bloody listen? Nothing I say is going to change her mind. In her head, she's finally hit the magic jackpot.

Mum wets her thumb with her tongue, then leans forward and rubs the spit-coated digit on my face. On. My. Face. I throw myself back away from her as I make a sound of disgust. "Mum, gross." I wrinkle my nose and scrub at my cheekbone. Ew. I can smell her spit and it makes me want to gag. "Why would you do that?"

"The marks are real?" she asks. "I thought they were some frivolous spell."

What? Marks? Oh, the glowing, swirling magical marks all over my face and body. "Of course, they're real."

"Mum, I don't think a spit bath is going to remove powerful magic," Jodie says with exasperation.

"Unless there's something in your spit that we don't know about," Diane snarls. She still hasn't let off her glaring.

"Tuesday, are you not going to offer us refreshments? I think we will be more comfortable sitting down in the lounge area. If you will all follow me."

Yeah, why not. Make yourself at home, I think as Mum sashays across the room and Dad, my sisters, and Heather obediently follow. Andy and his trainers squeak along at the rear.

"Andy has been so helpful while we've been dealing with this nightmare. He has really stepped up, hasn't he, Dad?" Diane says to change the subject. Dad makes a noncommittal shrug and mumbles what I think is an agreement beneath his breath. As if on cue, my magic pings with the lie. Huh. Interesting. I'm not the only one who thinks Andy is a dick and my sister is waaay out of his league.

But Diane is an adult and if she wants to love a man-child, that's up to her as long as he doesn't hurt her. I hope the creepy shit doesn't hurt her.

The shifter must also be on Owen's shit list, as when Andy attempts to take a seat next to me, he has to scramble out of the massive hellhound's way. Instead of standing behind me like an anonymous bodyguard, Owen sits down on the sofa, placing himself between me and my coven. He tugs me against his side.

This is all nice and cosy.

I let the magic of the realm pick my coven's brains and an assortment of food and drink clatters on the surrounding tables.

"What? What is this? I have never seen magic like this before."

"This is all very special."

"Whoa, can we eat this?"

I can't help but grin at my coven.

"Yes," I say, shuffling a little in my seat. "The magic of the realm can be a bit jarring. I woke up to the smell of bacon and fell out of bed."

"You know that this is beyond the coven's expertise, beyond anything we've experienced," Dad says, his voice soft.

"I know. I think it's beyond anyone's experience. I don't even think the other hosts know what they are doing."

"Oh my, afternoon tea," Jodie whispers at the full tea set and fancy tower of plates overflowing with mini sandwiches and cakes.

Heather squeals and gives me a toothy grin at her bowl of spaghetti. "Auntie Tuesday, your magic is epic."

"Perhaps we can sit in the dining room?" I ask, frowning at all the plates. Gosh, they are hungry.

"No, we are fine here," Mum replies. Dad grunts when she pulls the massive bacon cheeseburger from his hand and then loudly lectures him about his cholesterol.

"Yes, dear," he grumbles.

I roll my eyes as if Mum couldn't knock up a potion to counteract anything negative in his diet. Another burger appears next to his outside hand, with a pint of Carlsberg lager to wash it down. I snort and Owen's lips twitch. Without my mum noticing, Dad bites into his new burger. He closes his eyes on a silent groan. I help him out by getting Mum's attention as I feed Daisy a slice of cucumber with a "here comes the aeroplane" noise.

"A dragonette familiar," Mum declares as she takes a delicate sip of coffee. "It has been staring me in the face this entire time. I cannot believe the most important thing in the history of our coven, and I did not see it. Mainly because you avoid spending time with your coven."

Yes, yes, it's all my fault.

"Familiar?" I frown.

Familiars are scarce, to the point of being sacred to witches. Even in my coven, no one is strong enough to have one. There hasn't been a new familiar bond in over a century. I might be out of the loop with the witch community, but I know that.

"Do you think dragonettes are that friendly? It's a wild animal, girl. Of course, Denny is your familiar."

"Daisy."

"Oh yes, Daisy. Lovely creature." Daisy lets out a hiss and tries to bite Mum's finger as it waggles in front of her nose. Dad swiftly pulls Mum's hand out of the way of her snapping maw.

Mum's eyes are glazed over, so she doesn't seem to notice, and even after the close call of almost getting bitten, she doesn't drop her manic smile.

"You have a point. The dragonette is showing actual signs of a familiar bond. How interesting." Mum nods at Jodie's words and her smile grows even bigger. "She also adores Owen. Which is wonderful. She must see you,

Owen, as Tuesday's mate." Owen grins and Mum's smile vanishes as Daisy hops onto Owen's chest and rubs her muzzle underneath his chin with a happy chirp.

"Jodie?" I ask.

"Hmm?" She places a hand over her mouth as she chews a delicate-looking sandwich.

"Is it okay if I try to link a portal gateway to the shop?"

"You can do that?" Andy's nasal voice pipes up, butting into the conversation. He bites into an apple and peers at me over the shiny green skin, his face a mask of disbelief as he chews obnoxiously. *Chomp-chomp.* I wince at his mouth sounds.

"I think so... I'd like to try it."

"You aren't a gateway witch." My nose crinkles as I get a glimpse of chewed up apple as he speaks. "Someone is getting a little bit full of herself." He chuckles mockingly and opens his mouth to say something else, but then thinks better of it when Owen turns to stare at him. He looks away and takes another bite of the apple.

"Of course. That's a wonderful idea," Jodie says.

"I think it would make a good escape hatch,

in case anything were to happen again, you know, like the mercenaries."

"That's a great idea," Dad says. He leans forward in his chair. "So, did you use the escape ladder when the mercenaries came to your flat then?" I nod and Dad looks all too pleased with himself.

"Yeah, yeah," I groan and wave my hands in submission. "Yes, Dad, you were right about having an alternative exit." Dad grins but doesn't rub it in. "I am reformed and from now on, I solemnly swear to always have an alternative escape route."

"Why the shop?" Mum asks. "You should put one at the house so I can come here directly. I don't want to have to wait around for your wonky portal service."

Wonky portal, have you heard her? Yeah, that's never going to happen. A doorway directly to her house? Gah, I have to repress a shudder.

"So, I am going to do that today if that's okay?" I ask Jodie.

"No problem, the wards will let in you and anyone with you of your choosing," Jodie replies with a not so subtle nod at Owen. Andy grunts and we ignore him.

"You can always make your own portal, Mum," Diane says sweetly. Uh-oh, her smart mouth is going to get her into trouble. Mum can't make portals, only a gateway witch can, and only with fixed gateways that are attached to ley lines.

Mum ignores Diane's dig.

As a host, I don't use ley line magic. I think I just rip a connection through the dimensions as I make portals out of thin air. If my school's magical theory books are right, I should be able to open and fix a portal to go anywhere. That is a cool piece of magic.

I guess I have only just scraped the top of the iceberg on things that I can do. My tummy flips, and suddenly, I am overwhelmed and a little bit sick.

Another thing that is making me sick is all this marriage malarkey. Distance and running away has always been my thing, a simple but perhaps unhealthy way of protecting myself. I learned long ago no one was willing to listen to me, so there was no point in opening my mouth. Now, here is Owen. We've just had our first kiss and I am already head over heels. This time, I can't sit back and nod my head when my mother says I will marry a stranger. Owen doesn't know that I will agree, only to avoid my coven for as long as it takes for my mum to give up her wild notion. Another eight years if needed. But instead of it being me and Daisy against the world, I must take another person's feelings into account. I've got to think of him.

What does he think? What would I think if his pack insisted he marry... mate with somebody else? I'd be devastated. It would break my heart.

To not say something would be the worst thing I could do. Disrespectful. What kind of person would I be if I did that?

So, I do something I haven't done since I was sixteen years old. I fight my corner. I get a bright idea and send a blast of magic out into the real world.

Huh, it worked. I sit back, feeling a tad smug. Ah, heck... I might as well get this over with. I don't want this hanging over me and Owen. I have the urge to roll my neck like a fighter going into a ring.

Ding, ding.

"So, Mum, this whole marriage thing..." Owen's thigh brushes against mine. I nibble on my lip. This will be like removing a wax strip, unpleasant but worth it in the end. But like a wax strip, it must be done quickly. Not that I've used a wax strip. We have spells for that. Even though I hate magic—or I did—I'm not opposed to cheating when it comes to body hair.

"Not this again." Mum groans and dabs her mouth with a napkin. "I have decided you will marry one of those boys. There is no choice, no discussion. You will, for once in your life, do as you are told."

Well, there might be a teeny tiny problem. I try again, doing my best to hold in my smugness. "I appreciate the time you have spent on this, and I understand how important it is to *you*, but I am not marrying a stranger just to make you happy."

"I'm right about this. You'll see. I know what is best for you. I am your mother."

Owen grunts.

"How dare you interfere?" she snarls at him.

Owen just sits there and stares back at her. His silence will drive her bat shit crazy. She isn't his mum or his coven leader, and he doesn't have to learn her rules or play her games.

"Mum, you are being rude." Diane puts her steak knife down on her plate, abandoning the huge steak she is eating as she stares Mum down like she is dealing with a charging minotaur. "You have to stop." Mum blinks at her and then slowly takes in the angry faces of her coven.

"Carol," Dad growls. "That is enough."

"Well, it's a good thing then that I have magic," I say as I blow on my nails and then buff them against my dress. "'Cause I sent a magical announcement to both men, thanking them for their kind consideration, but I'm not and never will be available for an arranged marriage." Mum grows pale. Diane grins at me with approval, picks up her plate, spears a piece of steak, and chews happily.

"Oh, and I also sent an announcement to the rest of the community, so there will not be any further misunderstandings." For the first time since they arrived, my smile is genuine.

"You did what?" Mum croaks out.

A packet of crayons and a colouring book pop out of the ether and slap onto her lap.

CHAPTER TWENTY-EIGHT

Everyone gasps and Heather snorts out a laugh. Mum opens and closes her mouth a few times. I have rendered her speechless. *This might have been the best thing I have ever done in my life. Or the worst!*

Mum, seemingly no longer interested in the conversation, fiddles with the corner of the colouring book. The strange expression on her face makes me feel guilty. No doubt her brain is going a hundred miles a second. I cringe. Psychological warfare is her thing, and I am sure she will get me back, and oh boy, it will be a doozy. I gulp. It is the first time I have acted on the naughty voice in my head and... it felt amazing.

Which, of course, is very, very bad.

So now I have the overwhelming need to get the hell out of here before the shock wears off and she screams.

Uh-oh.

"I, erm, have lots of things left to do today," I say, as I jump up off the sofa like my bottom is on fire. I can't even look at Owen in case he thinks I behaved like a brat. "I am sure you also need some time for yourselves. Larry?" My voice is slightly squeaky. Larry appears at my side with a bright smile. *Run-run-run!* My head screams as I quickly introduce him to my coven. "This is my friend, Larry. He is the heart of the hotel."

If Larry could blush, I am sure his freaked face would be rosy red. He beams a smile at me, and I smile a shaky one back.

"I will get everyone settled, mistress," he says with a clap of his hands.

Jodie mouths the word *mistress* at me. I roll my eyes and shake my head. I quickly turn to Owen and grab his hand, tugging the huge hellhound to his feet.

"...we have a wonderful pool, and the leisure centre is divine..." Larry continues. His red hair glows from a strip of sunlight that beams through the window.

My mum lifts her head, and my heart misses a beat.

The last thing I hear as I fold the air around us is Diane's shocked voice. "Whoa. Did she just Step?"

* * *

"You Step, huh?" Owen asks when we arrive in my living room. I smile and look at my feet, suddenly shy. I should have asked him first instead of just grabbing him and running. "That's pretty cool."

"Yeah, it happened when the dryads came. It almost scared the poop out of me."

Owen grins. "Are you going to explain the dryad story?"

"You heard that, huh? Yeah, I will. It was horrible and sad... But first, I want to say sorry about beaming you out of there without asking and also thank you for... for you know... I am sorry about my mu—"

"It doesn't matter," Owen interrupts and wraps his arm around me. "She loves you." I want to deny his words, but I can't. I know she loves me. It's just hard to believe it sometimes. The hellhound hugs me to his chest and kisses the top of my head. Between us, Daisy licks my face. Her barbed tongue takes what I'm sure is a tongue's width of the skin off my cheek. Ouch and ew.

Thanks for that, Daisy.

"I didn't want to interfere too much, as I know they are your coven. I hope you don't think I overstepped."

"No, no, of course not." I can't help feeling all warm and squidgy. "You were amazing. It was nice to have you in my corner." Someone who genuinely cares. Although my sister's outrage on my behalf was a big surprise.

Yeah, he's amazing until he sees what you are really like, the nasty voice pipes up. What if that is true? What if he leaves?

I cannot control what Owen feels or does. All I can do is be me and if I am not good enough, well, it was not meant to be.

"Talk about amazing. I had to bite my tongue and channel nine hundred years of military training to stop myself from laughing when you slapped down those crayons and that colouring book." Owen guffaws. I huff out a mortified laugh at his expression. "That was priceless."

"It was mean," I whine. "She's going to kill me."

"Worth it." Owen's eyes sparkle with mirth and we both grin at each other. I drop my head and giggle into his chest. "Nah, she will not kill you. I think she was quite proud of you. It was an epic comeback." I shake my head, then lean back in his arms and take him in. The poor man looks exhausted. I sweep my thumb across his cheek.

"You're not going to lick it first?" he asks.

I giggle again and comically widen my eyes. "I can't believe she rubbed her spit on my face. When is that ever a good idea?" Owen smiles down at me.

My laughter fades and I bite my lip. He almost died a few hours ago. And after all that trauma, he then gets roped into my coven mess.

"When did you last sleep?"

"A while," he grumbles.

"Let's get you settled. Maybe you can have a few hours to catch up."

"No, it's okay. I can wait until tonight." Daisy, who is snuggled up against his chest, yawns, and Owen catches her movement and automatically yawns back. He sheepishly rubs his face. "Perhaps a few hours might do me some good. What about your coven?" *He doesn't want to leave me alone. My heart puffs.*

"Larry has got them, and I promise to keep out of their way while you sleep. Okay?" I reassure him.

"Okay," the hellhound says gruffly.

"Right then, well, let's get you to bed." My horrified eyes shoot to his. Oh crap. "Urm... I mean, show you to your room, on your own to, urm, sleep." I close my eyes. *Oh, for crying out loud. Shut up, Tuesday.*

Owen chuckles.

I really need to leave.

I show Owen into one of the spare bedrooms. Daisy wiggles out of his arms and throws herself down onto the bed. I stand awkwardly as I watch him remove all his weapons from magic only knows where. He's wearing trousers and a shirt you would think he wouldn't be able to hide anything in, but they just keep appearing. It's as if he is carrying enough weapons for ten men.

I run a finger across the hilt of a pretty but sharp-looking silver knife. "Silver," I mumble. I think I've seen enough silver for today, especially when I was pulling it out of him, dragging it particle by particle out of his bloodstream. I still can't believe I did that.

"Yes, it's a throwing blade."

"Why do you carry silver? Doesn't it make you tired? Why would you use a weapon that could also hurt you?" The hellhound pulls out another two blades. They clink against the bedside table.

"Over the years, I've become immune to some of silver's effects." He gently pulls me into his body and his arms wrap around my waist.

I could get used to him holding me. I'm not a tactile person, but I think being in his arms is now my favourite place to be. The fabric of his shirt rustles as he leans down and oh so gently kisses my neck.

My heart slams in my chest and I shiver.

"Oh," I say eloquently.

"Every weapon can be used against you"—kiss—"no matter what metal it is made from"

—kiss. Oh, my... He makes a good point about the *weapons*. My skin is on fire, and I want nothing more than to spin around and jump his bones. Climb him like a tree. Tackle him onto the bed...

I cough to clear my throat. "I will leave you to sleep." I reluctantly slip away from his arms. "Come on, Daisy." I wiggle my fingers at the sleepy dragonette, but she turns her nose up at me and snuggles more into the duvet.

"It's okay. She can nap with me."

"Are you sure?" Owen nods. Wow, that is sweet. "Okay. Well, I will get out of your hair and see you both soon."

I smile. The sexy, beautiful hellhound unbuckles his belt and smiles back at me.

Bloody hell.

CHAPTER TWENTY-NINE

I Step to the office and frantically wave my hand to fan my fiery face. Whoa, the look in his eyes when he undid his belt... I dreamily sag against the desk and swallow the copious amount of spit in my mouth. *That was hot. So hot.* The urge to go back and help him take off the rest of his clothes is huge.

I want to snuggle with the hellhound.

I groan and look up at the ceiling for divine intervention. Fate only knows I need help. Loved up, I might be, but I am annoyingly cautious. Stepping away from him—I shake my head—is a moment in my life that I will no doubt regret. Forever. On my deathbed, I will tell anyone who will listen, "I should have banged the hot hellhound when I was in my twenties." I snort and groan again.

No. I know I am impaired with this magic battering at me. I cannot think straight. My head is full to bursting with everything that has happened these last few days. It has been nuts, and here I am, throwing a new relationship into the mix. There is no way, no way, I can *nap with Owen*. It is unfair to him, and I can't do anything naughty until I sort my head out. I roll my eyes and rub my face.

Okay. I clap my hands like Larry does. I want to see if I can figure out a permanent portal to the real world. If anything happens to me, people in this dimension need to be able to leave. I have been reprimanded already by Mum for not having an adequate emergency plan in place, so an emergency exit is a priority.

Jodie also wants me to make her mini pocket dimensions. I know she only mentioned it in passing, but it would be lovely to give something back. She is always helping me, so I might as well work on that. I mean, how hard can it be? Nyssa makes them... I can Step. I should be able to stuff some magic into an object and make it its own dimension. No biggie. I slump against the desk.

I sigh and grab the datapad that was once that giant, dusty book and do a quick search and... there is nothing. Nothing.

Great.

I throw my hands in the air and push the datapad away. What is the point of this thing if it doesn't work? I will have to do this the old-fashioned way, by trial and error. Yeah, I am going to wing it. Magic on a wing and a prayer. What can go wrong?

I need to keep listening to my magic. Trust myself. I didn't know how to heal, I didn't have a bloody clue and yet, I did it. I saved three people. Three. With no training. That is amazing. If I take the time to listen, the magic tells me clearly what I need to do to get it to work.

I tug at my dress. First, an outfit change. With just a thought, my clothes change from the navy dress into a comfortable, soft-knit jumper and jeans. I roll up my sleeves and I open a portal to Jodie's shop.

I wander into the stockroom. Behind me, I keep the portal open; I have no idea if I can re-open it. *Shit.* I huff out a self-deprecating laugh. *I would look like a proper idiot if I couldn't get back in.*

The room is stuffed to the brim with witch paraphernalia—all things recognisable from my childhood. Instead of happy memories, the sight invokes a sickly sense of fear.

Everything in here has a terrible memory attached to it. I dig my nails into my palms to stop myself from being unwillingly dragged into a nasty memory. I do a full-body shudder to shake the feeling off as I push the thoughts away.

I scan the shelves and find what I need, which is a plain black drawstring bag with the shop logo. Ah, it is perfect.

I grab it, slip back through the portal to my office, and throw myself into the chair. *How the heck am I going to do this?* I turn my full attention to the cloth bag in my now sweaty hand.

Okay. I wipe my hands on my jeans. *What do I need it to do?* The bag needs to expand to store things, so the person using it can put things into the dimensional space and, with just a thought, bring them back out again when needed.

The weight cannot change, and the shape of the bag in the real world can't change either. I puff out my cheeks. No biggie. My leg bounces and my hand trembles as I fiddle with the bag's string. *What if I mess up?*

Oh no. I really don't want to blow up the cotton bag, myself, or the realm. I drop the bag and lean away.

Whoa, Tuesday, don't freak out. You improvised an entire realm. I think you can deal with one small cloth bag. "I just need to have a good imagination, that's all," I mumble. "Oh, and completely ignore physics." My other leg jiggles. *Stop it.*

I have all this negativity swimming around in my head. I flick the bag. I cannot let my past magical prejudice interfere with what is happening to me now. I can't let my old fears impede this strange new version of myself.

But it is so bloody hard.

I blow out a breath and twist my fingers. I have been doing some snazzy things, impossible things. I don't think what I can do has really sunk in. Snapping magic out on the fly with all the crazy life and death pressure. It is okay and perfectly natural to be a little nervous.

Okay, back to the pocket dimension and basic rules: living creatures are not allowed inside. I give the bag a poke. I know it is only a bag, but it could be the width of some kid's shoulders. I can't be responsible for asphyxiating some poor sod. I don't mind people stuffing their limbs in. That's understandable. But not an entire air-breathing person.

I nibble on my thumbnail. Size... the size inside. Does it need to hold stuff like an immense bag? Or does it need to hold the contents of a house? I tug the bag open and stare inside. It can only fit things under about ten inches wide, so there is no way anything big like a sofa will fit.

My mind immediately goes to Mum's magic bag. She lugs that thing everywhere. I click my fingers. *Magical wardrobe. No, that's not right.* My heart jumps with excitement and my eyes widen. *A stockroom.* A grin tugs at my lips. So, a magical stockroom, a pocket dimension roughly four-foot-square, should do it.

Once I get to grips with this, I will have to make Mum a replacement bag, or add a dimension to her existing one. If she will let me.

Okay. I narrow my eyes. The top of the bag will act as a mini portal, and the items will be stored inside the storeroom. What if items are small or super big? I don't want to put a limit on the pocket dimensions usage. So, I won't. I don't need to design things like shelves. Instead, why can't the person using it make it how they want? Self-designing. Oooh. I explore the idea of adding a choice. Once the owner bonds with the bag, their intent can shape the room within the original footprint and design rules. Oh my gosh, that is so cool.

To bond, the owner will need a drop of blood, and if anything happens to them, a simple incantation, like a pin code, will re-set the bag.

I nod. Yeah, that will work. I blow out a breath.

No pressure.

Sweat tickles my neck. I feel like I'm disarming a bomb. Small beads of sweat dot my upper lip. I use my sleeve to wipe them away. *It's okay, Tuesday, you can do this.* I press my jiggling legs into the chair to keep them still as I concentrate. I stare at the cloth and unfocus my eyes. I see the little filaments of realm magic float around in the air like energised dust motes. As they drift around me, I allow myself to zone out and drift with them.

It's as if I am not in control of myself, but a higher power is helping me, guiding me. My pounding heart settles into a steady rhythm, along with my breaths. I am in a weird, magical zone where nothing exists but the magic. I do what I have done for years. I first build the storeroom in my head.

When I am ready, I go with my gut and pull the magical dust towards me and the bag. I feed the magic, both my magic and the dust, into the black fibres with the intent to allow the space I am creating to be flexible. But also strong enough to hold the walls of dimensional space. When I feel like it is working, I expand the walls, making them wider, bigger, and stronger. I set my rules into the magic, layer by layer. When I think I have finished, I test everything. then come back to myself with a sigh and flop back in the chair with a satisfied hum.

Phew, it's good. I did it.

I eye the bag and let out a huff of surprise. *I bloody did it.* I squeal and do a little wiggle. The chair squeaks, and I do a full bum dance on the seat. I did it!

I carefully fold the bag and stuff it into my back pocket. I will give it to Jodie later and let her test it out to see what she thinks. I am sure my smart sister will have ideas on how to improve my design.

In the hallway outside my office, but closer to reception, I add a random door so I can use it to make a fixed portal gateway. I've seen these in a few posh houses—a portal room. Using the doorway as a guide, I open a new portal, this time to the inside of Jodie's stockroom.

I search the shelves and grab a finger prick lancet. I twist the top to break the seal and hold the plastic lancet with trepidation over my poor, innocent index finger.

"It's like a hole punch," I whisper. "A teeny tiny skin hole punch." I roll my eyes. Yep, that makes me feel so much better. Not.

A hole punch. Bloody hell, Tuesday. A hole punch? Really? Now all I can see and hear in my head is the crunch of the round metal prongs cutting through the paper and leaving those perfectly cut, *large* circle holes behind.

I gnaw on my lip and, with a gasp and a full-body cringe, I press the lancet down. A teeny tiny bit of pain derives from my finger. That's it.

I blow out a breath. That was a little anticlimactic. I then sternly remind myself to squeeze my digit. I squeeze until I have a good drop of blood balanced on the tip. I don't want to be doing the entire hole punch thing again today if I can help it.

With blood drop balanced, I carefully shuffle to the empty back wall of the stockroom.

Now comes the gross bit. I smear it onto the wall, tracing around the still open portal, but being careful not to touch the magic or get the blood inside the dimensional gateway. I have no idea what nightmare situation that would cause. I know it's gross and wiping an open wound onto the wall of my sister's magic shop is not exactly hygienic, but I am again going with my gut and what I am doing feels right. With another few squeezes, I finish the freehand rectangle.

A doorway.

I move back to eye the now fixed doorway that leads into my pocket realm. Perhaps I should say some witchy words? My lips twitch. A fancy incantation to lock it all into place. I know there is no need. My blood has done the trick. I stand and stare at it. Huh. My mum said my portal was wonky and look at that. A real wonky portal. It's like what she said was a premonition. I tilt my head. Yeah, it might not be the best thing I've ever done. Mum will moan that I should have outlined it first in chalk and perhaps used a ruler. The shape will irritate her.

It couldn't be more obvious that I made the portal unless I scrawled "Tuesday was here" in blood. I grin and shake my head. Yeah, I'm not going to do that.

Am I nuts, giving my coven direct access to me and my pocket world? Maybe. Although, it could be worse. I could have gone with Mum's suggestion and put the doorway at my parent's house. I snort and dramatically shudder.

I will have to pop a ward on the door at my end to make sure no one comes through to do some sneaky shopping. The shop has enough wards. No one but coven can access the portal, so at least I don't need to mess around with it on this end.

Blood is one of the scariest ingredients in witchcraft. Even trace amounts can be used against you. I press and hold a small button on the side of the lancet, and something hidden inside the plastic breaks. With a puff of smoke, the entire thing vaporises. I brush the ash off my hand into the bin. I should now use a medicated wipe to clean the wound, but with the portal open, there is no need. My finger has already healed.

I shuffle away and direct the pulse of magic that emanates from my chest at the portal. The blood trail around it glows, and with a flash of light that momentarily blinds me, the gateway seals.

The fading buzz of power tickles my skin, and then the portal closes, sealing the doorway into the very fabric of the building. The room transcends into darkness.

All I can hear through the pounding of my heart are my raspy breaths.

Dizzy, I sag against the wall and a few unseen items fall to the floor. I rapidly blink. *Whoa, that was a bit of a shock.* I have to lock my knees so I don't fall over.

It is not the power I used to make the doorway that is affecting me. To anyone else, using power like that would be a momentous challenge, if not an impossibility, but the power I used to make the fixed portal? Well, it didn't even register.

No, the reason I feel like a wet balloon that's been popped is that I have gone from immense power to *nothing*. Nada. Without the doorway open, I am back to being plain old me, and wow, I do not like it.

Staying in my pocket realm, I can see, will be addictive.

I was right. I do need to gain some perspective, take that fresh air break I promised myself. I will also not let this powerful magic control me. I need to make a decision that is right for me and not just go along with everything like a proper numpty.

I am no one's puppet. I need to be here. I need to think with no magical influence and be reminded of what being normal feels like. *Crikey, if I feel like this after a few days? What am I going to feel like after years?* What a terrifying thought. That is why I am going to stay here for at least a few hours.

I force myself to move my feet. The wooden floor creaks underneath me as I leave the dark storeroom behind. I come out into the homely-looking backroom, which I ignore, and instead, I enter the shop.

The smell of magic is more potent. The strangeness of the foreign energy wiggles across my skin like ants crawling. It tickles the back of my throat and I have to breathe in shallow gasps to stop myself from gagging. It is so gross.

I hate this shop.

Yet, I cannot stop my fingers tracing across the shelves, shelves packed to the brim with magical items and artefacts. The store's name is everywhere. 'TINCTURES 'N TONICS' - SPECIALISTS IN PORTABLE POTIONS. My lip curls with deep-rooted disgust.

This shop is the accumulation of everything that was wrong in my old life.

All I see when I come in here is my failure.

And I need to make peace with that. It is not the magic in this world's fault that my strange host magic was not compatible. I have blamed magic, school, the witch community, my coven... I swallow against the growing lump in my throat. *Everyone. I blamed everyone.*

Diane was right. I was bitter. I was jealous.

Those imaginary fairies bounce around in my abdomen as I come to a horrid realisation. *What type of monster would I be if I had all that power to begin with?*

I have been given a unique perspective that I would have never had if I had not lived it. *A gift.* I have had years of being weak and powerless. Perhaps I needed to learn through my experience to gain empathy and compassion. *Perhaps everything does happen for a reason.*

I roam around the shop, the retail manager in me mentally rearranging things to make more sense of the higgledy-piggledy way items are stuffed onto the shelves.

I itch my arm. The layout is going to give me hives.

There is an enormous mirror alongside a display of pretty jewellery. According to the labels, they contain powerful disguise spells that can change appearance, Diane's speciality. I glimpse my reflection and notice the lack of glowing marks on my skin. My stomach dips.

They mark me as different, alien, so how can I miss them? Of their own accord, my eyes drift back to the hidden portal. A sharp urge for *home* thrums through me. I need to get my head on straight without the pocket realm's magic mojo messing with me.

CHAPTER THIRTY

The door to my sister's magic shop clicks closed and I wander down the street. I take careful note of the people moving around me. Somehow, I am almost convinced some creature will stop, point and shout that I am the host everyone is talking about. I shake my head. I know the idea of that happening is ridiculous. Witches are incredibly private. They might be the worst gossips imaginable, but they keep what happens within the community to themselves. It's like some unwritten rule. Security is important.

I avoid the shopping centre where my department store is located. I don't want to see anyone. *My old department store,* I amend with a frown. I know the Hunters Guild already did a lot of the legwork, but I will still need to give them a call and officially hand in my resignation. No matter what, I can never go back. I would be too much of a security risk.

There is still a huge amount of guilt. I think I will always feel guilty. I know it is only a job and that everybody is replaceable, as bad as that sounds. At least I know I established a great team who will step up; it will be like I was never there. My tummy dips. Gosh, these changes are so hard.

Running feet have me turning. "Stop where you are!" bellows a male voice. I flatten myself against the glass of a shop as three hunters barrel toward me. Their weapons glint and jingle in time with the beat of their feet.

I only breathe a little easier when they run past. The wind stirs my hair in their wake. Everyone on the street has also frozen. Well, everybody but one guy. He takes off at a loping run.

"Stop. Niles Bradbury, you are under arrest!" The yelling hunter pulls out a potion. The crowd ahead parts and people scramble, disappearing into shops and doorways. The man, of course, doesn't stop, and with impressive aim, the potion hits his shoulder and bursts open.

The man takes a few more steps, seemingly unaffected, but then he falls to his knees with a muffled groan.

Like a well-practised team, one hunter steps forward and a null band is slapped onto the guy's wrist. The other hunter slaps silver handcuffs on him, pulling his long arms behind his back. *Long arms?* I let out a shocked gasp. His arms are super long. The null band must have erased the guy's appearance-masking spell.

His arms and legs are now super long, with his trousers halfway up his calves.

"You are here on Earth illegally, Niles Bradbury, and you will come with us to be processed."

"Nooo. Click-click." The prisoner's speech becomes garbled and his—mandibles?—clack together.

His face now resembles an insect.

An unmarked van pulls up from the closest alleyway and the guy is hauled to his feet and shoved unceremoniously inside.

I must make a noise as the hunter that threw the potion ball turns his head and looks straight at me. He closes the van door, and the bang makes me jump. The hunter narrows his eyes and glares.

My eyes dart about. Oops. I am the only one stupid enough to be left on the street. With a squeak on the glass, my hand frantically searches for the door of the shop. If I am not careful, my nosiness is going to get me killed.

The back of my left hand smacks into a handle. I grab it, push the door open, and I stumble gracelessly inside.

The bell above the door chimes a cheerful welcome. I hunch as I wait for the hunter to come and get me. But he doesn't, thank goodness. Self-consciously I stand a little straighter and look about. The delicious smell of cakes and coffee hits my nose and my eyes widen.

* * *

I balance the plate in one hand and keep one eye on the full mug as I shuffle across the room. I am conscious that if I am not careful, I will splash a trail to my seat. My hand-eye coordination is horrendous. I find the perfect spot for people watching—no, I have not learned my lesson— and I settle down next to the window with the bookshelves at my back.

The bright, winter sunset is hitting the table just right. It slashes across my arm and face. I lean back in the chair a little, so the light doesn't blind me. With a deep breath, I lift my eyes to the tree above my head. It has branches across the ceiling. Glorious pink blossoms entwined with twinkling fairy lights. *It's a dryad's tree,* I think with recognition. *I wonder if she's related to or knows Erin?*

If I breathe deeply enough, I can just about smell the sweet scent of blossoms above the coffee and cakes. The café is enchanting. I can't believe I've never been in here before. The smell of pastry alone makes my tummy grumble.

I turn the mug so I can get at the handle, and it catches on some bumpy lines on the table and wobbles. I move it to the left and run my finger across the gouged marks.

Huh. It's a name.

I tilt my head as the words are upside down. Liz. I wonder why someone wrote that? Perhaps this is a favourite table of someone's lost love. What I wouldn't give to be a fly on the wall when the person wrote that. I grab the spoon to start on the hot chocolate.

I bought Owen's favourite more-dessert-than-drink, with marshmallows, whipped cream, *and* a chocolate flake. I'm hoping it and the enormous slab of chocolate cake will pep me up. I guess it's over the top and will probably make me sick with a chocolate overload rather than fix my mood. But the cake looks amazing and I couldn't resist. I'll do my best to finish it all, as it would be a crime to waste it.

Across the road, a troll scratches his bum and shoots me a glare when he notices I am watching. I shift my eyes and let them go unfocused, hoping he thinks I am staring into space. I am a pro at people watching. No way do I want an argument with a troll. With an angry, if somewhat confused glare, he stomps down the street. I smirk when his hand goes back to itch. I bet that is the work of a potion.

From inside Jodie's borrowed coat pocket, I pull out my mobile, a notepad, and a pen. I slap them down on the table. Writing helps me think, so I've gone all old-fashioned as I enjoy jotting down my thoughts. If it all goes wrong, at least I will get some pleasure from ripping the page up into tiny little bits. Much more satisfying than a datapad.

I plant my left elbow on the table, lean over the pad, and I plop my head on my hand. *Okay, let's do this.* I draw a wobbly line down the middle of the page and scrawl on the top of the two columns: To stay. To go.

Okay, that's simple enough. I tap the pen against the pad. My rogue left leg bounces, and I puff out my cheeks when I catch myself humming the song *Should I Stay or Should I Go* by The Clash. With a groan, I sit back in the chair and rub my face. This is harder than I thought it would be.

I look about, hoping for inspiration. The café is almost empty, with only three other customers.

My eyes drift to the two human ladies sitting near the toilets. Their heads are close together as they enjoy each other's company. I can't help my smile at their raucous laughter. They giggle over a flowery blue teapot, and their words drift towards me. The conversation is about a dog called Tobie peeing on a nightmare neighbour's leg. *Go Tobie.*

Movement in the cake display area catches my eye. A sapphire blue pixie, in a protective suit, clutches a small paintbrush in her tiny fist as she climbs a wedding cake, like she's scaling Mount Everest.

Wow, the thing has got to be seven tiers. I can just about make out she is painting each flower with gold glitter. The attention to detail is astonishing, and I find her fascinating. I dig into my drink and pop the spoon loaded with a pink gooey marshmallow into my mouth.

The girl next to the pixie, the one with the rainbow hair who served me, groans. Hands-on-hips, she looks around the café—at us, her remaining customers, and then back at her watch. Her face scrunches up with a scowl.

I guiltily nudge my phone to check the time.

Phew, I'm okay. There is still an hour left until close. I am not keeping her from going home. From her expression alone, I am guessing it must have been a long day.

Crikey, how many times have I done that myself, looked at my watch with my feet and body aching. My poor brain buzzing with overstimulation and the overwhelming need to go home. A minute feels like a lifetime, like the working day will never end and when the second hand of the watch doesn't move, it's the worst. Especially when you are finally about to close the doors and a random customer strolls in. Why? Why do they do that?

"I'm so bored," she grumbles at the pixie.

"Well, no wonder," the Pixie huffs, wiggling her paintbrush at the girl's face. "You are so busy with the excitement of saving the world, no wonder you find being stuck here boring. I know you want to help Tilly out with a couple of shifts, but you have better things to do." She climbs up another tier.

"Yeah, I guess. I just wanted some normalcy, you know."

"I know you don't want to let things go," the Pixie says as she raises a tiny blue eyebrow meaningfully. Ooh, I bet there is a story there.

Heck, Tuesday, you are so nosy.

I lean forward in my chair and tuck my hands underneath my chin.

"But sometimes you've just got to move on. You live in the past too much." The pixie shakes her head when all the girl does is scowl at her words of wisdom.

She opens her mouth—

Clink, clink, clink.

Ahh, nooo! The lady furthest away sure likes to stir her cappuccino.

I rub my forehead as she irritably cracks the spoon against the cup a few more dozen times. I can't hear what they are saying. *I think you got it. What is she doing? Digging to Australia?* I hope she hasn't got anything to eat. She is probably one of those people that chews really loudly.

I glance down at my pad of paper and the simple words I've written scream at me. To stay. To go.

I say I'm a throwaway person, but if I'm honest, I run away before people get the chance. I keep away from people, so I'm less likely to be hurt. I glance down at the pen in my hands. I've picked at the rubber grip so much, it's falling apart, and the little yellow pieces are scattered across the table.

Emotional pain is my nemesis. It wiggles inside my brain, turning, twisting, rotting my sense of self. I sigh as I put the damaged pen down and slowly pick up each tiny, ragged piece of rubber. I collect them into the centre of my palm and then drop them into the coat pocket.

I think my mum always knew that there was something wrong with me. Something about me she didn't like. Even before she found out I had cheated at school, she treated me different. She dotes on my sisters.

I love her.

I love her, but I hate her too. How horrible is that? How can I hate my mum? I'm not even sure if she consciously knows what she is doing. I hope not. No, I don't hate her. I just hate some things she does. There is a difference.

The noisy cappuccino drinker stomps across the café and leaves. The girl with the rainbow hair moves like a dancer. In a few short silent strides, she is at the cappuccino lady's table, removing the cup and giving the table a quick wipe.

She goes back behind the counter as I take a huge bite of the cake. I groan as the taste of chocolate fills my mouth. I should really use the cake fork. I am eating like a savage. Oh, but this cake is divine. No wonder they boast the best chocolate cake in the city. This is—

I jump when the door cracks against the wall and the bell above chimes in distress. I close my eyes for a second and then place the cake gently back on the plate. My hypervigilance kicks into overdrive.

Uh-oh. I hope this isn't about me.

CHAPTER THIRTY-ONE

A dark-haired vampire angrily strides up to the counter and points at the girl. No, it's not about me. "You, abomination," he snarls.

"You just had to say it, didn't you? You had to say you were bored and tempt fate," the pixie says in a singsong voice from the top of the wedding cake.

In response, the girl rolls her eyes, casually leans against the counter, and crosses her arms. With her top hand, she dramatically points her thumb at her chest and flutters her multi-coloured eyelashes. She manages the best 'who me?' face I have ever seen. I can't help snorting.

"Yes," the vampire snarls. His teeth elongate and prick against his bottom lip. "Prepare to die."

Whoa. My eyes widen. That escalated quickly; things are about to get real.

The girl, seemingly unaffected, smirks and holds a hand up. "Hold on a minute. That's against the health code. Sorry, they are pretty strict with the no dead bodies in the café rules. We'll have to take this outside."

Wow, how cool is she? My eyes automatically drift to look outside and I frown at the busy street. It's bustling with people going home after a busy workday. She must spot what I have seen as she huffs, "Perhaps we can go out the back."

"No," the vampire bellows.

It appears he has had enough of the conversation and to make a point, he swipes his arm across the till display, sending things flying. Leaflets scatter, and an empty sounding tip jar crashes to the floor. His fist then heads for her face.

Oh no.

I watch as she blocks the vampire's strike with an almost lazy movement, as if fighting is so easy for her, she could make a cup of coffee while she's doing it. The vampire *really* does not like that, and he lets out a dramatic roar. She rolls her eyes.

Then his hand heads towards the cake masterpiece. My eyes almost pop out of my head. *No, not the cake!* The pixie squeaks out in horror. "Tru, stop him!"

The girl, Tru, grabs his wrist. "No. Bad vampire," she scolds.

Gone is the amusement and in its place, with a flash of red eyes, the girl transforms into something *other*.

What the heck is she?

I thought she was human. She must have him in a bone-crunching hold as the vampire winces. Like Owen's friend, Forrest, who has all that crazy power packed inside her, this girl has a serious hidden strength that makes me feel a bit like wet lettuce.

Two more vampires aggressively crash into the café.

Double oh no.

It's a full-on party. Like a wimp, I sink lower into the chair, and with shaking hands, wipe my chocolate frosted fingers on a napkin. I puff out my cheeks and try my best to control my rapid heartbeat. It's all going to kick off and I don't want to be ringing the dinner bell with my heart racing and my tasty blood rushing through my veins.

Not that vampires are allowed to go around chomping on people, but I wouldn't put it past them to say my neck got in the way of their teeth.

The old ladies also sink in their seats. We are all scarcely breathing. They look so frightened.

I grind my jaw. The rainbow girl is going to struggle against three vampires. I don't want to see her get hurt.

The first guy smiles smugly at his backup and puffs out his chest. He yanks his wrist out of the girl's grip as the other two vampires spread out about the room with the bigger of the two blocking the door. He cracks his knuckles.

Err, I hate bullies.

When I was younger, I always expected people to have the same level of morality as my own. To understand wrong from right, to value life. It was a shock and a big lesson to learn. Other people do not play fair. They do bad things and sleep well at night. As long as they are alright, the world they live in is perfect.

I can't do that. I cannot sit back and watch

bad things happen when I can do something, try to help. I think my life would be easier if I minded my business. The problem is... I care too much.

Gosh, after everything I have been dealing with, I'm going to die by vampire in a tiny café.

Boy, my mum is going to be pissed.

All I'm missing is my raging temper. I didn't realise how much of a buffer it was. I think I prefer to be angry than feel this kind of powerless fear. *If only I had my magic, if only I had access to my power...* An idea tickles at the back of my head. It is such a silly thought. I have to be in my realm to use my magic, but perhaps I can use it another way. I do have an item coated with magic in my pocket. The portable dimension. Nah, I shake my head. No, it will not work. It can't be that easy.

Can it?

Tru might not even need my help. My eyes flick back to the vampire as he continues to shout out murderous threats. But we all know what happens to witnesses of a crime and if she fails... she isn't the only one who's going to get hurt, or potentially die. I can't help looking at the two old ladies. One whimpers and the other shushes her, reaching over to hold her hand.

No, I will not sit and watch this happen without at least trying to help. I make sure the vampires are busy and, millimetre by millimetre, I lift my hips and from my back pocket, pull out the empty storeroom bag. With a hope and a prayer, I unravel it and without giving the game away, I stuff my left foot into it.

My leg tingles with pins and needles. Okay, that is something.

The vampire grabs hold of Tru's hair and, at the same time, sticks his dirty finger into the cake. The pixie, with a kamikaze scream, throws herself at him and bites his hand. He hisses and bats her away. Her tiny body flies across the room and hits the café window with a bone-crunching crack.

"No!" Tru cries.

Oh my.

"That's enough!" I yell as I slam my hands on the table and stand up. The chair scrapes the floor and rattles as it impacts the bookcase behind me. My leg continues to tingle as familiar energy zips across my body and settles into my chest. Relief makes me almost dizzy as my glowing tattoos reflect in the window. It's working! The two vampires turn and one of them, the big one, rushes toward me.

Oh heck.

With a fancy parkour move, the rainbow-haired girl leaps over the counter and spins on her toes. With unnatural speed, a blade appears in her hand and she stabs the closest vampire in the chest, just as I throw my hands up to cover my face.

There is a moment where it feels like time slows down as I wildly fling out my magic.

The seconds tick.

When nothing happens, I peek from behind my quivering arms. The knuckle cracking vampire's fist hovers inches from my face.

Ooh.

I don't know why, but I reach out a shaky hand and poke at the dinner plate sized fist. *If he had hit me with that... Hell, look at it.* I gulp. *He would have mashed my face.*

Luckily, I have frozen the vampires in place.

Tru circles the frozen vampire she stabbed and pokes his cheek. "Huh." His blood didn't freeze with his body, and it drips down his chest onto the floor. "Shit, Tilly is going to kick my arse. I hope you have got some cash on you," she says to the now presumably dead vampire. "You're paying for the clean-up spell, buddy."

I wince.

She moves, graceful and lithe, like a dancer, to the next vampire. When she isn't leaning against the counter, the rainbow-haired girl is super tall. Beautiful but... with a sleek predatory quality I didn't see when I first spoke to her. All I saw was the girly hair. I guess that was all she wanted me to see.

I shiver.

With a shrug, she grabs hold of the next vampire's head. With one hand gripping the back of his dark hair and the other on his chin, she breaks his neck with a crunch. She does the same with the third. The one near me. I swallow down bile. I'm not used to this kind of violence.

My wide eyes meet the girl's.

"It's okay," she whispers. "Vampires can't be killed by a broken neck. They will heal. Well, those two will. The one I stabbed..." She pulls a face. "I hit his heart. You can let them go now." I release the freezing magic, and like puppets with their strings cut, all three of them flop to the floor. I shiver.

"Thanks. Shit, are you okay?"

I nod.

Across the room, there's a tiny rasp. Even from here, I can see blood bubbling between the pixie's lips with each of her struggling breaths. "Oh no. Please, no." The despair in Tru's eyes makes my abdomen clench as she spins and hurries back across the café toward her friend.

I don't know how long the power in the bag will last, so without losing time trying to move and worrying I'll dislodge the bag from my foot, I direct the magic to heal the pixie.

I cringe and cross my fingers. I am all so new to this, and I've never healed without touching someone before. My magic flies like an arrow from me to the pixie without issue. It takes seconds to heal her. Then because I can, I fix the beautiful wedding cake that the vampire damaged.

With a wobble, I lift my foot and pull off the bag. My trainer smokes. It also looks a completely different colour than the other one now. Whoa, I must have pulled in some power.

I scrape it against the floor, and it leaves a rubber residue. At least it didn't disintegrate.

The bag still bubbles with power. I can feel it, but I have got no energy left to access it. Working magic in the real world is exhausting.

Dizzy, I slump in the chair and, with trembling hands, take a mouthful of the now cold drink. Black spots dance across my vision. I need to eat something. My stomach growls and aches like it's eating itself. I take a big mouthful of cake.

"Hey, thanks," the pixie shouts. Standing on the glass dome that surrounds the cakes, she grins and waves. "You healed me and saved the cake. Thank you so much. It took me so many hours to make."

I finger wave, finish my mouthful of cake and wipe my lips. "Oh, you're welcome. I'm just glad you're okay." The bell chimes above the door as the old ladies leave without a word. I try not to watch as Tru unceremoniously drags the dead and unconscious vampires outside.

I duck my head and shovel in more cake.

"He will know about this. I bet he's already on his way," the pixie whispers.

"Yeah, I know. That is why I've texted Tilly that I'm getting the hell out of here. I'm so done for the day. I need to go to the gym and smash things."

"We can close early. It's almost time."

I jump in my seat when the rainbow-haired girl appears. Crikey, she is freaky quiet. She must have glided over the floor like an apparition, making little to no noise at all. I know 'cause I was listening so hard to their conversation. It's another little detail that affirms her deadly nature.

"I owe you one. You stepped up even when you didn't know us. You saved my friend's life. Thank you." I blink. Her warm orange eyes take in my trembling body.

I must look pathetic.

I shuffle uncomfortably in the seat. "It's no bother," I say with a shrug. "It was the right thing to do."

"Yeah? Well, thank you. You are a total badass."

"Me?" I squeak. I point at my chest and shake my head in disbelief. "I was so scared."

"You could have fooled me. I loved the whole 'that's enough!' scream. It was very scary. Here. It's on the house." She slides a replacement hot chocolate on the table.

"Thank you," I mumble.

"My name is Tru." She taps the table twice and raises a rainbow eyebrow.

Oh, she wants to know my name. "Tuesday," I splutter. Seemingly satisfied and finished with our conversation, with a nod and a warm smile, she pirouettes on her toes and goes back to cleaning up.

Huh. Tru didn't ask any awkward questions. She didn't even care what type of creature I was. She just appreciated my help.

That was nice.

My trembling disappears, and my pounding heart settles. Bloody fate. Looks like I'm exactly where I need to be. Back in my pocket realm, helping people like Erin. For the first time since this wacky adventure started, I can take a full breath. This vampire fight has settled something inside me.

I'm enough. I am strong enough, and if I can pull magic out of my arse to deal with raging vampires, I can deal with my mum and running a hotel in another dimension. I dab my finger onto the plate and sweep up a dollop of chocolate frosting.

Perhaps I can be a badass. *Yeah.* I grin at the plate. *Piece of cake.*

CHAPTER THIRTY-TWO

"Jodie." I knock. "It's me. Have you got a sec?" I love using my magic to pinpoint my sister's location—I can't seem to find Larry but I'm sure he will pop up—and the more I use the magic, the more natural it feels.

Coming back from the real world, I am energised and emotionally lighter. Gosh, who knew this ordeal could be so cathartic? My head is clear for the first time in years.

"Tuesday." The door flies open, and Jodie blinks at me, then peeks over my shoulder with a salacious grin, which then promptly drops.

"Oh, no hunky hellhound?"

"No, he doesn't follow me around all the time."

"Could have fooled me," she says under her breath. Louder, she says, "I've known that man for years and how he looks at you..." Jodie grins and fans her face.

"I like him too," I say softly. I can feel my face going a nice, bright red. I guess I will have to get used to many shades of red when conversation steers towards Owen. I rub my damaged trainer against the carpet and the rubber peels back.

Oh, yeah, the reason for my visit. "Here." I shove the mini pocket dimension into her hands. When I returned, I checked the mini pocket dimension over in case I had damaged it with my foot. Strangely, the power inside had increased, so much so that the bag was practically vibrating. Whatever I did in the real world, it liked it.

Freaky magic.

Jodie's smile dims. She tilts her head to the side and frowns at the bag. Visibly confused, she opens it and peeps inside. "Oh," she gasps.

"Oh my, Tuesday this is... wow." She looks up at me, dumbfounded.

I rub the back of my neck and chuckle. I then quickly explain how to use it with the blood and stuff. "It's a tester, so let me know what changes or improvements you need."

"I will. Thank you so much."

"No problem. I made the fixed portal too. I placed it on the back wall of your stockroom. But now I am thinking it was a stupid idea, what with all the wards in the shop. If anyone unauthorised goes through, they are going to get a nasty zap. So, I might see if Dad has an alternative location, and we can just use that one for the coven."

Jodie nods and waves a hand; she's not listening to me. She's staring at the pocket dimension bag with gobsmacked awe. I roll my eyes when she hugs it to her chest. "Mum is on the warpath," she mumbles between bag hugs.

"She's always on the warpath," I scoff. "Okay, see you in the morning. I'm going to hide out in my roo—" As I am walking away, I stumble, and full body smack against the wall.

Oh! Well, that isn't good.

"What's wrong?" Jodie asks, rushing towards me. "Tuesday, you've gone white as a sheet."

What the heck was that?

I press my forehead against the wall and groan. Jodie grabs my elbow and I lock my knees to hold myself up. The magic inside me is screaming a warning. "Someone has just ripped a bloody big hole into the realm," I say in disbelief. Horrified, I stare at Jodie, my eyes wide. My ears ring, and my head pounds from the attack. "I don't know what's happening. No one should be able to come here like that," I rasp. "You aren't safe. I don't think anyone is safe. I need to lock down the portals. Please grab our coven and get to the new emergency exit while I deal with this. It's the door behind reception, near my office. I will let you know when it's safe."

"No, no, I can help you." I shake my head and somehow send her the location of everyone in the coven. I can't find Andy, which is strange. I hope he is okay. "No. Come with me. We can get them together." Jodie tugs at my arm.

"I can't. I am so sorr—"

"Please," she begs.

I made a choice in the café. I chose this new life and the realm. Now here is some wacky cosmic test to prove my mettle. I will not fall at this first hurdle. I won't.

Lives are counting on me.

"I have a responsibility to my guests, to the realm. I know where this person is. I still have strong magic, Jodie."

Jodie takes in my determined face and, for a second, she closes her eyes and sags in defeat. "You are so bloody stubborn."

"If Owen won't go with you, tell him to head East."

"Okay, okay, go kick their arse. I've got this, sis. I will get everyone to safety. Go. Go!" Jodie runs to my parents' room and bangs on their door.

With the magic's insistence pulling at me, I Step.

CHAPTER THIRTY-THREE

I arrive at a dark place that I didn't even know existed. It looks like a dead corner carved out in the world. The surrounding air is heavy and stagnant. The elf who tried to kidnap me is standing in front of me. "You," I say in shock. When he sees me, his overlarge bright blue eyes widen with surprise.

Yeah, I can Step just like you. I might not be able to in the real world or use my magic without a bag on my foot, but in this world, I'm golden.

"Hello," he says politely. "What a lovely surprise. It's nice to be greeted."

"You," I sneer. "Did you think I wouldn't notice you ripping a hole in my realm? What the heck do you think you're doing? What are you doing sneaking about? You are so not welcome."

"I seek sanctuary," he says in a low, smug tone.

My lip twitches into a snarl. "Sanctuary denied. Go away."

"Okay, you got me." He holds his wrists out together mockingly as if I'm going to whip out some handcuffs. "No, I don't want your stupid sanctuary. But thank you for making everything so much easier. You've Stepped right into my hands."

I huff and roll my eyes. "Do you know what the definition of insanity is, elf?" My hands go to my hips as I channel my mum. "According to Einstein, it is doing the same thing over and over again and expecting a different result. Have we not done this song and dance before? It was only a few days ago." The massive elf looms menacingly over me and I instantly regret my snarky words, and I quickly scramble back.

"Don't you dare come any closer." I wave my hands in the air to frantically warn him away. His deep chuckle makes me want to bop him in the face.

Oh my goodness, could I be any more pathetic?

I have magic. I have an entire dimension at my fingertips. *Why do I always forget?* I pause my retreat. I gather my magic and feel more confident. "I have friends coming who are going to lock you up." I continue with a little bit more bravo. "You made a huge mistake coming here. By doing so, you've handed yourself over to the fae warriors." Smugly I freeze him in place like I did the vampires.

"Do you mean the useless group of fae warriors and shifters that I iron and silver bombed? Those friends?"

Oh no. That was him?

The elf smirks and itches his nose. *Wait... what? That isn't right.* How is he talking, moving? My heart misses a beat when I realise the magic has done nothing. Nothing. The elf isn't frozen.

I try to grab the magic of the realm as this guy is strong and I need the big guns. But it's kind of unwilling. Sluggish. I huff, and nervous energy skitters down my spine, as goosebumps erupt on my forearms. Perhaps I can't use the magic so soon after I've Stepped? Or maybe there is an issue after he ripped his way into the realm?

I swallow my panic and continue talking to keep him busy. "What do you want with me? Why did you attack my coven?" I ask as I wrangle the unwilling magic, I need to restrain him. The fine strands of magic finally slide ever so slowly around his body like I'm a spider and he's a fly in my web. "Is it because you knew what I was? A host?" There, sorted, he shouldn't get away from that.

Phew, I was worried there for a second. Then it clicks in my head. "Are you a member of the sealgairí? Are you a sealgair?"

He chuckles annoyingly, and with dancing blue eyes, drops his head to observe the magic as it wraps around him. "Is that what they are calling me a sealgair? A hunter? How fitting."

"If you know what I am, that I am a host, why are you attacking me here, where I'm the most powerful? What is wrong with you?"

"Are you? Are you really?" He lifts his chin and smiles manically. "Are you really the powerful one here, little lost host?" He drops the smile, and my tummy drops along with it.

"The magic isn't playing ball with you, is it?" He waves his hand and the magic web crumples away.

'Ecky-thump, that's not good.

"You think I dumped you here for you to ruin everything I created?" His eyes narrow, and he slinks closer. I want to move away, but the ground underneath my feet will not let me. Oh my goodness, my feet are glued to the floor.

"THIS IS MY DIMENSION, YOU STUPID GIRL!" he screams. His face is so close to mine droplets of spit spatter against my cheek, and his voice echoes around us. I tremble. His nostrils flare as he takes a deep breath, and once he is back in control, his voice drops. "You are here because I brought you here to drain your magic." I stare at him with absolute horror, and he wrinkles his nose. "Not for you to play hotelier and set yourself up as a benevolent fucking hero. You shouldn't have made it through the first night. Isn't that right, Larry?"

Larry manifests next to the elf. He stands, head down, hands in his pockets, and kicks at the ground.

"Larry?" I rasp.

I catch the horror and worried expression as it crosses Larry's freckled face. His green eyes meet mine and the light in his eyes goes dead.

Oh Larry.

The elf reaches out. I finch away but he grabs the back of my head. His hand tangles in my hair and he violently yanks my head back. I wince as my scalp burns and my neck aches. At a painful angle, the elf holds my head still and brushes away an escaped tear that was rolling down my face.

With an unnecessary slurp, he licks the tear off his finger.

"He was supposed to get you here so the realm could drain you dry," he whispers into my ear, pressing his face against my cheek. "Not make friends with you." The elf's other hand whips out and Larry stumbles sideways as the elf cracks him across the back of the head.

"Larry, you lured me here to drain me?" I rasp around a growing lump of terror in my throat. I have never in my life been so frightened. I strain my eyes to the side. The way I am being held means I can only move my eyes to look at him. "You're a bad guy?"

No shit, he's a bad guy, Tuesday. Didn't the incident with the dryads not teach you anything? Why did you think he acted as if it was same old, same old? Because it bloody was.

I didn't see it.

I didn't want to see it.

I attributed it to him being non-human and

his construct nature. Why did I assume? I'm such a fool. How could I be so trusting? *Unless he doesn't have a choice and he's being coerced?* Gah, there I go again, making excuses. I am so bloody stupid.

Oh gosh, I hope my coven has left. I can't feel them anymore. My connection to the realm has been ripped away. I cannot believe I brought them here. I presumed the place was safe. Even when my instincts knew something fishy was going on, with everything thrown at me, I didn't have the time to work it out. If something happens to them, it's my fault.

It's then I notice that I can thankfully still feel Owen. He is in his wolf form and rapidly heading this way.

"I thought we were friends?" I whisper.

"He's a magical construct, you stupid girl." The elf gives me a shake and yanks my head sharply to the side and I can't help whimpering. "He is my magical construct. He isn't real. The red-haired guy you see before you is what works to lull my victims." He lets go of my hair and grabs hold of Larry's face and drags him towards me. The elf squeezes Larry's cheeks till his mouth bulges. "Everyone loves this handsome, freckled face." The elf speaks in a cutesy baby tone and pouts his lips, mirroring Larry's squeezed face. "His bright smile is the perfect lure." With a dark chuckle, the elf slaps his hand against Larry's face and roughly palms him away.

It's all been an elaborate trap.

"If you are a host, and if this is your dimension, why was it dying?" I need to keep him talking. I need to give Owen time to get here and help me. My hellhound will rip him to shreds.

"The power is mine, silly girl. I control the dimension; it doesn't control me. I used way too much magic making this world. I will not spend energy making it pretty. It's a tool."

"But... but Nyssa told me about the man who created this sanctuary, that he made it to help people."

"That old spiel?" he scoffs. "Smoke and mirrors, girl, smoke and mirrors. I wanted to help myself, not other creatures. Now, this little chat is nice and all, but I'd prefer to drain you now. You will make such a pretty husk."

Husk.

Oh God.

CHAPTER THIRTY-FOUR

"There is nothing sweeter or more powerful than draining a host. Our magic is delicious." He licks his lips.

"You cannibalise your own people." To understand what this creature does is an alien concept in my head. It is horrific. Another realisation comes to me. "There are no sealgairí, is there? No big bad killing hosts. It's you, isn't it? It has always been you. You have pulled the wool over everyone's eyes." I shake my head. "Not only are you a mass murderer who has taken our race to the verge of extinction, you have been draining other creatures, while blaming it all on the realms."

"Not so stupid after all." He creepily tilts his head and taps his lips. The man is a bloody psychopath. His expression is thoughtful as he shakes his head. "Tell you what, I will indulge you just this once, as what does it matter? A last wish. The hosts left alive are too wily, too embedded in their little realms, hiding like little mouses. So, I hunt the young ones. The ones like you."

He bops me on the nose. "Baby hosts, yet to get their power. I scare them enough that they run and I trap them in my dimension. It activates their magic and then... bam! I simply drain them dry." He shrugs as if he's not talking about ending innocent lives. "It all worked perfectly." He scowls. "Until you."

He leans closer again and breathes me in. A shiver of revulsion trickles down my spine. "So much magic," he whispers. His tongue flashes out of his mouth as he gazes at me like I am an extra delicious cheeseburger. "You know, it has happened once or twice when the magic hasn't drained my prey completely overnight." He smirks. "They spent the time they had left flapping around, panicking, crying, freaking out. They couldn't even leave their room. After a day or so, when I finally got to them, they were practically basket cases. So deliciously frightened."

I feel sick. This guy is a monster.

"What they didn't do is take over. YOU TOOK OVER MY FUCKING WORLD! LOOK AT IT!" I flinch as he roars, sweeping his arms around to encompass the realm that peeks out from behind this dark horrid corner. He lowers his voice and, somehow, it's more menacing. "Trees, flowers, butterflies, a lake? I left a rotten hotel and a barely functional car park. You've been busy making yourself a true sanctuary when you should have been a good little girl and laid down dead. This isn't fucking Disneyland," he spits. "This pocket dimension is not yours. It is mine. *Mine.* This place was made to be a prison."

In a panic, I send my magic out and try—like I'm pulling strands of string that are tangled—to gather the realm's magic, but it is as if I'm trying to touch through glass. I keep hitting a wall.

"Girl, stop trying to manipulate the magic. You have had days to try and learn something I've been doing for millennia. Quit it. This pocket world is not yours."

It wants to be.

"That's the problem though, isn't it?" I rasp. "This realm *likes* being a sanctuary. It does not enjoy being a trap." *Sentient.* I know it sounds crazy. The magic is sentient, and that is the reason I am still alive. He's been killing people for centuries, sucking out their life force, abusing the realm's magic. Like me, the magic doesn't want to hurt people, it wants to help, and perhaps it found that spark of possibility within me. We align. The magic stepped up and protected me. "That is why you are so pissed. The realm locked you out." My released host magic combined with the dimensional magic healed the world and pulled it right out of the rogue host's hands.

"Oh, will you just shut up? What does it matter, Nancy Drew? Just shut up and die already." He groans. "It will take me years to get your stink out of this place. Do you know what? I'm going to drain you slowly. It will take weeks." He runs his finger across my lips. "I will cut out your tongue to halt the incessant chatter and put you in a tiny pocket cell, safe and away from my realm. While I drain your magic, I will enjoy watching you slowly go mad."

Pain screams inside me. *Is he draining me already?* Ouch.

"You feel that, don't you? The tickle underneath your skin." A tickle? More like my stomach and bowels have been put into a meat grinder. "Danger will do that. The magic doesn't like it. So finicky in its attempt to be so pure."

My vision flashes to black and I am forced to close my eyes. Creatures pop up on the magical map inside my head, and it pounds with the overload of information. I take the opportunity to frantically check on Owen, Daisy, and my coven. For the moment, they are safe. I can feel my hellhound's concern and determination. But then I see what the rogue host wanted, the reason why he is allowing me to see, to torture me with the truth. Eight—no, ten people that shouldn't be here. Mercenaries.

The first thing I did when I felt someone rip a hole in the realm was lock down all the portals. He has yet to re-open them.

I locked down every portal, except for one.

I didn't lock down the emergency one leading to Jodie's shop. Nobody but a member of our coven could gain access to her shop. *Yet they have.* Perhaps the rogue host destroyed the wards? But Jodie would have known.

"I brought along some friends." Despair fills me. His *friends* are surrounding my coven. They didn't make it out. I failed. The magic screams at me to do something, but the rogue host cuts my connection. It is down to just a whisper.

My voice cracks. "How?"

"I didn't even have to pay them," he says, all jolly. "You killed a dryad, and some guy loved her. He went a bit nuts when her tree disappeared. The poor love-blinded fool thought he had a hope of saving her—save the tree, save the girl."

Erin.

"When the whole clan up and left, he knew something bad had happened. So he did a little digging. A kind-hearted soul—that would be me—whispered your name in his ear. I helped to stir him up and push him in the right direction. Towards you. I also helpfully gave him the number for an excellent mercenary firm as professional backup. The rat shifters are wonderful soldiers and so much easier to manipulate than the wolves."

Yeah, the same rats that ransacked my flat.

I don't bother telling him that Erin is still alive and well. It's not something he'd understand. Undoubtedly, he thinks everyone is a soul-sucking monster like him.

"I needed a backup plan in case you were more difficult to deal with. Waste of effort, really. I thought you would have at least offered me more of a challenge, but..." He huffs. "Never mind. By now, the rats will have gathered all your guests, including your pathetic little coven, for me to eat. Even if they kill everyone before I get there, the power, their souls, are mine."

I force my face to look appropriately horrified. The host has made a mistake. He should have used a null band on me. He should not have left the tiny little spark of access to the realm's magic.

Using that magic, I initiate a change of plan. Instead of letting Owen come to me, I need him to help the guests, help my coven. With the access to the realm's magic drifting ever so slowly out of my grip, I get a message to Owen, to tell him what is happening and to give him access to the realm map and the location of all the mercenaries. Within the message, I lie and tell him I have got everything under control, and with a blast of magic, I Step him back towards the hotel. I breathe a silent sigh when it works.

The host does not notice, as he is still waffling on with his villain speech. "...I must say, I do so enjoy the thought that so many creatures will add up to a real feast."

"Can you remember who you've killed?" The host scoffs and tightens his hand in my hair before wrapping the other one around my throat. "What about Rebecca Lynch? She was a—"

"Dead." He squeezes my throat. "Any creature that stumbles into the hotel and isn't useful is dead. A mere snack. Unlike you. I'm going to feast on your power, little girl. I will be careful to drain you so slowly you'll be kept alive for months."

"What about Atticus? Does he not care about you killing hosts, killing guests?"

He laughs. "No, you naïve little fool, of course not. He doesn't know. What do you take me for, an amateur? I control everything he sees. Pureblood vampires are selfish. He doesn't care about others."

"That's where you'd be wrong," says a cultured voice behind us. "I care, and I quite like having a swimming pool."

CHAPTER THIRTY-FIVE

Atticus's fangs flash, and he buries his teeth into the host's neck. His black eyes glisten with satisfaction as they meet mine. The ground beneath my feet lets me go and I stumble away.

When I sent a message to Owen, I also sneakily sent a message to Atticus with two questions: what was his girl called, and did he want to meet her potential killer? My magic brought back his answers: Rebecca Lynch—and if I gave him Rebecca's killer, he would be eternally grateful. When my magic moved Owen to where he was needed, it yanked Atticus here.

I look away from the vampire and block out the noise of his feeding. I don't like violence, but I understand justice.

Even if justice makes me a little queasy.

My knees knock together, and I rub my throat, then my aching neck. I never want to be in that position again, with an enemy's hand wrapped around my throat.

I need to be better, stronger.

"Tuesday, I did what I could to protect you. I am sorry I could not tell you," says a pained voice. I raise my eyes from a spot on the floor and meet Larry's pleading green gaze.

Oh no, Larry! The magical construct is *translucent*. "Larry? What's happening?"

Why does he no longer appear real?

"You freed me from a monster. Please forgive me for my treachery. I am glad you are safe." I watch him fade into nothingness. "Thank you for showing me what it was like to have a friend..."

"Oh, Larry, of course, I forgive you." I reach out and brush the empty air. My hand trembles.

I fold my arms underneath my chest, so I am hugging myself. I hear a thump, like something heavy falling to the ground. Like a body. I gulp, hunch, and keep my back turned. I have already seen a dead person today. I do not want to see another. A second later, the magic of the realm floods into me. My connection to the realm is restored, and it is stronger than ever. The feeling is so powerful, I stagger. I have to peek at my feet to double-check I'm still on the ground, as I could swear that I am floating. My hair follicles tingle and when I pat my head, my hair crackles with power.

Freaky.

Oh gosh, what am I doing? I need to help my coven, is my next urgent thought.

Eagerly, the realm's magic hunts down each trespasser. The mercenaries do not stand a chance. Removing their weapons, we pluck them up as if they are just pieces of a board game and Step them to the hotel reception, where they are frozen solid in place while they wait for me to deal with them.

"Tuesday," Atticus says.

I can't. I can't turn around. I'll vomit. I hunch into myself. "Yes," I answer him with stiff lips.

"Here." His hand reaches over my shoulder and a heavy bronze ring settles in my palm. "He was wearing it. It is rightfully yours as it is full of magic—your realm's magic."

My precious, Gollum from *The Lord of the Rings* coos in my head. *Crikey, I am such a weirdo.* The ring is so heavy in my hand. I frown down at it and give it a poke with my index finger. The power inside gives me a little nip.

"Thank you, and thanks for coming to my aid." I decide to put the ring in the little pocket of my jeans for safekeeping. I flip it between my fingers so I can slide it inside. When it touches the fabric, the ring comes apart and becomes a single piece of metal. I freeze. *Oh, that's not...* The ring, like something from a horror movie, jumps and wraps itself around my right ring finger. It tightens.

A whimper leaves my throat as I come out of my strange paralysis and then, as if my hand is on fire, I flap it about like a crazy person. *Get off, get off, get the fuck off!* Yeah, as if shaking it will dislodge it. I go to yank it off. I yelp. The little bugger shocked me! Ouch, that was more than just a nip.

My hand shakes as I hold it as far away from my body as I can. I hiss and brace it with my other hand when what feels like a thousand barbs dig into my skin, muscle, and then the bone of my poor finger. "Ouch, ouch, ouch." My stomach twists and the pain makes me want to vomit.

When I am about to hyperventilate and do something stupid like, I don't know, grab a blade out of the ether and chop my damn finger off with the sheer overwhelming panic I'm feeling, the pain stops.

I lick my dry lips.

"I have seen nothing like that before. Jewellery is not normally that rambunctious," Atticus says.

My wide eyes swivel towards him. "Yeah, no kidding. It really wanted on my finger." My chest aches. Cautiously, as if the ring is a dangerous animal, I remove my stabilising hand to rub my chest. My heart pounds underneath my palm "Crap-on-a-cracker. That was scary." I clear my throat and blow out a breath.

After a few more seconds and no further pain, the previously inert silver swirls on the back of my hand get in on the action.

Uh-oh.

They pulse in time to my pounding heart and then they change direction. They straighten and flow towards my abused finger and the ring. Like an electric circuit.

"Do you want me to cut it off?" Atticus asks matter-of-factly.

"No!" I squeak as I tuck my hand against my chest. "I don't think so. No. At least it's no longer hurting me." It's not draining my power either. Somehow it makes me feel more centred. The power of the realm is now crystal clear. Honestly, can this day get any crazier?

Atticus tilts his head as he stares at my hand. "I believe this might be how he used his magic outside the realm."

"Oh." Atticus is right. The ring is packed full of magic, and things that were bugging me now make sense. Answers slide into place. "I forgot he was Stepping in the real world." And smashing powerful wards in minutes, destroying magic that would have taken anyone else hours, if at all. I then remember crocodile lady smirking at me when she noticed I didn't have a ring. "The other hosts have the same ring," I mutter.

The silence stretches between us.

"Do you urm… want the body?" I ask awkwardly.

What the feck, Tuesday?

Well, I don't know what the hell I am doing. This is stressful and I have no idea about revenge protocol!

"No. No, thank you." Atticus smirks.

I rub my face. "Okay." I then nod my head like a nodding dog and allow the magic of the realm to absorb the dead host's body. Without looking, I somehow know he's disappeared.

I stare down at the ring. As he was the original host, the realm should technically die with him, but because of me, the realm is stronger and healthier than ever.

Gosh, I still have so much to learn. Everything written about hosts seems to mislead or be outright lies. I have so much to do... Wow, it is going to be an adventure.

"I need to deal with everything."

"Of course. Oh, Tuesday, I would prefer you not transport me. It makes me want to vomit," Atticus says, looking a little vulnerable trusting me with his honesty.

I nod. "Okay."

I wonder if my Stepping makes others sick or if my new friend, the big bad pureblood vampire, has got a weak stomach from all the blood. I will have to ask Owen.

Owen. My mind and magic automatically go to him. He has tracked the mercenaries back to reception and is guarding them, still in his wolf form. I can feel how anxious he is, so I send reassuring thoughts through the magic.

Right. I better get to it. I need to deal with the mercenaries. The longer they stay, the more at risk we are of them combating my magic. Boy, they have some questions to answer. I already know, or can guess, most of what's happened. The host's slimy fingerprints are all over everything.

"Tuesday, thank yo—"

"Think nothing of it," I rudely interrupt, my voice squeaky. "Really don't."

The scary pureblood vampire chuckles, and I turn and hurry away. I leave him standing there to make his own way back.

Just before I wrap the magic around me to Step, I send a magic call to everyone in the realm to let them know everything is safe, and the emergency is over. I then send another magic message to my coven, for them to meet Owen and me at reception.

CHAPTER THIRTY-SIX

The foliage crunches underneath my feet as I carefully pick my way between the trees. I have to make a quick stop to collect Erin before I deal with the mercenaries.

I am glad it's only my coven, Atticus, and the dryads staying. If I had more guests, the reputation of the realm as a safe place would be ruined after today. The dryads have made zero sign they even heard the warnings, as they didn't stir from their trees. They must be in some kind of deep, regenerative sleep. I will have to check on them in person. My anger over Erin's situation has made me negligent and I let Larry deal with them... Shit, what was I thinking? Yeah. I shake my head. *I wasn't thinking.*

Yep, good call there, Tuesday. I give myself a hearty mental thump on my back. *Great job.*

Hindsight is a wonderful thing.

At least the realm's magic tells me they are safe. Otherwise... I puff out my cheeks as something inside me cracks. This entire situation with the rogue host will have me waking in the middle of the night for years with thoughts on what could have gone wrong and what I could have done better. I can't believe it has worked out so well, unless he has more surprises waiting for me. I glance at my right hand. As soon as I think about it, the ring on my hand weighs a tonne. I squeeze between some branches, and shuffle around a thorny bush.

The realm was a bloody prison, so it is only up from here, right? Ah bitterness, my old friend. A prison. Then there was me, all lah-di-dah and butterflies. I thought the realm would be a fabulous safe space while knowing nothing about it. Like I invented the wheel and a brand new six-star resort. Crikey, I allowed my coven to come. I put them in danger.

Right, shut up with the self-flagellation. Now isn't the time.

I mentally duct tape my insides and tuck away the horror and panic I feel until I am ready to deal with it later.

"Erin." I reach out a finger and brush the rough bark of her tree. I then instantly feel weird. Is touching a dryad's tree like touching them? I don't know the protocol, so I drop my hand and scoot a little further away to what I hope is a more appropriate social distance.

Erin's tree looks amazing. It is even healthier than when I first healed it, and the entire forest appears to be better. Yesterday, the forest was more open. Now it has grown thicker, like a protective barrier has grown up around Erin's tree.

"Erin?" I try again. "I know you want to be left alone, but something has happened. I need your help. I haven't spoken to him yet, but from what I have been led to believe, a man you know, a man who claims to be in love with you, has infiltrated the realm with mercenaries looking for justice as he believes you are dead. He thinks I killed you. Erin? Please, I need your help."

I feel stupid talking to a tree, and when nothing happens, I doubt she has even heard me. Then the tree shimmers, and Erin's pretty face appears. Her long eyelashes flutter and pieces of bark attached to them drift into the air with each blink.

She yawns. "Pardon? Did I hear you correctly? A man claims to love me and has tried to kill you?" Erin pulls away from the tree with a pained gasp. First, she wiggles her arm free and then her left leg. She has to forcibly yank herself from the tree's clutches as if it does not want to let her go. "Mercenaries?" She stares back at me with frightened, horrified eyes. "Jeff came to find me?"

Jeff. I file his name away. "It is more like he came to kill me. I have not had the pleasure of his company yet. Fortunately for him, he hasn't hurt anybody, and I have him detained." I add on quickly, "He is safe," in case she is worried about him.

"He came to avenge me? He thinks I'm dead? Oh, no." Erin rubs her forehead. "What was he thinking? We split up over a month ago. We are not together. He... he told me he couldn't deal with the whole tree thing, and he wouldn't let me explain that without my tree, I am dead." She presses one hand to her heart and the other behind her on the tree. "He said I was overreacting and that my dramatics were interfering with his game time. He was more interested in his game console than my life. Can you believe that? Overreacting to my pending death. I'm so dramatic.

"We had a huge fight, and I left him. Then everything happened. My tree got knocked down, and that was that. As my tree slowly rotted on the ground in our decimated forest, I slowly rotted alongside it. The other dryads panicked. They had no choice but to ask for help as they could see what was happening to me and they knew they were next.

"An elf pointed us in the hotel's direction and said it was a safe place for our trees. As we are earthborn, we are not allowed in any of the fae realms." Erin frowns and rubs her head. "I don't know why I didn't tell you any of this before. It's... it is like my tongue was tied and it didn't seem important. All I wanted to do was sleep." She drops her hand and shakes her head. "The elf told us we would have to make a sacrifice. I was told I would be that sacrifice, as I was already dying. Friends, creatures that I had loved and known my entire life, turned on me. I was told my death would have meaning.

"But when we got here, you healed me and saved my tree. I didn't have time to let Jeff know what was going on. Not that he would have cared." Erin laughs bitterly. "So, now he loves me? What is that all about?" She gazes down at the ground and toes a few rotten leaves. "I didn't think he cared. I am so sorry; I can't believe he came here. After everything that you have done for me, I pay you back by bringing trouble to your door. I'm so very sorry, Tuesday. Geez. Did he think playing combat computer games made him a mercenary?" Erin pulls away from the tree. "Love?" she huffs. "I didn't think he even liked me."

"It is clear the elf set you all up. That is why your friends acted out of character and why you did not tell me what had happened. Until now. The horrible guy is dead, so he can't manipulate anyone anymore." *I hope.*

This is why asking questions is important. If I had not been so shocked when the dryads arrived, I might have saved myself some heartache. If I had asked them simple questions, I might have realised things didn't add up.

"Will you come with me to speak to him?" I ask, holding out my hand.

"Of course, I will come."

I drop my offered hand as a thought enters my head. I need to tell her now before she sees him and perhaps changes her mind. "I must warn you, even if I think Jeff was manipulated, I have to treat him like a threat. He came here intending to hurt people, so he won't be able to stay with you in the realm."

"I completely understand. Believe me, I don't want him to stay either. I don't know why he thought coming here with a group of hired thugs would be a good idea. Avenging my death... when he left me to rot." Erin looks up from the ground, her eyes pleading. "Y-you won't kill him, will you? Please don't—"

"No, I won't kill him," I say, horrified. I feel a little disappointed at her insinuation. Although I can see why she would be concerned, she can probably see the anger radiating from me. I'm pissed. But that anger is aimed at me. I am so disappointed in myself. "I also don't blame you for his actions." And in all honesty, I don't blame Jeff either. That host was a master manipulator.

"Come on, let's get this mess sorted out." I hold my hand out again and Erin takes it.

CHAPTER THIRTY-SEVEN

Erin and I are the last to arrive. The frozen mercenaries immediately draw my attention. My magic has just plonked them together in a rough grouping. A couple of them are even facing the wall. Seven are standing, and three are unconscious. *The Power Rangers.* "Has no one ever told you guys that your Power Ranger outfits are ridiculous?" Of course, the frozen men can't reply, they can't make a peep. For extra safety, and not willing to encounter any more surprises, I lock the entire reception down.

The huge black wolf's grey eyes land on me, and he shifts. What I can only describe is a look of pure relief crosses Owen's handsome face as he prowls toward me. His entire focus is on me. His enormous hands land on my hips and he lifts me into his arms. The cinnamon and vanilla scent of him fills my lungs. One arm is underneath my bottom—like the best kind of seat—and it holds me up against him while his other hand cradles my face. My tummy flips as I am engulfed in his heat and his perfect bumper car lips find mine.

He kisses me sweetly, reverently, as if I am the only person who matters to him in the entire world.

When I reluctantly pull away to take a breath, my breasts brush against his chest. His pecs are hard. Steel beneath silken skin, reminding me of the power of the man that holds me. We breathe in unison for several seconds and unfortunately, my head screams a warning that we are not alone.

Oops.

I am now very aware we are kissing in the same room as my parents and a bunch of mercenaries.

I glare at him ruefully. Owen returns the look with a soft smile, so I allow myself the luxury of leaning against the hand that is cupping my jaw for a few more precious seconds.

When I finally lift my eyes, I peek over his shoulder. My coven is milling around; they appear relaxed considering the current situation and the earlier excitement. My attention lands on Mum. She isn't so relaxed. Her eyes are politely averted, and her hand is firm across a grumbling Heather's face, blocking her view.

In the back of my head, I acknowledge my hellhound is, um, naked, having just shifted. Even though I love his soft skin underneath my fingertips, and I know he isn't shy, nor does he mind everyone checking out his bare bottom, I tease, "I'm not the only one who should be called Flash.'" I wrap him in his combat style clothing and include his weapons for good measure.

"I was so worried," he whispers. "I am so glad you're safe." The rough stubble on his jaw scratches against my hair as he kisses the top of my head. Owen gently places me on the floor and pulls away just enough, so he can check me over.

The bruising on my throat where the host grabbed me must have faded. But it still doesn't stop my hellhound from homing in on the area. Probably scenting the host on my skin. "Where is he?" he growls.

"Dead." My mouth goes dry with the words and my throat aches. "He is dead." Owen's eyes soften with compassion.

"Good. Did you kill him?"

I shake my head. "Atticus."

"I owe him."

I don't bother correcting him that the vampire still owes me, but it is a long story and I'll tell him when we have privacy and not an entire reception full of frozen but listening mercenaries.

"Daisy?" I don't wait for his answer as my magic finds her automatically. She is swimming in a lava pool with her fake dragonette friends. "Found her," I mumble.

"She kept trying to bite your mum."

"Oh." I can't help but grin and Owen's eyes sparkle. "I will have a stern word with her to not bite grandma." As if we conjured her, Mum tugs me away from Owen and hugs me.

Oof.

"The dragonette is not my grandchild. I am so glad you are okay. Please don't do that again. I was worried. Tuesday, you don't have to prove you are the strongest person in the room. We all know it. Next time, let us help you. You don't have to do things alone." She gives me a shake and then Diane, my protector, pulls me away from her tight grip.

"Now is not the time, Mum," Diane chides. "Glad you are okay, sis."

I expect Mum to say something else, to reprimand me, but she doesn't. She gives me a small smile and... is that respect in her eyes?

Nah. Now I know I must be seeing things. Her concern has shocked the stuffing out of me.

"Is everyone okay?" Andy, as usual, is scowling.

"Yes, we are fine," Ava says.

"Hellhound"—Mum clears her throat—"perhaps we need to discuss a spell that will retain your clothes while you shift. While you are a fine-looking man, we do not need to see you in all your glory. Especially when there are children present. We are witches, not wolves, and we have standards."

I snort and Owen and I share another look.

"I don't know," Jodie whispers to Diane. "I don't mind." Diane shushes and elbows her, while Andy looks appalled.

I turn back to our prisoners. "So, you got three?" I ask Owen, acknowledging three of the mercenaries who are unconscious and a little bit worse for wear. I look a little closer and spot the odd man out. I should say, two mercenaries and one lovesick young man are unconscious and frozen on the floor.

"Oh, hello, Jeff."

Erin's takes that as permission to hurry towards him and drops to her knees beside him on the floor. Her hands flutter about as if she doesn't know where to touch him. "I don't know whether to ask you to slap some sense into him or help him," she whispers. When she catches my eye, she blinks back tears. "Please, please help him. I know it's wrong of me to ask, but can you please heal him as you did me?"

I can see he's a little beat up. Claw marks rend across his chest and his abdomen. The eyes of my coven and the frozen mercenaries track me as I shuffle toward them. As I kneel in front of

Jeff, I whisper, "Erin, will you please stay out of the way for a second? Just so I can talk with him without interference? I promise I won't be long." Erin nods and scrambles out of Jeff's sightline.

"I am going to heal him first." I keep him frozen as I send my magic into him to heal the superficial wounds. Well, superficial to a creature. But not to the pale young man before me, who has the markers of a person who spends all his time inside.

Jeff is human. Which makes what he did, coming here for revenge, more impressive—I frown—if not more stupid. What was he thinking? Was the host's influence that substantial? Or is Jeff the gamer a closet Rambo?

Gosh, he has been very lucky to have only got away with a few nasty scratches. As my magic finishes healing him, his eyes flutter open.

"Hey Jeff," I say, all friendly-like.

I remind myself that the rest of Jeff is frozen, so I unfreeze his mouth, allowing him to speak.

"Bitch," he snarls. Erin gasps. I wave the hand that he can't see at Erin, in a silent request for her to keep her mouth closed until after I have finished talking to him. Thankfully, she listens.

"It's you, isn't it? He told me you had freaky purple hair. You killed my girl and I'm going to end you."

I slow blink. He is going to *end* me. My lips twitch. That was kind of adorable.

"I am going to rip you apart with my bare hands and shit down your neck."

Ew. Lovely. That was not quite as cute. "Are you now? Well, alrighty then," I say with zero aplomb. "That is kind of a dramatic statement, Jeff, considering you are frozen to the floor. I healed you and you are so welcome." I rub my eyebrow and wrinkle my nose when Jeff roars.

He grits his teeth and grunts with a bold but bizarre attempt to prove me wrong. I watch as his face goes bright red and a little blood vessel in his temple throbs as he struggles to make good on his threat.

Gah.

I tilt my head to the side and wait him out. After a few more grunts and groans, he settles. "Are you done?" I quietly ask. He glares at me and then looks away. "So, Jeff, who told you I killed Erin?" The same eyebrow I've been scrubbing rises with my enquiry.

"Everybody knows. Everybody knows that you're a murderous bitch. And if I don't get you, someone else will."

"Okay, that's nice." I nod sagely and then ask the same question. "Who told you I killed Erin?"

"An elf did."

Ah, now we're getting somewhere. His explanation doesn't seem to differ from the host's villain speech. "What did he tell you?" Jeff clamps his lips closed, and he stubbornly closes his eyes. I sigh at his childish antics. "The elf lied to you, Jeff. He used you and you put Erin in danger by coming here all potions blazing."

"Liar!" Jeff yells. "You're a lying evil bitch." Owen growls, so I freeze Jeff's mouth before Owen can come over and pull his head off.

I get off the floor and wipe my sweaty hands on my jeans. I am so completely out of my comfort zone in dealing with this. I know I'll get nothing out of him. He is too angry. At least it is easy to prove I'm not lying. "Wow, Erin," I mumble, "you have a real winner here. No wonder you broke up with him." I nod and wave my hand in a "have at it" gesture. She falls forward, shuffling on her hands and knees towards his inert body.

My eyes go to the mercenaries. Perhaps by speaking to them, I will have more success?

"What did you do?" Erin cries as she grabs hold of his shirt. The shock in his eyes is worth taking his vitriol for a few minutes. "Tuesday saved my life, you idiot. She saved my tree, and you want to shit down her throat? Are you for fucking real? What the hell did I see in you, you weasel?"

Jeff's eyes almost bug out of his head, and I again allow him to speak.

"What? You're alive? How? What? Erin! Erin, I love you so much. I had to come here, as I couldn't live without you." I sigh as he blubbers. I don't think Jeff will want to kill me anymore, so I unfreeze him. His arms snake around the dryad and he clutches her to his chest, raining her with snot and tears as he cries.

I catch Erin's mortified look. I wince.

While trying to push him off, Erin tells Jeff about how I saved her and her tree. Jeff tells her about finding her missing and then being unable to find the rest of the dryads.

And *then* he talks about meeting an elf who offered him a chance for revenge, which he couldn't pass up.

To give them privacy, now that I've got what I need, I move them to a new build cabin in the woods, close to Erin's tree. I make sure that Jeff cannot go wandering about, confining him to the cabin. After all, he hired a bunch of mercenaries and led them to my realm to kill me. I'm not a horrible person and they need privacy to sort stuff out. So, I will give him an hour and then stuff him in a portal. Then the human police can deal with him.

I flick my magic over the two injured mercenaries, rapidly healing them. As shifters, they'd be able to heal themselves completely if I let them shift, but there is no way I am unfreezing them to allow that. Hands on my hips, I check out the mercenaries. Well, the ones that are facing in my direction. You can tell a lot about somebody's character from their eyes. One guy in particular makes nervous shivers run down my spine as his black eyes glare at me with uncontrolled hatred. He has the whole 'rough leader' vibe going on. Perhaps he might be the best person to have a little chat with.

Like I did with Jeff, I unfreeze his mouth and ask him a question. "Who do you work for?" He continues to glare at me. "Do you know what? Like you, I have had such a horrid day." I sigh and shake my head. "Today has been nothing but drama. All I want to do is have a nice bath and go to sleep.

"I could sleep for a week. I am sure you're the same, Green Power Ranger, what with getting set up, being treated like bait, and then getting your arse kicked. I bet you want to go home, get out of your little rubber outfit, and have a beer and relax." The rough mercenary's left eye twitches. "Please don't make me kill you," I whisper.

When I look back at this conversation, I'd like to think it was the soft appeal in my voice that made the green Power Ranger answer me. But I know him opening his mouth is probably more than likely because of the growly hellhound at my back. The world I live in is sadly patriarchal to its core, and no matter the power I have, I will always be viewed as a mere woman. Not that I care.

"I work for Rattan and Sons." *Bingo.*

"Perfect, thank you. Have you got their phone number?" I pull my phone out of my pocket. With an incredulous tone, green rattles off a number, which I promptly dial. The phone rings. "What's your boss's name?"

"Henderson," he growls.

"Thank you."

As the phone rings, I give the steely-eyed hellhound behind me a chin lift in appreciation. *I see what you did there, handsome.*

The phone connects, and a bored sounding receptionist rattles the company's name, with a not-so-pleasant "How may I help you?" added at the end. I guess it is getting late.

"Good evening, please may I speak to a Mr Henderson?"

"Mr Henderson is not available at the moment."

"I think he would *really* like to speak to me."

"Mr Henderson has finished for the day."

"Oh, okay. I just thought he'd want to know where his missing team was. I'm sure nine lives are easy to throw away, what with mercenaries being so abundant and easy to come by. I understand they must be such pesky employees, and not worth Mr Henderson's precious time." I pause and stare at green as I listen to the woman gasp and splutter.

"I will transfer you now. Please hold." Music plays in the background and I put the phone on speaker and tap my foot to the beat.

"Who is this and what do you want?" comes a gruff voice.

"Mr Henderson?" He grunts an affirmative. "My name is Tuesday Larson, and you must have been informed I have nine of your men in my possession."

"Are they alive?"

"Yes, and healthy."

"What game are you playing? What do you want?"

"I'm not playing a game, Mr Henderson. I will give your men back to you out of the goodness of my heart, but I need something from you first."

"What do you want?" he snarls.

"Mr Henderson, let me be clear on this. Their lives are on the line. All I ask for their safe return is for you to give me a promise, a single promise that for as long as you live, for as long as your firm exists, you will *never* accept a contract for my realm or a member of the Larson coven. Oh, and I'd like to add my boyfriend to that list. Owen—he's the hellhound. We are on your 'do not touch' list, do you understand? If you don't have such a list, you make one tonight. In exchange, I will return your men to you unharmed."

"So, I make a promise and you return my men? Is that it? Just like that?" He laughs. "And you said you weren't playing any games, Miss Larson."

"If you make this promise to me, Mr Henderson, let's just say I have the power to enforce it."

"Yes, yes. I am sure you do. Okay, we have a deal, for whatever it's worth," he finishes with a grumble and a disbelieving scoff.

"Perfect. Oh, and as a punishment and safeguard, every person linked to your company, including their families, they have a lifelong ban from The Sanctuary realm. If they try to enter, they will be refused admittance and if they somehow get inside under false pretences, I will kill them. Is that understood?"

Whoa, I am sounding very bloodthirsty this evening.

"Okay. Whatever. Who cares?"

"I have your word?"

"Yes." I feel the realm's magic pulse, and I watch as filaments of the magic shoot out like arrows and disappear into the mercenaries' chests. Oh, now that is handy. A magical tag, just so I can keep track of them. "What the fuck was that?" Mr Henderson yelps.

I open a portal behind the mercenaries and shove them through. As soon as I hear the thuds over the phone, I release the frozen spell holding them captive and snap the portal closed. Owen moves away from behind me with a relieved sigh.

"Nice speaking with you, Mr Henderson. Have a pleasant evening." If that didn't scare the shit out of them, I don't know what will.

"Oh, Miss Larson, don't go just yet. Don't you want to know who let my guys into your realm?" Oh, I do. There I go again, forgetting the important questions. "As you have returned my men safe and sound, I can afford to give you some free information."

"Call me pleasantly intrigued."

"Your rat—pardon my pun—the wolf with access to the magic shop and your fixed portal, was your sister's boyfriend, Andrew."

CHAPTER THIRTY-EIGHT

Owen's eyes widen, and my world slows down to microseconds.

A weight slams into my back, knocking me off my feet and sending me flying as a fifteen stone wolf hits me from behind. The phone clatters to the ground, followed swiftly by me. I hit the floor with a crunch and my ears ring as my head bounces off the wood. Ouch. I roll to avoid a heavy paw to my face, and bring my hands up just in time to protect my throat from the wolf's savaging teeth.

Bloody hell.

Underneath the wolf's snarls is the sound of Mr Henderson's tinny laughter.

Even though the wolf attack feels like forever, it is only a matter of seconds until the shifted wolf goes airborne and is yanked off me.

"Andy? That was Andy, right?" I say dazed. My vision is hazy, and I can see actual squiggly lines in front of my eyes. I must have really cracked my head if I am showing signs of concussion. I watch as a black fuzzy blob rushes toward me.

"Tuesday, are you okay?" Mum cries as she helps to sit me up.

"I am fine, Mum," I rasp with a fake smile as I move my head to knock her icy hand from my cheek.

The bloody magic lie detector pings. *Great.* The stupid magic won't even give me the peace to lie to myself.

I blink a few times and my head clears. "He just knocked the wind out of me, that's all. The realm magic will fix me right up." My tone is light and even, but my heart is slamming against my ribs.

I lick my lips. Blood coats inside of my mouth and the back of my head aches. I duck my head to cover my horrified expression, and madness bubbles inside of me. The shock I'm feeling right now makes me want to roll back onto the floor and laugh. Laugh like my entire world has not fallen apart.

Up. Get up.

My stomach churns with fear, and my body is rubbery with shock. My limbs are like a day-old Pot Noodle. I scramble to my knees and, with my left hand, I stretch out and grab the fallen phone. "Thanks for the heads up, Mr Henderson," I say pleasantly as I end the call.

With Mum's help, I stand. I fist my right hand behind my back.

"Flash, are you okay?" Owen asks over the ruckus of the brown thrashing wolf. He has a good grip on the wolf. He holds him by the scruff of his neck.

"Yes." I get the single word out before my throat locks up.

Liar, liar, broom on fire. The old nursery rhyme echoes around my head.

With Owen's attention on Andy, it is easy to pull the wool over his eyes. Plus, this is my realm, and reality can be altered. I make sure the scent of my blood goes nowhere near his keen shifter nose. The hellhound lets out a hair-raising growl and shakes the wolf like a puppy. His arm bulges with strength, but Andy's weight doesn't seem to affect the big man.

"Andy?" Diane whispers brokenly. "Why, Andy? Why would you do that?" I clamp my mouth closed, as it takes everything that I have not to say, "'Cause he is a dickhead."

Jodie tries to comfort our sister while looking back at Mum and me with frightened eyes. Ava and Heather are nowhere to be found. I don't need to ask my magic where they are as Dad is guarding the way to my office.

"Shift back, or I'll break your neck," Owen says. His voice is a deadly whisper in the snapping wolf's ear. Then it's as if Andy comes back to himself. He finally pauses his struggles, tucks his tail between his legs, and cowers.

With puppy dog eyes and pink spit dripping from his jaws, he inspects our angry coven. The realisation is dawning on his wolfy features. He has seriously messed up.

The wolf shifts.

I'm glad to see Andy isn't naked, having been gifted the coven's expensive clothing retention potion. I stand there quietly. I don't have the heart to interfere with this interrogation.

One thought keeps screaming at me. It bounces around in my head and I have to push it away, so it doesn't come spilling out of my lips in a devastated scream.

"You brought in the mercenaries," Diane says, shrugging off Jodie's arm and surprising probably everybody in the room as she steps up.

Her voice is clear. Gone is the pain, and it is replaced with anger. "You brought mercenaries here to hurt my coven. Why? Why would you do that?" Andy winces as Owen applies pressure to his neck. There are flames in my hellhound's eyes and is that... yes, his free hand is once again engulfed in dancing blue flame.

I love that I can see his magic. I am not in love with the circumstances, but I'm glad I get to see him like this again, for what undoubtedly will be the last time.

"I am sick of you and your fantastic, amazing, incredible coven looking down at me as if I'm scum. What are you without your potions? What can you do really? It was easy to make you think I loved you." Andy winks. "Any hole is a goal, am I right?"

Beside me, Mum lets out a disgusted sound.

Diane blinks a few times and then laughs. "You narcissistic, little shit. To think I thought your weirdness was endearing. You are a joke. Who told you any of this would be a good idea? When did you decide on this brilliant plan?" She waves her arm in the air and then nods at Owen. Owen's fiery hand drifts closer to Andy. A droplet of sweat from his hairline rolls down his face. Andy lets out a whimper.

"It was all Mr Henderson! He knew I was dating you and when you included me on the trip to the safe house, it gave the ideal opportunity to set things in place. It was a nice little earner. Kill two birds with one stone. It meant I was finally rid of you and wouldn't get my arse kicked by your bitch of a mother." Mum huffs. "Win-win. Until you all decided to move location and come here." He toothily grins at me.

He knows. He knows what he did.

"So, when your useless sister mentioned fixing a portal to the shop at lunch, I got on the blower and made the plans. It happened quickly after that."

Ah, this wasn't the work of the host. Good to know Andy was not a victim, brainwashed into doing something that was out of character.

I keep my injured right hand behind my back and a small droplet of blood splatters unnoticed on the floor. The realm's magic whisks the evidence away.

Andy looks again at me with a triumphant grin. I didn't get away unscathed and no magic on Earth will heal me. Andy bit me in his deadly wolf form.

He bit me.

"Tuesday. Will you open a portal?" I must have missed some of the conversation. Mum gently strokes the back of my head to get my attention. "Your dad and Owen are going to take Andy to the Hunters Guild."

I nod. "Sure," I croak. I need to mask what I am feeling, suck it up until they've gone.

I open the portal.

"Please don't take me there. I don't want to be locked up. Diane, tell them to kill me. Are you not going to kill me?"

"Kill you? No, that would be way too easy. Where you're going, pal, they will keep you alive for a very long time." Owen shakes Andy like he is a rag doll to get his point home. I am glad I've not said anything about the bite. Owen would rip Andy's throat right out.

Andy must have the same thought. "Tell him, Tuesday—"

I freeze his stupid mouth.

My breath shudders. It's probably my imagination, as I've always been a tad dramatic, but as the painful bite on my hand burns, I can already feel the poisonous shifter magic running through my veins.

"Love you, Dad."

Dad kisses me on the cheek and whispers, "And I love you. Please look after your sister." I can't speak the lie, so I nod.

I shuffle towards Owen and quietly mumble a goodbye. "See you in a bit. Be careful. Thank you for your help." Owen smiles at me in that way he does.

"Always."

My heart wails. *Why? Why couldn't I get my happily ever after?*

I'm dead, my body just doesn't know it yet. The small bite will kill me within seventy-two hours, and this is the last time I will see my hellhound. I don't want him to see me suffer like that.

I stubbornly lift my chin as they step into the portal, dragging Andy between them.

I love you. I love you so much. I scream inside.

Before the portal closes, I squeeze my eyes tightly shut and turn away so I cannot see the budding confusion in his beautiful grey eyes.

I can't watch him leave. I just can't.

When the portal closes, I lock everything down so he can't return. I am so proud that I held it together.

Now I have a decision to make. I can run, like the million times I have done before, or I can be honest. Tell the truth. Everything inside me wants to run away, wants to find some deep, dark hole to fall inside. But the selfish part of me wants my mum. It also wants Owen. But he is gone. It wants to be greedy, to have my coven and Daisy at my side.

My heart aches for my brave, beautiful hellhound to somehow fight this for me, to chase away the poisonous magic in my blood and rescue me.

But he can't.

A sob wrenches out of my throat. I cover my lips, and beneath my hand, an inhuman wail comes out of my mouth.

I never knew grief and horror had such a sound.

"Tuesday, Tuesday, please tell me what is wrong."

"Mum, I'm sorry." Blood dribbles down my wrist as I hold up my bitten hand.

CHAPTER THIRTY-NINE

The silence is so strange, ominous.

It is a silence that will stretch through time and be a clear memory for the rest of their lives as it implants itself into their soul with a vicious crack. They stare at me, shell-shocked, and I do not know how to comfort them. Diane is the first to react. She sinks to the floor as if her legs have given out, like she is a puppet with her strings cut. She pulls her knees to her chest and rocks. "No. This can't be happening. It's a nightmare. It's not real."

Mum freezes. Her violet eyes narrow, and

then a look of horror and pity flashes across her face. "No. Please, no."

I bet you are glad it's me and not them.

Jodie goes into nurse mode. She is suddenly there in front of me, holding my cold wrist between her warmer hands. She gently palpitates the skin around the bite. It is numb to the touch. I am glad the wound doesn't hurt. Though not hurting is probably a terrible sign. She then pulls the sleeve of my jumper up to my elbow, and there is a hitch in her breathing, and she visibly swallows. I glance down. The only reason I do not swear up a storm is 'cause of my respect for Diane. I don't want to upset her any more than necessary. I hold in my horrified gasp.

A spider web of red spreads from the bite. It wraps around the silver swirls on my wrist. It looks horrendous against my pale skin. And where the red web touches the silver swirls, they blacken. That isn't good. Jodie's compassionate brown eyes meet mine, her gaze holds such heart-wrenching sorrow that for a split second, it feels like I am already dead.

Diane wails behind us.

"Help her," I whisper underneath my breath.

"Okay," Jodie whispers back. We both know there is nothing she can do. I'm sure she has seen different versions of this scenario dozens of times before. I shake my arm until the jumper slips back over my wrist.

Jodie crouches next to Diane. She pulls out a familiar black bag and I can't help my small smile. It is the pocket dimension I made for her. She quickly pulls out various potions. "I am going to give you something to help you cope."

"Why are you not helping Tuesday?" Mum whispers.

Jodie shakes her head and pops the top off a pale lilac vial. Diane, between sobs, obediently sips.

I move toward her to help and—

It is then I recognise his heat. Before I can spin around, a solid arm wraps around me and gently grips my right arm. "Did you think you could hide that from me?" he says against the shell of my ear as he rubs the skin above the bite. "That I wouldn't see the overwhelming pain and fear in your eyes? That I wouldn't notice the woman I love is distraught?"

"Owen." My voice cracks, and I turn and bury my face into his abdomen. *He didn't leave me.* The indifferent, stupidly brave mask I'm hiding behind shatters. I thought I could only remain brave if I held on to pain and sorrow. *I was wrong.*

He holds me as I cry. His massive hand threads through my hair and the other rubs my back as he makes soft comforting sounds in the back of his throat. When I've thoroughly dampened his shirt and I don't think I can cry anymore, I lift my eyes.

"Y-you love me?" I whisper.

His eyes crinkle at the corners. "Since you shuffled to the bathroom with your trousers around your ankles." I laugh, and I don't care that, even to my ears, it is a retched horrid sound.

"I love you too. So, so much," I gush. And then I remember that isn't going to be enough. "I don't want to leave you."

"Do you think I will let you die without a fight?" His thumbs wipe away the remaining tears from my face, and he crouches so we are eye level. "Listen to me, Tuesday Larson, I've seen you do things that are solely confined to the history books. I've seen you do things— impossible things. You learned in days magic that would take anyone else a lifetime to master. So let me be clear, so you understand, and there's no mistaking my words.

"This. Is. Your. Realm. With your rules. The rules of Earth don't apply here. That is why you can create the things that you do, why you can pull things out of thin air. Why you can *heal* creatures when all hope is lost. You will *not* die."

"I won't?"

"No. I have so much faith in you. I know in my heart you have the power to heal yourself. This is not the end." He rests his forehead on mine. "I want our happily ever after," he growls.

Bloody tears. I swallow the enormous lump in my throat. What he says makes a strange kind of sense, but... the bite is a hundred percent fatality rate.

How can I beat that?

"That is an amazing idea," Jodie says, suddenly becoming animated and standing. A subdued Diane flops almost casually against

Jodie's legs. "You use the shifter magic, absorb it and mix it with your own. Owen is right. No one has ever seen anyone like you before. I bet you differ from the other hosts, too."

"I do differ," I mumble. "They resemble our elves. While I'm all witch."

"Exactly."

"You are way too stubborn to die," Mum snaps. I take in her red eyes from her silent crying and puffy face. Her hair is listing to one side. I have never seen her so not put together. Softer, she pleads, "Tell us what you need. We will help."

"Mum, what's happening?" Heather whispers. "I don't understand."

Aw heck.

I wince. I missed their return to reception, and the realisation wraps me with guilt. I didn't want Heather to find out like this. I did not want her to know until I was gone. She deserves to know from her aunt; she deserves to see, even in the face of such fear, I have dignity. "I'm so sorry, Heather. I have been bitten by Andy in his animal form. As you know from school, the bite is deadly to women."

Again, everyone is quiet while Heather absorbs this information.

"You are going to fight, right? You will not let the shifter magic win."

I shake my head as determination fills me. I need a little faith, belief. "No. I will not let the shifter magic win. I am a Larson."

Heather nods. "Okay."

"Forgive me. Forgive me for not being fast enough." I spin on my toes and look up at my hellhound.

"Forgive you for not having a crystal ball, you mean? Owen, bad things happen. This"—I wave my wrist underneath his nose—"was not your fault. It wasn't Diane's fault either. It was dickhead Andy who attacked me. He went for my throat and ended up chomping on my hand. Stop blaming yourself and put the blame firmly on him. The jumped-up little prick. Right..." I clap my hands. "Coven bedtime. Come on, everybody. Let's get some sleep. I know I'm exhausted and I cannot think clearly with all the snivelling."

Diane huffs out a laugh. "You are unbelievable. Do you ever take anything seriously?"

"Never. I will need your super smart brain and your witchy talents. You need to be at your best in the morning, so go and relax. I will see you soon."

I unlock the portal so Dad can get back after dropping Andy off. I also check to confirm that Jeff has gone.

"You won't do anything stupid, will you?"

"No, Mum." I ignore the magic ping. "I am sorry about the crayons, Mum."

"I'm not. I find colouring relaxing. Perhaps the swear word colouring book was a tad much. But you made your point."

"It was a swear word colouring book? Wow, is that a thing?" I grin. "Well, I am glad you will enjoy it." Mum nods as she helps a swaying Diane to her feet.

"I'm sorry. I am so sorry my horrible boyfriend hurt you. Killed you. I love you, little sister," Diane says as her head flops oddly from side to side.

"Stop that. I am not dead yet, so you can stop looking at me like that. Otherwise, I am going to moan the word *brains* and do the zombie shuffle." Heather opens her mouth. I hold up a hand. "No, I am not turning into a zombie. It was a joke. Sheesh. Diane can't control another person and what he did was on him. It was my fault for getting my hand in the way." I'm so glad that they are all safe, as it could have worked out so much worse. "I got some bad luck, that's all. Now please, go get some sleep."

"I'm going to kill him," Diane viciously whispers as she is sandwiched between Mum and Jodie as they wobble away.

"No, you are not. Think about how miserable he is going to be locked up. He doesn't deserve a quick death," Jodie tells her.

"I would not make it quick," Diane huffs back.

"Not tonight. You're going to get some sleep and then you are going to help our sister."

"Of course, I'm gonna help Tuesday. I'm going to fix this, but there's no way I am going to be able to sleep."

"Naturally, no, but I've got another wonderful spell you can chug."

"See you in the morning, Auntie Tuesday."

"Night, Heather."

The hallway door swings closed. "Now you've got rid of your coven. What are we really going to do?" Owen says once we are alone. "I know you will not have a nap. You have that expression on your face."

"What expression?"

"Mischief. Trouble."

"Oh." I shrug. What can I say to that? Although I'm less mischief and more shitting myself, what with dying and all. But my hellhound's attempt to lighten the mood is sweet.

"What are we doing, Flash?"

All the way through this rollercoaster journey, I have always felt as if the magic was guiding me. And I've concluded that the realm needs me just as much as I need it. So why not ask the realm what I need to do? The answer comes to me.

"I'm going to the heart of the realm and you're going to help me."

"Together?"

"Yes, together."

He gently kisses my cheek. "You haven't had a normal few days, have you?"

"No." If I survive this, I don't think I will have normal ever again. "I can feel the foreign magic, Owen. It is eating me up inside." I rub my shoulder and puff out a breath. I roll my sleeves up and the red spider web has already spread further up my arm. It is itching along my shoulder, pulsing as it threatens its way towards my heart. "There is a war going on inside of me. I think I have less than an hour."

"An hour?" Owen rubs his forehead and then presses his palm over his mouth. "How can I help?"

"Can you go get Daisy?" My voice breaks as soon as I say her name. I swallow a few times and cough to clear my throat. "Then can we go to the lake?"

I worry that Stepping will only exasperate the poison.

So, after Owen comes back with Daisy, he carries us both outside.

CHAPTER FORTY

The night is still and warm. With my arms wrapped around his neck and my legs around his waist, I nestle against him as he holds me with reverence to his chest. Daisy curls across his shoulders, watching me intently. She chirps her concern and, every so often, nudges my arm and face. I find it hard to look at her.

I have never seen a night sky like this. I tip my head back to investigate the blackness of the night sky, and, of course, there are millions of beautiful bright stars. Pinpricks of burning flame, circling overhead in a spiralling vortex. The stars, it is like they are almost following us. Perhaps they are? They are my stars, after all.

Even with me in his arms, his footsteps are silent. The hellhound moves like a ghost, like he is floating. His feet barely touch the ground.

With my eyes on the sky and the smooth, but fast movement of my hellhound, it isn't long before we reach the lake. He has chosen the spot well, where we had our picnic, close to the dock and our rowboat. Owen settles down onto the grass. My legs slide on either side of his hips.

My hellhound carefully arranges me. My body is so floppy, I have zero control over my limbs.

My thoughts wildly scatter. *Ah, fear, my old friend, so glad I can't make a fool of myself, as my body is now too messed up to deal with you.* My heart is sluggish and doesn't even pretend to care as my mind freaks out.

In the last few minutes, I'm finding it harder and harder to breathe. Each new breath is more laboured than the last. I am not in any pain. It's just the spreading numbness that is disconcerting.

If there is ever a time to keep my cool, it's now. If I don't keep calm, I'm going to spend my remaining time freaking out instead of finding a solution.

When I was a little girl, I had appendicitis and had to have surgery to remove the defective organ. I remember when the nurses used the anaesthetic potion. I could feel it burning and spreading through my veins. I could taste the spell underneath my tongue. Flooding my mouth with its bitter tang.

It is kind of similar to that, wrapping like a monster around my lungs, rushing its poison through my blood. A coldness.

Owen cradles the back of my head and Daisy quietly creeps as close as she can, her golden wings touching the both of us.

"Tuesday," Owen says, breaking the raspy silence.

"Just hold me. Please, if it doesn't work—"

"It'll work," the hellhound growls.

"I love you," I gasp out. Gosh, talking without being able to breathe is hard. "I am sorry we didn't have enough time." I wheeze. "I know... it's a lot to ask but please will you take care of Daisy? She is my heart."

"Please, Flash—"

"Thank you for not leaving me when you could, for staying..."

"You don't have to thank me, and this isn't the end," he whispers gruffly. His grey eyes shine with tears. "I believe in you. You can do this." He is so strong, my hellhound.

"Okay." I flop against his chest and listen to the steady beat of his heart. With his heart showing me the way, I close my eyes and let go.

I fall.

I fall into the magic and the life force of the realm embraces me. My soul peels away from my dying body. I perceive my essence as it shifts between dimensions to a crossroads linking all the worlds.

It is so dark here. Like how I imagine a sensory deprivation chamber would feel. The silence is so vast, it is never-ending and no matter how hard I strain my ears, I cannot hear a thing. No matter how much I strain my eyes to pierce the blackness, I can't see even the smallest pinprick of light. Nothing exists.

Have I made a mistake?

I was supposed to go to the heart of the realm, not here. Not this lifeless place. Then there is a whooshing sound, and I brace the body that no longer exists, but instead, my battered soul flutters, as vast power flows over my incorporeal form and... that is when the pain comes. Every previous hurt finds me, and I am torn apart.

Judgement.

My life flashes before me and everything I have done wrong is plucked out and put on display. Analysed. Set out before me is a loathsome, macabre exhibit of my past wrongs.

I see moments of small hurts that I caused, moments of long forgotten unkindness. There aren't many, thank the stars. But the careless words bite, and the careless actions sting. It's a wall of shame and it makes me ashamed.

I'm being judged, and I am found... *lacking.*

I am not good enough for the mystical heaven. Not bad enough for the mystical fires of hell. Some higher power communicates to me in feelings rather than simple words. I still have so much left to do. Two choices: purge the shifter magic or embrace it.

The choices come with knowledge, a knowing of future issues, and a knowing of future pain. I am stubborn, so of course, I choose the hardest, but most rewarding path.

I am remade.

Remade into something different, something that I was always meant to be. More than just a host, more than a simple witch.

The knowledge of my choice and what I learned fades from my mind, leaving no trace. And then, with rough dismissal, I'm thrown back into my body.

So much bloody pain.

A colourful array of magic bombards me; it oozes through my veins. Strangely, the taste of fruit fills my mouth, then the fresh almost tasteless coolness of cucumber, and the bitter taste of volcanic rock. Daisy? When flavours in my mouth fade, green magic joins that of the realms, washing away the pain and some of the darkness that is still clinging to me. Familiar magic. Daisy's magic mixes with mine and the realm's. It combines to batter the remaining numbness away.

Everything stops, it grinds to a halt when I hear a voice. "Come on, breathe. Damn you. Don't you dare die on us."

What is that?

There is pressure on my chest. "Please don't leave us. I love you." The ring on my finger burns a fiery path up my arm.

My body jolts.

The magic explodes inside of me and finally, the shifter magic is now *mine*.

I gasp.

"I've got her back. She's breathing," says a raspy voice. Jodie. My sneaky sister must have snuck out and followed us here, knowing I would need her help. My eyes flutter open. "Never do that again!" She slaps my arm weakly and then bursts into tears. "Three minutes. You stopped breathing for three minutes." She sniffles.

"Sorry…" I croak out.

"The ring on your finger started glowing, and it was as if the entire realm held its breath. The bite on your wrist healed and the red marks faded almost straight away, but they didn't go away fully until Daisy touched you. Tuesday, your little dragonette glowed like a freaky green star and then… that was about the time you stopped breathing…"

My sister continues to ramble. My hellhound is right next to me, stroking my face and hair. I cannot focus on his expression yet, as my eyes are kinda fuzzy. "...I did chest compressions, and I was about to use a spell to shock your heart."

I move my fingers; at least I am no longer feeling numb. I take a deep breath, ooh, and I can breathe without issue. Sweet oxygen fills my lungs. I am alive; I did it.

So why do I still feel a little spider webby? I frown.

The sticky new magic zips through me, vibrating the very cells that hold me together. The cells that make me, me. I sit up with Jodie and Owen's help and lift an unsteady hand to my face. The vibrations in my body are getting worse, and my right hand is tingling.

Time seems to slow, and goosebumps raise on my skin. My vision becomes clearer, and I watch in morbid fascination as tiny pieces of skin detach from my hand and float off. I blink. *What the heck is that? Does anyone else see that!*

The shape of my fingers is the first to disappear. It doesn't hurt and the cells don't go far, they hover above me in some sort of magic swarm.

Time speeds up, and it's not just my hand, it is my entire arm and then... it's as if I am made of sand. Everything crumbles.

And then there is nothing.

Blackness.

With a strange pop echoing in my ears, everything is normal again. *Well, that was weird, and a little bit anticlimactic. Did lack of oxygen do something to my brain? Has everything that has happened made me mad?*

I move my hand back in front of my face to check out the bite on my wrist, and... Oh boy, that's not a hand. Uh-no. That is a fluffy, violet *paw.*

I yeep. Jodie squeaks.

Beside me, I can hear Owen's shocked laughter and I kid you not, my left ear swivels toward the sound. It is the weirdest sensation I have ever felt. I am not even going to say anything about my tail. When I look at him, the stupid thing wags!

I clamber to my feet, all four of them. My ears fatten to the side of my head as I wobble.

"You are purple! Your fur is purple. I can't believe you are a bloody wolf. Oh my god. Wait until mum finds out!" Jodie splutters.

That last comment has my cells zipping and vibrating with panic. Mum is going to kill me. Then I am standing naked and shivering.

Did that just happen?

A warm top is slipped over my head, and the body heat clinging to the fabric engulfs me. While the scent of cinnamon and vanilla wafts around me, the smell makes me dizzy. My sense of smell is... wow. It is like I had a cold with a stuffy nose my entire life, and now I can finally breathe. Owen stands there, his gorgeous dark skin and rippling muscles on display.

"Hi," I whisper.

"Hi," he says gruffly. I force my eyes to leave his bumpy abs and his beautiful sparkling grey eyes capture mine. He has been crying. Oh, Owen.

"I am sorry I frightened you. Did that just happen? Did I—" My words abruptly stop. I stare at my hands as if I have never seen them before. My thumb picks at the ring still on my finger, not even changing shape will dislodge that sucker.

Change shape. My bare feet wiggle into the grass and I blurt out a weird-sounding manic laugh.

"Shift? Yes."

"Oh. Crap-on-a-cracker," I mutter.

Daisy does a running jump, and she hits me in the chest so hard I grunt—I'm so glad shifting has fixed my remaining aches and pains—then I am hugging her and kissing her scaly, adorable face. "Who is a clever girl with fancy green magic?"

"You're alive. I can't believe you're bloody alive! And you turned into a wolf!" Jodie says as she tackle-hugs my side. Daisy snarls. I hold my hand out to the side, and Owen's massive, warm hand engulfs mine. I squeeze and he squeezes me right back.

Jodie pulls away with a pat on my arm. "I think I need a shot of the same potion I gave Diane. It's going to take a full year for me to calm down." She rubs her face. "Blinking heck, I feel like I have aged ten years." She spots our clasped hands and smiles softly. "Okay, well, I am so done. I have had enough excitement for the night. I will leave you guys to it. I'll go get some sleep." Daisy yawns so big I can almost see her tonsils. Jodie giggles. "She is so cute. If you want, I can take her with me. Do you want to stay with Auntie Jodie for tonight?" she coos.

I shrug. Daisy lets Jodie take her out of my arms. Head in the air, she holds herself as stiff as a board, and more amusing, she keeps her wings and tail stuck out at awkward angles. *"I will allow you to touch me, but I don't have to like it."* Mournfully, her eyes roll in our direction. She wrinkles her snout and makes an unhappy sound at the back of her throat. Once Jodie hugs her, that is the extent of her objection. She yawns again and relaxes, bestowing her temporary permission.

Aw, my little dragonette is completely tuckered out. "Thanks, sis. See you in the morning." We watch as Jodie and Daisy trudge back towards the hotel. I don't want to Step them until I have tested my magic.

Owen pulls me into his arms and hugs me. I bury my face into the silken skin of his chest as he rests his chin on the top of my head. "You are a beautiful wolf."

"I am a bitten shifter who can shift, the first woman known to survive a bite," I whisper.

"The first of my kind. It's going to be a nightmare when people find out. They are going to lose their shit."

"They will wonder if The Sanctuary Hotel solves our dwindling numbers, if what happened to you will be the shifter's salvation."

I groan.

"It will not. This will likely bring evil into our lives. Owen, the crazies will come."

"Let them. Between us, we can take out the rubbish. The predators are more than welcome. You are not a simple shifter, and neither am I, and I am not going anywhere."

"Are you sure you don't want to tap out?"

He grins. "Hell no."

"So, are we going to do this? Run the hotel? What about your job?"

"You are my priority. So yeah, we are going to run the hotel."

A safe place for all the misfits and the rebels. I like the sound of that.

"Hey, Flash, will you do me the honour of coming for a run?" What? I pull away slightly and blink at him.

"A-as... as wolves?" I stutter.

Owen's grey eyes dance, and he smiles brightly. "Race you!" And within two breaths, his clothing flutters to the floor and a big, black wolf is bounding across the grass. He stops and turns his head; his tongue lolls out in a wolfy grin and he playfully yips.

I shift, and on wobbly violet paws, I join him.

THE END

Dear Reader,

Thank you for taking a chance on my book. This is my fourth-ever book! Wow, I did it again. I hope you enjoyed it. If you did, and if you have time, I would be *very* grateful if you could write a review. Every review makes a *huge* difference to an author—especially me as a brand-new shiny one—and your review might help other readers discover my book. I would appreciate it so much, and it might help me keep writing.

Thanks a million!

Oh, and there is a chance that I might even choose your review to feature in my marketing campaign. Could you imagine? So exciting!

Love,
Brogan x

P.S. DON'T FORGET! Sign up on my VIP email list! You will get early access to all sorts of goodies, including signed copies, private giveaways, and advance notice of future projects and free stuff. The link is on my website at **www. broganthomas.com** Your email will be kept 100% private, and you can unsubscribe at any time, zero spam.

ABOUT THE AUTHOR

Brogan lives in Ireland with her husband and their eleven furry children: five furry minions of darkness (aka the cats), four hellhounds (the dogs), and two traditional unicorns (fat, hairy Irish cobs).

In 2019 she decided to embrace her craziness by writing about the imaginary people that live in her head. Her first love is her ~~husband~~ number-one favourite furry child Bob the cob, then reading. When not reading or writing, she can be found knee-deep in horse poo and fur while blissfully ignoring all adult responsibilities.

Brogan Thomas
BOOKS

Printed in Great Britain
by Amazon

19605088R00274